NORTH
OF NEED

NORTH
OF NEED

HEARTS OF THE ANEMOI
BOOK ONE

LAURA KAYE

Entangled Publishing, LLC
2614 South Timberline Road
Suite 109
Fort Collins, CO 80525
Visit our website at www.entangledpublishing.com.

Entangled Publishing is a subsidiary of Savvy Media Services, LLC.

Edited by Marie Loggia-Kee and Heather Howland
Cover design by Heather Howland

eBook ISBN   978-1-937044-46-6
Print ISBN   978-1-937044-87-9

Manufactured in the United States of America

First edition April 2012

To everyone struggling with the loss of a loved one.
May you find your Owen when your heart is ready.

CHAPTER ONE

The cold scorched Megan Snow's throat, making it hard to breathe. Hard to think.

That was a good thing.

She tugged her scarf over her mouth, grateful for the expansive winter sky and crisp air, and set off on a trail walk. Four days alone in the cabin, and Megan was sure the walls were closing in on her. Outside, everything was bright and clean and open. Just what she needed.

She headed for the stand of trees off to the side of the house, hoping the snow might be more shallow under the thick canopy of branches that sheltered the woods. A creek sat a half mile in where, on warmer days, happier days, she and John had sometimes picnicked and made love. It would be iced over, of course, but having a goal burned off some of her restlessness.

Megan high-stepped through the snow until her thighs burned, gripping onto one tree after another. She tripped on buried branches and rocks until the trees were the only things keeping her upright. Hugging a hickory trunk for support, she glanced back over her shoulder and groaned.

The clearly visible cabin mocked her progress. Most of the twenty inches of snow blanketing the wide field in front of the house had made its way to the forest floor, too. She wanted a distraction, but she needed to be smart, safe. Damn. She retraced her path to the cabin.

But she wouldn't go back inside. Couldn't.

She grabbed the shovel from the covered porch of the story-and-a-half log cabin and dug into clearing the front sidewalk. *You know you're going stir crazy when shoveling backbreaking wet snow counts as entertainment.*

Her family was right. It was probably time to stop coming out here for the holidays. But she just couldn't give this place up. Not yet. Not when it was the only thing she had left of *him*.

Nope. Not thinking about that.

Sweat trickled down her spine under her cotton turtleneck and thick fleece with each scoop-and-toss. Blonde curls worked their way out from under her hat and hung in her eyes. She didn't mind though, because with each newly revealed foot of sidewalk, the ache in her muscles made it more and more difficult to wallow in memories.

The shovel hit something solid and kicked back against Megan's frozen hands. She groaned as the shock of thwarted forward motion rocked through her wrists and elbows. Gravel from the driveway spilled from the shovel blade into the snow. Huh. She turned and looked behind her, surprised to find she'd cleared the whole length of the twenty-foot path.

Without once thinking of him. Of the anniversary.

Progress.

And proof that manual labor was her friend. There'd be

no more sitting around with books or music or TV shows she couldn't concentrate on. She'd just exhaust herself into a mindless oblivion.

She looked to her left, down over the expanse of shimmering white to the distant forest that marked her property line. To her right, her now-hidden driveway formed a curving path two-thirds of a mile to the main road and civilization. Shoveling *that* mess certainly would require manual labor, but Mr. Johansson would be up here with his plow as soon as the weather broke. How would she explain to him she'd tried to shovel it by hand? She imagined the confounded look on his craggy face.

So, what next? After returning the shovel to the front porch, she stood and surveyed the Western Maryland landscape. The low peaks of the ancient Appalachian Mountains rose around her, the firs and hardwoods for which these forests were famous veiled by two days of nonstop blizzard conditions. The only sound besides her labored breathing was the occasional whistling of the wind through the snow-burdened forest. For all Megan knew, she was the only person in the world. Sure felt like it, these days.

What to do?

God, I'm so lonely.

She sighed and shook her head.

The wind moaned. *Then do something about it.*

Heart pounding, Megan jerked around, her right boot skidding against a slick spot, pink scarf fluttering out around her like a ribbon. Who'd uttered those last words?

No one, of course. The silence and stillness were complete, as was her isolation—exactly the qualities she and John had always loved about this place.

"Jesus, I'm losing it," she murmured out loud, just to create the impression she wasn't so alone. Her gaze returned to the snowy field in front of the cabin. Trimmed by a dense line of firs at the far edges, the clearing was big, clean, empty…

Do something about it, the mysterious voice had said. Oh, she'd do something about it, all right.

Back to the high-stepping routine, Megan trudged out into the front yard. Any spot would do, she supposed, so she stopped and mashed two mounds of snow into a sticky white ball. The lull in the storm had allowed the temperature to creep up into the high twenties, so the snow was good packing quality. She rolled the ball over the powdery surface, intent on making it as big as she could. After a while, the thing started to fight back when she pushed, but she wanted the exertion. Digging her toes in, she fought for every additional inch in diameter until, finally, she was done.

She stood with snow-crusted gloves on her hips and admired her work. "That's one big ball ya got there." She sniggered, then shook her head.

Now, for the next two. She set about the packing-rolling-grunting process again until she created a sizable middle and the head. Lifting them into place proved a challenge, but with a lot of grunting and a few choice expletives, she lugged the heavy masses where they needed to be.

"Now, to transform you from androgynous snow person into my snowman." Megan jogged back to the house and didn't even worry about tracking snow inside. Moments later, she reemerged with an armload of supplies she dumped at the foot of her creation.

"First, we gotta give you a face, mister." Emptying the bag of buttons on top of the flannel shirt, she sorted through with glove-thick fingertips. She wanted bigger ones for the eyes, and found two. She frowned. They weren't the same color, but she wouldn't be able to tell from a distance. She plugged the biggest navy and chocolate-brown buttons into the face as eyes. A light brown button made a cute nose, and a row of mismatched reds made a friendly mouth.

The red and white plaid flannel shirt was a big don't-even-let-your-thoughts-go-there, but she couldn't allow the poor guy to go without clothing. Besides, she had a closet full of them. She wrapped the soft fabric around the middle section. The snowball was wide, but the shirt closed. After all, he'd been a big guy, hadn't he? She tugged off her gloves so she could do up the front, then trudged to the oak tree on the corner and snapped off two branches. With cold, shaking hands, she threaded the twigs through the flannel sleeves until Snow Man was inviting her in for a hug. She finished him off with a blue tartan wool scarf and a thick black knit beanie she stretched down as far as possible.

Standing back, Megan admired her work. He was the best snowman she'd ever built. Tall. Well proportioned. Handsomely attired. "Now I'm not alone."

Inspired, Megan fished a dry pair of blue gloves from the supply pile and collected more snow, beginning again before her brain could assess and refute her pronouncement. She packed, rolled, and lift-grunted until another, somewhat smaller, snow person stood beside the first. Back at the tree, she broke off more branches and gave the second person arms. She slid her soaked-through pink gloves on the end of each stick, then wrapped her own matching pink scarf around the snow woman's neck. Perfect.

Hands on her knees, Megan rested and struggled to catch her breath. Her lungs burned with the frigid air, her lips chapped and cracked. Her body ached from the heavy lifting. Definitely the route to a decent night of sleep. God, how she needed that. She plunged into her third creation.

The temperature dropped and the biting wind picked up. Big, wet snowflakes fell in a heavy blanket, darkening the afternoon sky. Her flagging energy and the deteriorating conditions made the work harder, and this snow person ended up much smaller. On her knees, with wet gloves and cold hands almost too numb to do the job, Megan set its little head in place.

Breathing hard, she staggered to her feet and studied her afternoon's labor with her hands on her hips.

She'd made a snow family.

A snow *family*. A snowman, a snow woman, and a snow child.

A sob tore up her throat and echoed into the stillness. What the hell was she thinking?

She stumbled, gasping at her own stupidity. The emotional scab ripped open. Hours of effort came undone. Her boot stuck in a deep drift and tripped her. Her body fell hard at the base of the snowman and her breath whooshed out. The sobs choked her as she crawled to her knees and slumped against the man. She yanked off a glove, needing to touch something he'd touched, something that had been his, but her frozen fingers could barely feel the soft cotton of John's favorite cabin-wear. She buried her face against the worn material. He'd been gone too long to be able to smell him on it, but that didn't keep her from inhaling deeply to try.

"Why did you leave me?" she wailed, her tears soaking through the cold shirt. "Why?" Her fists curled into the flannel. "I need you."

The wind swallowed her words and carried them away. John was gone. And they'd never have a family of their own. They never even had the chance.

CHAPTER TWO

"Merry Christmas," Megan murmured to the empty bedroom the next morning.

Gray light filtered through the two windows on either side of the king-sized bed, enough to illuminate the outlines of hundreds of glow-in-the-dark stars on the ceiling. She'd once remarked offhandedly that her favorite thing about spending time at their cabin was the huge glittered dome of the rural night sky. Up here, no city lights dimmed the stars' brilliance, so even the smallest, most distant ones beamed and twinkled. The next time they'd visited, John redecorated their bedroom ceiling. Just for her. He wanted her to have her stars, inside and out.

She didn't bother wishing on them anymore, though. Not in two years. Two years, today.

In spite of the circumstances, the holiday filled the air with a special, magical buzz that set her stomach to fluttery anticipation. A ridiculous reaction, of course, since she was alone. No surprise gifts or family-filled dinner awaited. Just a quiet, empty house.

Wallowing in bed all day sounded appealing, but a burning sensation on her cheek demanded attention. She patted the area. The skin felt rough, like a scab. *Lovely.* Turning back the cocoon of the thick down comforter, she slipped out of bed. She followed a path from one hooked scatter rug to the next, avoiding the cold, wide-planked wood floors.

The navy, mahogany, and white color scheme of the bedroom carried into the adjoining bathroom. Megan squinted against the brightness of the mounted light and leaned toward the mirror. Her left cheek bore the deep, dark red of frostnip. Her skin looked almost sunburned, except the angry mark was localized to the cheekbone. The spot where, yesterday, she'd leaned against the snowman, crying until the unceasing flow of her tears froze the wet flannel to her face. At least her nose and other cheek, pink from windburn, didn't hurt.

She gently prodded the mark with her fingers again. Last night, it had been cold to the touch, but now it was hot, chafed. So stupid. She slathered moisturizer over her face and smoothed ChapStick over her dry lips, and brushed and clipped her loose blonde curls on top of her head in a messy pile. What did her looks matter?

Megan slipped a pink fleece robe on over her flannel pajamas and threaded her way across the large great room, past the grouping of buttery leather couches and the floor-to-ceiling stone fireplace, to the open kitchen. Coffee was a must. She tapped her fingers on the counter as she waited for it to brew. Giving up, she walked around the long breakfast bar to the one concession she made to Christmas.

There, next to the raised stone hearth, a small potted Douglas fir stood in darkness. She reached behind and found the plug. A rainbow of colored lights shimmered to life, brightening the dim gray that still dominated the room despite the number of large windows. She stepped back and gazed at the small tree. Plain balls of every color mirrored the riot of lights, but the basic ornaments also spread an impersonal cast over the tree. She hadn't unpacked their collection of ornaments—where every one had meaning or told a story—since her last Christmas with John.

She turned away, sucked in a deep breath, and promised herself she wasn't going to think about that. Not until she had to. And she had almost eleven hours.

She curled into a wide armchair with a warm chenille throw and a mug of strong coffee. The ringing phone startled her and she almost spilled it in her lap. "Oh, hell," she murmured as she unburied herself and rushed for the cordless.

She knew who it would be before she answered.

"Merry Christmas, dear."

"Hey, Mom. Merry Christmas." She settled on the edge of her seat and dragged the blanket over her lap.

"How are you doing up there? The weather looks bad."

Her mom wasn't really worried about weather, today of all days, but Megan permitted her the ruse. "I'm just fine. It's been snowing steady. We've got well over two feet, I'd guess." An earlier peek out the front window revealed the storm had undone all her hard work from yesterday, reburying the stone sidewalk she'd shoveled. The snow family still stood there, though.

"I wish you weren't up there alone. You should be with us. Especially today. I mean, who's going to keep your father and brother from sneaking bites of ham and stealing cookies while I'm trying to cook?" Her chuckle sounded forced.

Restraining her emotions made Megan's throat tight. "I just…I'm not ready." Not ready to walk away from the annual holiday tradition of a cabin getaway she and John had created, even before they were married. Not ready to be around people actually happy it was Christmas. Not ready to pretend so others could be comfortable.

Her mother's sigh made its way down the line. "I know. I know you have to grieve, and I know how hard this has been. But, damn it, it's been two years. You're twenty-nine, Megan, so young, so much life ahead of you, so much to offer. You can't spend the rest of your life mourning John." She paused. "Nor would he want you to."

Megan forced her eyes to the ceiling to pinch off the threatening tears. "I'm trying, Mom. I am. But, please, I can't do this. Not today."

"I'm sorry. I told myself I wasn't going to say anything. I'm just so worried about you."

Megan nodded and swallowed around the lump in her throat, unable to do much more in the face of her mother's emotional outpouring.

"Oh, shit," her mother muttered.

"What happened?"

"That was uncharitable, wasn't it? Mrs. Cooke is tottering her way up the front sidewalk, annual fruitcake in hand."

"You need to go?" Their neighbor had been dropping by the inedible bricks since Megan was a kid, though this was probably the first time Megan felt grateful for it—Mrs. Cooke's timing provided the perfect distraction from this line of conversation.

"Yeah. I'm sorry, dear. Let me go help her. Your father hasn't been out to shovel yet, and God help me if she falls and breaks a hip on Christmas morning."

"Okay. Enjoy your fruitcake."

"Keep it up, smarty. I'll save you some."

Megan managed a small smile. "No, please. Don't do me any favors."

"I'll be thinking about you, Megan. I'll have Dad give you a call later." The squeak of her mom's front door sounded in the background. "Hello there, Mrs. Cooke."

Their quick good-byes overlapped their neighbor's high-pitched chatter. Megan could so easily imagine the scene unfolding at her parents' house. Christmas there was comfortably predictable. An enormous real tree filled the living room with the scent of fresh-cut pine. More decorations than a Hallmark store. Mrs. Cooke's visit. Her dad's buttermilk pancakes for anyone who had stayed the night before. The savory aroma of baking ham. A small army of visitors—Megan's older brother and sister with their spouses and kids, occasional aunts and uncles with their families, and even a few neighbors without other plans. Enough food to feed said army, and then some. A mountain of presents. More food. An evening of games around the big farmhouse table.

Much as she had always loved it, she couldn't face it. Not yet.

By ten in the morning, she'd talked to her sister Susan, amazed to learn her two nieces had been done opening presents for hours already, and her brother Aaron, who quickly handed her off to his wife. She liked Nora well enough and enjoyed talking to her, but knew her brother's cursory greeting stemmed from his continued discomfort around her. He didn't know how to make things better for her, and his instinct, as a man, as the big brother, was to *fix* it. Not being able to help her put him at a complete loss. Megan didn't hold it against him.

As noon approached, Megan talked herself into getting

dressed and having a bite to eat. She was about to dig into a bowl of chili and homemade cornbread when the phone rang again.

"Megs! Merry Christmas!" came her best friend's voice.

Megan smiled. Kate always did that for her. "Merry Christmas to you, too. You just wake up?"

"Damn straight. Well, Ryan woke me up with some yuletide cheer earlier, but we fell back to sleep after." Kate snorted.

"Aw, too much information, woman. I don't need to know about his little yuletide cheer."

"Who said it was little?"

"Argh. La-la-la, so not listening."

"All right, all right," Kate said. "So, how are you? The truth."

"Meh."

"That good, huh?"

"Pretty much."

"Oh, Megs, what the hell are you doin' way up there by yourself?"

"Honestly? I couldn't face Christmas at my parents'. I know they want me there, but I hate feeling like the elephant in the room. Everyone tiptoeing around me. It sucks."

"Big hairy balls."

"Exactly." Kate's goofy side had often been a lifesaver, but not today. Megan sighed. "I can't believe it's been two years."

"Me neither. It's so hard to imagine."

"They say the first year is the worst, because every sunrise represents the first time you experience that date without the person you lost." The first Valentine's without him, the first birthday without him, the first summer alone, the first Thanksgiving without him to be thankful for. The first Christmas. Megan stirred her cooling chili and struggled to put her thoughts into words. "But, honestly, the only thing different about the second year is you feel like you can't talk about it anymore. Everyone expects you to move on."

"You can always talk to me. You know that, right?"

"I do. Thanks." She huffed. "Jesus, I'm sorry to be so damn morose. Maybe we should talk about Ryan's yule log again."

Kate barked out a laugh. "Hmm...yes, that is a *big*, happy subject."

"Shit, on second thought."

They hung up with promises to talk later in the day. After.

Despite their joking, the honesty of the conversation chased away Megan's appetite. She wrapped the bread and chili for later and wandered around the cabin, relocating from one seat to another without any real purpose. A lull in the storm brightened the afternoon. Needing fresh air and a little distraction, Megan bundled up and shoveled the sidewalk for the second time, estimating perhaps ten new inches covered it.

She was officially snowed in.

As she stomped back up the cleared path, her eyes looked where her mind told them not to. The snow family remained, though the constant snow had weighed so heavily upon the woman's arms that they'd collapsed to her sides, her pink gloves presumably buried somewhere beneath the new snowfall. Megan frowned when she looked at the man. Both his hat and eyes were gone. Blown away or, like the gloves, buried.

Back inside, her eyes drifted where she didn't really want them to go, to the clock on the microwave. Little after four. Her stomach clenched. About two and a half hours until the anniversary came and went, until John had officially been gone for two years. She found herself glad she hadn't eaten that chili.

Mismatched picture frames drew her to the mantle. Smiling

faces shined out from the past. A candid of her whole family. Her and Susan kissing Aaron's cheeks at his wedding. Mom and Dad's portrait from their twentieth anniversary. And half a dozen shots of her and John — their wedding, skiing, her sitting on his lap. Happy and healthy. Alive. She turned away, but he was everywhere. In the rustic moose throw pillows he insisted they had to have, despite the fact no moose resided in these mountains. In the beautiful Mission-style lamps they found at an antique store outside D.C. In the stars on the bedroom ceiling, in the closet full of his clothes.

By five o'clock, the snowstorm returned with a vengeance, dumping more white fluff while the wind whipped through the surrounding trees. When the lights flickered for the first time, Megan groaned. No way the electricity would hold against the storm's relentless onslaught. At least she'd stocked the firewood rack when she first arrived. She built a strong fire, providing a blazing source of illumination should the lights fail completely.

The flickering continued at uneven intervals. She'd never seen the electricity falter so much without simply failing altogether. Despite the crackling heat of the fire, the great room air chilled. She tugged on a fleece hoodie and checked the thermostat. The LED screen flashed. She frowned as she reset the program, but the screen just kept flashing. Jeez. First the Freon leak in the air conditioning unit and now the heat was on the fritz. Not much she could do about it with this storm, though. She'd have to schedule a repairman before she headed back to D.C.

A fresh pot of coffee would ward off the chill. She wandered to the kitchen and froze. "What the hell?" All the LED screens — on the microwave, the oven, the coffeemaker, the digital alarm clock on the counter — blinked. Odd. Especially since the clock had a battery backup and, like the thermostat, the coffeemaker wouldn't reset.

A high-pitched tinkling, like a small ringing bell, sounded from somewhere outside. Goose bumps erupted over her arms. She didn't have a wind chime, and the next nearest house was over a half mile through the stand of trees to the west.

The hair on the back of her neck prickled.

She dashed to the entryway and peered through the glass panes on both sides of the door. Without light, her effort was useless. A wall of darkness swirled beyond the glass. She reached to the side and tripped the light switches, then turned back to the window.

A strangled scream stuck in her throat.

CHAPTER THREE

Out of the darkness, from the heart of the howling snowstorm, a hunched-over man staggered up Megan's front steps. She wrenched back from the door, her heart pounding in her chest. Panicked, she skittered behind a couch.

Who the hell could he be? Nobody could have walked or driven here in this weather. Her breath came in fast rasps. The lights flickered again, then again. Her eyes trailed to the fireplace tools on the hearth. Maybe she should grab the iron poker. Just in case.

The lights wavered, struggled to hold on. From outside, a solid, deadweight thump startled a gasp from Megan.

Help him.

The words were so quiet they might've been a thought, but in her current state she still whirled, fully expecting the impossible—that someone else was crouched next to her behind the sofa. Of course, she was alone. She peeked around the corner of the couch, her panic subsiding into a feeling of absurdity.

Help *who?* The man. Just a regular, ordinary man. Who must be in trouble. She remembered how he seemed to stumble on the steps and the thump. He'd fallen. She rushed from her hiding place like a sprinter at the sound of the gun. Peering through the sidelight, she whispered, "Oh, shit." She was right.

She tore open the door. Jesus, he was big. No one she knew from the neighborhood, though there were always tourists renting surrounding cabins to take advantage of Deep Creek Lake and the Wisp Ski Resort. God, he wasn't dressed to be out in this weather. No coat. No shoes. What the hell was she going to do with him?

Cold wind buffeted her and nipped at her skin, making her nearly frostbitten cheek tingle uncomfortably. Her hesitation wavered, then dropped away completely. What choice did she have? She couldn't leave him out in this blizzard.

The bitter wind sank into her bones as she stepped shoeless and coatless—like him—onto the porch. She didn't have to check for a pulse. Each shallow breath sent up a small fog from his mouth. Megan crouched behind his shoulders and wedged her hands underneath. Two fistfuls of red plaid flannel in hand, she pulled. He barely budged as she grunted and tugged. She tried two more times.

Shit, but it was mind-numbingly cold. "Come on, dude. Work with me, will ya?" she muttered, her hair whipping around her face.

Megan rethought the problem and stepped around to his bare feet. How could someone walk to this cabin without shoes? She shook her head and crouched, back facing him, between his legs. Securing an ankle under each armpit, she cupped his heels and pushed herself into a standing position. This time, when she moved, he moved. The guy was so big and heavy, she felt like

Rudolph pulling Santa's sleigh without the help of the other eight reindeer.

The warm air from inside the cabin embraced her body, its comforting tendrils drawing her over the threshold and into the slate-covered foyer. The lights flickered again, sending out a quiet electrical hum that raised the hair on her arms and the back of her neck. She tried to drag the man carefully, but his head still thumped as it crossed the shallow ridge of the doorjamb. She winced. "Sorry."

As soon as he was clear of the door, she set his feet down and ran to close it. The indoor temperature had probably dropped twenty degrees while she'd been outside figuring how to lug his sorry butt in. She engaged the dead bolt, and the lights died. She gasped and pivoted, flattened her back to the door. He lay, right where she left him, melting snow all over her hardwoods.

Knowing he needed warmth, she recommenced with the lift-and-drag routine until she had him right in front of the fireplace. The crisis of his exposure to the elements behind them, she looked him over more closely. The first thing her eyes latched onto was the shirt and scarf—John's clothing. The pieces she'd used on her snowman. Was it possible this guy had walked here…in what? The pair of faded jeans he wore and nothing else? And then…he'd grabbed the clothes in desperation before collapsing at her door? Everything about that was two kinds of strange.

Well, she wouldn't know anything for sure until he woke up and could tell her what had happened to him, so for now she'd concentrate on warming him back up.

She grabbed the thick chenille throws from the sofa and draped the first over his torso, tucking it as far under his body as she could. His crisp, clean scent, like snow on a spruce, filled her nose. Long as the blanket was, it still didn't reach below mid-shin.

With the second blanket, she started at his feet. Amazingly, while his feet were red, they didn't seem to suffer any of the telltale signs of serious frostbite. She wrapped his legs completely, trying to give him a little extra cushion against the floor's hardness. While she was at it, she sacrificed her comfy down pillow to the cause, flattening it out with her hands before sliding it under his head. His hair was a mess of longish strands that hung onto his forehead and down to his collar. It looked pitch black, but then it was also sopping wet.

Maybe she should call 9-1-1. Could an ambulance even get here in this weather? She shook her head.

Megan stood and stretched, admiring the man's surreal good looks. Even asleep, unconscious, whatever, the guy was ruggedly handsome. Mop of shiny black hair, strong brow, square jaw, fair skin, full red lips. A male Snow White.

Her eyes traced down. Very male. No wonder she hadn't been able to lift his shoulders. They were broad and well muscled, which the tight wrap of the blanket emphasized.

Jesus. She hugged herself. What was she doing? She was all alone, stranded in a blizzard, with a strange man in her cabin. A why-this-was-stupid ticker ran through her mind.

But did she have a choice?

୫୦୯୫

Hot. Too damn hot.

Sweat soaked into Owen's shirt and jeans, making the latter rough and heavy against his sensitive skin. His hair was heavy and damp where it covered his forehead. He tried to lift a hand to wipe his forehead, but it wouldn't move. Something restrained him. He struggled, moaned.

"Hey, hey, it's okay. You're okay."

Owen's eyes snapped open at the sound of her voice. An angel hovered over him in the darkness. He sucked in a breath and flew into a sitting position, tearing out from under the tight blankets. She gasped and yanked herself back from him.

"Where am I?" He looked down at his hands, turned them over, practiced flexing his fingers and making fists. He wiggled his toes against the weight of the blanket.

"You're at my cabin. I found you on my porch."

He dragged his gaze over her. The fire illuminated the halo of loose golden curls that framed her face and covered her shoulders, made her inquisitive blue eyes sparkle and dance. He frowned at the crimson puffiness of her cheek. His fingers itched to trace the wound. His lips puckered as he imagined kissing it. Her beauty reminded him of the first snowfall of winter—clean and new and bright. Full of possibility. Far from diminishing her, the injury highlighted her fairness by contrast.

"It's Christmas," he said.

She eyed him and nodded. "Uh, yeah."

He pushed the covers off his lap and yanked the suffocating wool from around his neck, relieved to be rid of their warm weight. The fire crackled beside him, drawing his gaze. He shrank back and swallowed thickly.

"How about something nice and warm to drink?" She rose to her feet, words spilling out of her in a rush. "I've, um, I've got a Coleman coffeepot just, uh, out in the garage. Operates on batteries, so—"

"I'd like something cold. If you don't mind." He followed her movements with his eyes. She was tall and thin. Too thin.

"Oh, okay. No problem." She turned and strode into the

kitchen.

Following her lead, he stood, testing his body, getting his bearings. He took a few tentative steps, enjoying the chill of the floor against his bare feet. He rolled his shoulders, twisted his neck from side to side. His muscles came to life as his body made its first halting movements.

He glanced to the kitchen and found her watching him. Her gaze lit on him like a caress.

"Want water, juice, or soda?" she called.

"Water, please."

She returned with the glass immediately. He downed the whole thing in one greedy gulp.

"May I have another? Colder, if you can?"

She gaped at him. "Ice?"

"Mmm, yes."

A blush bloomed on her face. Curious. He liked it. Wanted to touch the flushed skin.

She handed him his second glass and gestured to the couch. "Would you like to sit down?"

He took a smaller drink, his eyes following the sway of her hips as she walked around the sofa. After a moment, he joined her. The leather was cool and comfortable.

"So"—she clasped her hands together in her lap—"why were you out in this storm?"

He frowned. Tried to think. "I don't know." He couldn't remember much before waking to the vision of her over him.

"What? You mean, you don't remember?"

He dragged a hand through his wet hair. Concentrating made his head ache. "Uh, no, I guess not."

"Oh. Well, are you hurt anywhere?"

He looked himself over, moved the parts of his body in

sequence. "I don't think so."

"You collapsed on my porch. No shoes or coat."

The image of a swirling snowy nightscape flashed behind his eyes. He blinked, tried to hold on to the image. "I did?"

She nodded. Fidgeted with her fingers. Stuffed her hands between her thighs. "So, uh…"

He watched, fascinated by all her small nervous movements. Such a pretty woman. "Why are you here all alone on Christmas?"

She paled, her mouth dropping open. Then she gasped. "Oh, my God." Her eyes cut to the dark components under the TV. She cursed and flew from the couch. More curses came from the kitchen. He rose, regretting his question, and went to where she was rooting through a bag on the kitchen counter. She pulled out a small cell phone, pushed some buttons, then groaned. "Why is nothing working?"

"Can I help you?" A pit of guilt took root in his stomach. Though he didn't understand the urge, he would've done anything to ease her apparent panic.

"The time. Do you know the time?"

He shook his head. "Sorry."

"I can't have missed it. Please tell me I didn't miss it." She ran across the broad open space and disappeared into a dark room, then returned moments later carrying a small glass-domed clock with a shiny brass pendulum. She placed it on the stone hearth, face toward the undulating flames, and settled onto her knees.

Something stirred deep in his gut, niggled at the back of his mind. A feeling like déjà vu gripped him. His forehead ached as he struggled to concentrate, to make sense of the odd sensation.

A low moan yanked him out of his thoughts. The woman curled over the stone hearth in front of the clock, her head buried in her arms, her shoulders shaking.

Her tears called to him. Down deep, on some fundamental level of his psyche.

Just as he stepped toward her, images and words flooded his consciousness. The panel of gods, the pleading man. He sucked in a breath.

All at once, he remembered his purpose. He remembered himself.

CHAPTER FOUR

She'd missed it. She'd missed the anniversary of John's death. While she sat admiring *another* man in the cabin she'd only ever shared with John, 6:37 p.m. came and went.

Shame and guilt soured her stomach. She wept into the arms of her sweater. When she'd placed the battery-operated clock on the hearth, her pulse had raced in anticipation. And then the fire had flashed off the ornate brass face. The curling arrows of the hands pointed out 6:59. Her breath stuck in her chest as she clutched the glass casing in her hands. No. She couldn't have missed it. But the big hand snapped into its most upright position, chiding her as it signaled the top of the hour. And she'd lost it.

She'd missed the anniversary. For more than an hour, she'd forgotten it altogether.

Big hands squeezed her shoulders. "Megan?"

Her lips formed words, but she couldn't quiet her sobs enough to muster a response.

A thick thigh brushed her own as the stranger settled beside her. A large palm smoothed soft circles over her upper back.

I'm sorry, John. So, so sorry. I will never forget you. Never.

"I know," he said.

Megan whipped into a sitting position with her butt on her heels. "What did you say?"

"Nothing." The man dropped his hand and leaned an elbow back against the hearth. "I wasn't trying to be forward, I just hated seeing you cry after you've been so kind—"

"No, you said 'I know.'"

He shook his head and held up a hand. "I didn't say anything. Promise."

She buried her face in her hands, mumbled against her palms, "Oh God, I really *am* losing it." No. Wait a minute. She gasped and slapped her hands against her thighs. Her heart beat in her throat. "You said my name."

His red lips twisted. He narrowed his gaze, appraised her. But he didn't speak.

She scrambled to her feet, stepped back, fists clenched. "How do you know my name?" Her grief bloomed into rage, a white-hot maelstrom swelling in her chest.

In a blink, he stood. She wasn't short, but he towered over her. Dark eyes peeked out between his long black bangs. He held out a hand. "Megan—"

"No!" She skidded backward until she put the length of the leather sofa between them. "Were you..." She pointed toward the door. "How did you...I mean, what are you doing here? How do you know me? There's no way you just randomly appeared at my door, not in this weather." God, this was exactly what she'd worried about before she'd opened her door and dragged his sorry stalking butt in.

"You're right."

She gasped. "Oh, shit." She'd let a strange man into her cabin. A man who knew she was here, probably knew she was alone. The weather had her trapped, the power outage left her unable to call for help. Jesus, he knew her name. It was horrible to admit, but over the past two years she'd more than once flirted with thoughts of death, of joining John wherever he was. But now that her life was in danger, her soul screamed to survive. "What do you want?" Her voice trembled, cracked.

He shook his head, moved slowly toward her. "Please don't be frightened. I would never harm you."

She scoffed, circled the couch in the opposite direction. "I'm sure that's what all the serial killers say, right before they slam a bag over your head and stuff you in the back of a nondescript van."

They continued their tense dance around the couch until she stood closest to the fireplace. Blood pounded through her veins, whooshed through her ears. The fire popped behind her. The sound gave her an idea, and she whirled and grabbed the iron poker from the rack. She gripped it tightly to hide how much her hands trembled.

He held his palms up in the universal gesture of reassurance, but continued toward her. "I don't blame you for your fear, but tell me what I can do to allay it."

She brandished the poker in his direction. "Don't come any closer."

He didn't listen. "I'm here for you."

"What? Why? What does that even mean?" Poker held high, she stepped backward toward the couch.

His dark eyes blazed in the fire light. Their depths flashed with wisdom, purpose, setting off butterflies in her stomach.

"You're not ready for the rest yet."

She snorted, stepped backward again. "You suck at allaying fear."

One corner of his lip quirked up. He raised his shoulders. "I'm new at this."

"Whatever. It's time for you to go."

"You don't want me to go."

"Yeah, I really do." Wielding the poker with one hand, she pointed at the door with the other. "Out."

"Megan, if you'd just let me—"

"Out!" she shouted, waving the poker as she retreated from his continued advance. Her calves backed into something low. Her knees buckled and she waved her arms to maintain balance. The poker dropped, clanged against the hardwood.

Big hands wrapped around her waist, catching her from falling over the coffee table. Her heart thundered against her breastbone, making it hard to breathe. "No. No, no!" She pounded the man's broad chest. Forceful though her blows were, they made little impact against the firm muscles under the thin shirt. *John's* shirt.

"It's okay. It's okay." One arm still around her, he grabbed for her hands to prevent the pummeling.

She squirmed and pushed against him, punched, swatted her way out of his grasp. Her hand gripped the placket of John's shirt and wrenched at it. If he was going to hurt her, kill her, he wasn't going to do it wearing John's clothing. Two buttons popped off as the fabric gave way. She grunted and yanked again, feeling near crazed with her determination to get that shirt off him.

"Stop. Stop, it's okay." He released his grip on her waist and, with two hands, finally captured her wrists. She continued to struggle. "Please stop fighting me. I don't want to hurt you."

It's okay. The words curled around her body.

Megan whimpered. Her eyes locked onto the man's unmoving mouth. She'd heard the words, just like before, but this time she knew, she'd seen, that he wasn't the one who'd said them. The fight drained from her body. Grief and confusion swamped her. What was happening? Maybe you really could go crazy from grief. A sob tore from her lips just as her knees gave out.

The man caught her and lowered them to the floor.

෨ඏ

As he cradled her in his lap, Owen was torn between the intense pleasure of holding this woman close and a soul-deep yearning to ease her devastation. How could he make her understand?

He only knew he had to. It's why he was here. Why he'd been sent. Her acceptance was his greatest need.

He laid his cheek against the soft waves of her hair. "I'm here for you," he whispered. "Let me help." Her body heat felt like life against him, especially as his own body in this form possessed the same warmth—so unusual for him.

"I...don't...understand," she stuttered between shuddering breaths.

"I know."

"I thought you didn't remember anything."

He sighed and rubbed her back. "Talking to you, touching you, I'm starting to remember."

She leaned back, looked up. Her gaze scanned his face for a long moment. He hoped she found the sincerity he felt. "This is...I don't..." She shook her head. "You have to explain all...

this."

"I know. And I will."

His chest swelled at the cautious hope that framed her lovely face. "Promise?"

He nodded. "Yes. In time." He gently wiped the wetness from under her eyes, the simple act of providing care for another felt so odd, yet so welcomed. Her tears tingled against his skin, and he curled his hand into a fist, wanting to hold onto the curious sensation. As he studied her heart-shaped face framed by all that wavy gold, his lips twitched at the thought of kissing her wounded cheek. He wanted to make it better. To make it all better, for her.

Her gaze drifted down to the stretched and torn flannel. "I'm sorry."

"Don't be. It was your shirt anyway."

"Yes, about that."

He shrugged one shoulder. "It was there."

She rolled her eyes. "You are the master of the vague. You realize this, right?"

"If you say so." Her unexpected playful chiding appealed to him, made him want to push her so she'd keep pushing back.

"I really do." Her gaze fell to his chest. A blush colored her cheeks a sweet, sensual pink. "Um, sorry." She pushed off him, attempted to rise.

He helped her to her feet, his eyes trained on the pink, and yearned to know the meaning of it. The relaxed atmosphere between them disappeared. She crossed and uncrossed her arms.

He sighed, eager to ease her. "I will leave the cabin if you still want, but I won't leave you. I'll wait on the porch until you're more comfortable with my presence."

"You're not going to hurt me." Her tone was a mix between statement and question.

"Never."

"But, if you do, I reserve the right to make use of that poker."

"If I ever hurt you, I'd use it on myself."

Wary amusement played around her expressive eyes. "And you're going to explain… all this?"

He nodded and hope filled him with a wonderful feeling of levity. "Soon." Once he figured out *how* to explain it.

She groaned. "I can't believe I'm saying this, but you can stay."

A small victory. His first. "Good. I'd rather be with you."

She looked away to the fire. "M'kay. Well." She shifted her stance, once, twice, then stilled and cocked her head. "Since you're going to be staying and all, any chance you got a name?"

"Owen. Owen Winters." He stuffed his hands in his jeans pockets.

"Owen Winters."

He was immediately in love with the sound of his name rolling off her tongue. "That's me."

"All right, then, Owen, how about I get you some dry and, uh, not torn clothes?"

He nodded, enjoying the repetition of his name and taking in every small movement of her body, all long lines and curves where they counted. "That'd be great."

She grabbed a flashlight from a kitchen drawer and disappeared into the dark room where she'd found the clock. Her muttered musings warmed him with good humor, an unusual sensation in its own right. Gods, she made him feel so alive.

For good reason.

CHAPTER FIVE

Not letting herself think too much about what she was doing, Megan returned to the great room with a pile of clothes. Now that she was making nice with the guy, an unsettled flutter rippled through her stomach.

He accepted the items and looked around. "Thanks. Um, where—"

"Oh, right. Sorry. Here, take the flashlight. That door over there is the bathroom. I grabbed a bunch of stuff, not sure what you might want."

"Sounds good." The yellow glow of the flashlight swung back and forth as he crossed the great room to the single bathroom in the cabin.

As soon as the door closed behind him, she threw her head back and whispered to herself, and to who-the-heck-ever-else was listening, "What the hell is going on here? What the hell am I doing?"

This time, she listened for a response, but the oh-so-helpful

voice she'd been hearing, the one that encouraged her to accept
the stranger, remained quiet.

"Got nothing to say now, huh? Figures." She snorted.
Hearing voices was one thing, but talking back to them probably
hiked her up to a whole other level of psychosis. Awesome.

Across the room, the fire had settled into low-burning
embers. Since it was their only heat and light for the foreseeable
future, she piled on more logs, then sat back and stared as the
low flames erupted into a great blaze. The heat eased her aches.
Her muscles were still sore from yesterday. She was just weary.

Two years without him. Two-*plus* years without him, now.
But she was still here.

The bathroom door clicked open, and Megan turned her
gaze to find Owen in clean jeans and a short-sleeved black shirt.
The shirt was tight through the chest and shoulders, in a totally
good way. Jeez, did he look hot in black. Skin fair but not pale.
The dark eyes and long-layered jet hair swept over to one side
gave him a dangerous vibe. Though, he'd already proven he
wasn't. She was completely mystified by his presence, but there
was no denying he'd been gentle and respectful.

"Find something?" she asked.

He walked into the firelight and held out his hands. "Yes.
Thanks."

She pressed her lips together to restrain her smile.

"What?" He looked down at himself. "Oh." He stuck out a
white foot and made a face. "Little short."

"Yeah, just a bit." The jeans were about three inches too
short. John had been trim through the middle like Owen, but
definitely not as tall. "You didn't want the socks?"

"Nah, I'm good."

Megan pushed up from the hearth and stretched. "Can I get

you anything? Are you hungry?"

Owen rubbed his stomach. "I could eat."

Megan nodded toward the kitchen. "Let's see what I have. I can get the camping stove from the garage if you want something hot."

He followed her into the kitchen. "Don't go to any trouble."

Megan opened the refrigerator. She felt Owen's presence behind her, looming over her shoulder. "Uh, hand me the flashlight?" He pulled it from his back pocket, and she shined the light into the fridge. "Well, I can make turkey and cheese sandwiches and a salad. It's not fancy, but it's quick and easy."

"Sounds great."

Megan piled all the fixings onto the breakfast bar and collected plates and utensils. Busying her hands took her mind off how damn weird this all was. "Have a seat. More water?"

He settled onto one of the stools. "Yes, please. Can I help?"

"Sure." She poured them both glasses of water, lit a few candles on the bar, and sat on the stool next to Owen.

Outside, the wind howled against the side of the cabin. They prepared their meal in relative silence as Owen built the sandwiches and she chopped some veggies for the salad, only exchanging words to ask what the other wanted or liked. After a few minutes, working with him felt more comfortable, which was totally absurd given the situation. Something in her gut said to just go with it, so, for now, she would.

"Looks good." Owen lifted half a sandwich, took a big bite, and moaned.

The sound of his pleasure drew Megan's eyes. She swallowed, hard, and she hadn't even eaten anything yet. His obvious enjoyment of the food sharpened the angles on his face. Jeez, he was hot. She could hardly believe her own reaction, but there it was. This whole situation was so bizarre. "Glad you like it."

Owen finished his turkey and cheese and moved on to the salad before Megan had finished her first half.

"Hungry?" she asked.

"Starving."

"Been a while since you ate last, huh?" The words resonated with her. Having put the chili away earlier, this was actually her first meal of the day. God, her aborted lunch seemed like days ago, not hours.

Owen froze, his hand midway between the salad bowl and his mouth. "Huh. That, I can't remember."

Megan finished her sandwich, sneaking glances in Owen's direction every so often. Aside from eating a little fast, he was perfectly polite in his table manners. But for all the little moans and words of appreciation, he acted like he was dining on filet mignon. Megan's stomach flip-flopped. Having provided him with a meal he so obviously enjoyed set off a warmth in her chest. It had been a long time since she'd fixed a man a meal and watched him devour it, a long time since she'd felt that kind of satisfaction. A wave of guilt immediately washed away her pleasure. What was she doing?

When not a speck of food remained, he pushed his plate away. "Thank you for a great dinner."

She nodded. "You're easy to please."

"Just appreciative."

His intense gaze brushed over her face like a caress, raising the hair on her arms. The candlelight played games with his eye color. She couldn't quite make it out. But she didn't need more than the candlelight to admire Owen's rugged handsomeness. Her eyes couldn't decide whether to focus on his thick shoulders or smooth, square jaw. Her fingers nearly twitched to learn if his hair was as soft as it looked. She gripped her plate. She was lonely, just lonely. That's all this was.

"Now, you eat."

"I'm eating." She made a show of picking up her fork and taking a bite of salad.

"Good."

Under his intense observation, her face flamed hot. "You're watching me."

His eyes fixed on her mouth. "Mmhmm. You're nice to look at."

She shook her head and took another bite. All of a sudden, the candles made the dinner feel intimate, charged with some unnamed energy. It took concerted effort to stay on that stool, to not flee from his straightforward compliments, from her enjoyment of them.

"What happened to your cheek?"

"Oh, uh." Her fingers grazed the mark, which still tingled and was starting to itch. She waved her hand. "Nothing. Stupid."

He frowned. "I sincerely doubt that. Does it hurt?"

"Not too bad." She emptied her plate, tilted it toward him. "You approve?"

"Mmm. Very much so."

His words made her stomach flutter. What was wrong with her? She hopped off her stool and rounded the breakfast bar to escape his intensity. Grabbing the empty plates and perishables, she asked, "You have a sweet tooth?"

He cocked his head and narrowed his eyes.

His quizzical expression was so damn adorable. "You know, do you like sweet stuff? Desserts?"

"Oh. Like ice cream?" His dark gaze brightened.

Megan smiled, the rare expression drawn out by the

sincerity of his enthusiasm. "For one, yes."

"Aw, yes, ice cream, please."

She shook her head. "So easy to please." The flashlight revealed half gallons of chocolate chip cookie dough, chocolate chunk, mint chocolate chip, and peaches and cream. A girl alone in a cabin couldn't have too much ice cream. She turned to him for his preference.

"Scoop of each?" He rocked forward on his elbows like a kid hoping his mom would say yes.

It was such an incongruous action given his size and age—a little older than her, she guessed—that she laughed. She covered her mouth with her hand, unused to the sound, unfamiliar with the lightness of being it caused. "Okay," she finally managed. "Why not."

Bewildered by her own reactions, Megan chose peach for herself and prepared his sampler bowl. She nodded him over to the sofa with their dessert and curled into her favorite corner. How odd to be so comfortable with him when just an hour ago she'd been prepared to assault him with an iron poker. She couldn't explain it, but felt the rightness of it down deep.

80G8

Owen watched Megan's lithe form retreat from the kitchen before springing into action and following her. Her actions, her words, the flash of her blue eyes and heating of her soft cheeks—everything about her already intrigued him.

She was so much more than he'd been shown.

Bowl in hand, he sank into the opposite corner of the couch. He waited until she had her first spoonful, then dug into the ice cream with fervor. He tasted a little of each. The flavors exploded on his tongue, the cold creaminess filled him with strength. Gods, between the coldness and the sweetness, he couldn't get enough. He looked up when Megan chuckled. "What?"

"I take it the ice cream is a hit?"

Damn, what he wouldn't do to see more of that smile, reserved as it was. "So good." He stretched closer and peered in her bowl. "Is that the peach?"

She nodded and spooned the cream between her lush pink lips.

His spoon sagged in his hand as he watched. He stifled a groan when she licked her lips and he added another attribute to his newfound favorite dessert: dangerous. Because it made him want to throw his peach ice cream away in favor of tasting it from her tongue. He looked down into his bowl and decided to save the peach for last. So he could savor the same flavor coating the inside of her mouth.

Once he refocused on the ice cream, he became a man on a mission. He plowed through the mint, then the chocolate chunk, then the chocolate chip cookie dough—ice cream and cookies together? He was powerless to stop the little moans that escaped his throat as he ate. Between the dessert and his company, he was in heaven. Well, heaven on earth.

And, oh gods, the peach ice cream was the sweetest sin. The thought that *this* was what she tasted like, right now... He had to shift in his seat.

When had he last taken such pleasure in the world? In another being? He savored the dessert, forced his thoughts to focus on the goodness of it. Because the last thing he wanted was to focus on the answers to those questions.

When the scoops were all gone, he tilted his bowl to spoon

out the melted cream.

"You *so* want more."

Owen's gaze cut to Megan's face, painted with humor and a challenge to deny her words. He couldn't. "I do. But I'll hold off for now." He rubbed a hand over his stomach, stretched in satiation. Her smile grew, and it touched him in strange places. And he thought he'd enjoyed the ice cream.

She twisted her lips, but her eyes danced with amusement. "You sure?"

"For now."

"Okay." Megan carried their bowls to the sink and returned to the couch, picking up the discarded blankets in front of the fireplace as she moved. She curled back into her seat and draped a blue one over her lap. "So." She picked at an invisible thread in her lap. "Is it soon yet?"

"Soon?"

"Yeah, you know, you said I'd get some answers 'soon.'"

"Ah." Her expectant gaze pushed him to open up, no matter his hesitancy about overwhelming her by telling too much, too soon. "Well, what would you like to know?"

She stared at him a long moment. "How did you end up on my doorstep tonight? How did you know my name?" She scooted toward him as she spoke, readjusted the throw over her legs.

Owen debated, then took a leap of faith, hoping she'd leap with him. "I know what this sounds like, Megan, but I was sent here. For you." He released a deep breath. "A Christmas gift, of sorts."

She shook her head. Her brow furrowed over narrowed eyes. Her fingers massaged one temple. "What does that even mean?"

"Just what I said."

"But, who would send me a"—she gestured to his body—"man? As a Christmas present?"

He swept his hair back off his face. The breathy way her voice had lowered when she'd said "man" made it necessary to shift in his seat. Again. He dropped his hands to his lap. Damn borrowed jeans. "Well, when you say it like that, I might as well be the hired entertainment at a, uh, what do you call it? Oh, a bachelor party."

"I didn't mean it like that." She looked away and smiled. "And I think you mean bachelorette."

Soft pink bloomed over her cheeks. His fingers itched to know if the skin would feel as warm as it looked. "Perhaps. And, I know you didn't." The smile melted off his face as he recalled what he'd learned about her, *before* his arrival to this place. "You've had a rough go of it, Megan."

Her whole body stilled. "And you...*know*...about my rough time?"

"A little."

"Like you knew my name without my telling you?"

Owen nodded, appraised her reception of this information. Her thought process worked out in her facial expressions, but she wasn't running for the hills. Or grabbing the fire poker again. So far, so good.

"You realize this is all totally weird, and a little creepy?"

"I can see how you'd feel that. I'm not trying to frighten you, though, just being honest."

Megan traced a seam in the blanket, picked at it. "And, uh, how did you come about this information without my sharing it?"

"From a mutual friend."

"A mutual friend."

At the tremble in her voice, Owen moved closer on the couch and grabbed the hand twisting the fabric in her lap. He squeezed, hoping the gesture gave her some reassurance, then intertwined his fingers with her smaller ones. For a moment, he got lost in the sensation of touching her. His senses thrilled. She was so warm, so soft. His heart yearned. Amazing how important, how necessary, physical connection to another was to the soul.

Why had he denied himself this for so long? How many winters had he remained elemental to avoid the awkwardness and betrayal he'd been certain awaited his homecoming to the Realm of Gods? Isolation had become his own personal brand of hell. Made no difference that it had been self-imposed. Then, he'd felt he had no choice.

"And who might that be?" Her voice drew him from his thoughts. She brushed her thumb against the heel of his.

This was where it would get interesting. He took a deep breath, fully prepared to tell her the truth.

She scrambled up and jumped away from the couch. "What the hell? Again? Really? Now you have something to say? Get out of my head already!"

Alarmed, Owen sprung to his feet. "What's the matter?"

"Oh, nothing," she said, her voice shaky and exasperated. "Just going crazy over here. Don't mind me."

He rubbed his hands against her biceps, trying to ease her. "I don't—"

She waved a hand. "I know. Never mind." She sagged within his grip. "Apparently, I'm not *ready* for this conversation." She said the last part louder, and directed it out into the empty space of the room instead of to him.

Owen squeezed her arms, ignoring the physical urge to pull her into his, and bent down to look her in the eyes. "Okay, then. Well, you just let me know."

CHAPTER SIX

Megan stared at herself in the mirror, the flashlight throwing up a long oval of gold from its perch in the sink. She'd had enough weirdness for one day and promptly announced she was tired and going to bed after the annoying voice-from-beyond butted in with his two cents again. She froze. Since when had she decided the voice was a *him?*

She half believed she would wake up any minute and find this had all been one bizarre-o dream. Except for the little, er, big problem of the very real, very flesh-and-blood male currently parked on her couch for the night.

Peeking into the living room through the bathroom's connecting door, she called out, "You gonna be okay out there, Owen?"

He was lying on his back, long flannel-pajama-clad legs crossed at the ankle and arm up over his head. Cover off to the side. No shirt. Jeez, his chest was broad and defined, stomach cut with ridges of muscles. He turned a lazy gaze from the fire to where she stood in the doorway. "I'm good. Thank you, for everything."

Good, indeed. She'd never look at that couch the same way again. She hugged herself. "Okay, well, give a shout if you need anything, or just help yourself. G'night."

He nodded. "Good night, Megan."

Megan ducked back through the door, leaving that one open in case he needed the bathroom in the night. She trailed through the bathroom out to her bedroom—the cabin's only bedroom—and closed the door behind her.

She frowned. It locked from the inside, so there was no locking him out. Which, *hmm*, now that she thought about it, kinda negated the fact that she'd locked the main door to her bedroom.

"You better be right," she said, head tilted back to the ceiling. "It better be 'okay,' just like you said it would be." She stilled, listened. Of course. Never talkative when she wanted. Stupid voice. She climbed in bed and arranged the covers. "And don't even think of pulling any Dickens-esque ghost tour tonight, either. You'd be a day too late, anyway."

With a huff, she settled back into the pillows. Aah, so warm, so comfortable. God, she needed some rest. Everything would look clearer in the morning.

Her eyes trailed to the ceiling, but the glow-in-the-dark stars didn't shine tonight. There hadn't been enough light to set them to glowing for her. She felt John's presence anyway. Here, in this place that had always been just their own. "I miss you, John. I'm sorry there's a strange man in our house. But I couldn't leave him out in the storm, ya know? Hope you don't mind too much. He's kinda nice."

She turned on her side facing outward, punched the pillows

to get comfortable. Her mind wouldn't settle. She flipped to the other side. Closed her eyes. Concentrated on falling asleep, which chased it further away. She couldn't even pretend she didn't know what the problem was though, because she had no trouble concentrating on the man sleeping on her couch.

Owen. A complete stranger she'd met so recently she could count the hours on one hand. It was ridiculous she was giving him any special thought at all. But the more she told herself that, the more her brain conjured images of their evening together. The timbre of his voice complimenting her. The intensity of his dark gaze. Those little moans of pleasure he made over their dinner, and the ice cream. The way she forgot she was alone.

Owen made her think things, feel things, *want* things she hadn't allowed herself to even consider in the previous two years. Things in her darkest hours she couldn't have even conceived of having again. On the one hand, it felt like she'd just lost John yesterday. But, on the other, sometimes it felt like he'd been gone forever. Like maybe he'd never really been here at all. Was two years enough time to let her eyes—her heart— open to the world around her again?

"Stupid," she mumbled into the pillow. "Way to get ahead of yourself, Megs."

Sleep eluded her for a long time. She tossed and turned. Her ears strained to pick up any telltale signs of Owen's movement, but everything was quiet. At one point, she toyed with the idea of going out and stoking the fire. The air was downright cold, though she was comfortable in bed with the covers piled high and deep. With only those chenille blankets, though, Owen would get cold if the fire died completely, but she hated the possibility of waking him. Finally, she settled for just checking on him. If she could see he was asleep like he was supposed to be, maybe she could settle herself.

Megan crept from bed and threaded through the bathroom. She couldn't see his eyes from across the great room, so she tiptoed closer until she could confirm they were closed. His soft, slow breaths told her he was out. The chenille lay twisted around his calves and feet, leaving all that broad, toned flesh of his chest and abdomen exposed to the chilled air.

Her fingers itched to pull the cover up over him. Hmm. Probably overstepping. She nodded to herself and returned to bed. This time, she fell right to sleep.

ଓଓଔ

Her cries woke him. He flew into a sitting position and listened as she whimpered and called out plaintive, half-formed words.

Owen debated for only a moment before hauling himself off the sofa. He strained to read the clock on the hearth, and barely made out it was a little after two. Except for a few orange coals on the bottom, the fire had gone out.

In the darkness, Owen cut through the bathroom and pressed his ear against the door to her room. She let out a high-pitched cry. His chest tightened. He was here for her, and she needed him. Quietly, he turned the knob and stepped into her room. He stilled as he made out the arrangement of furniture. "Megan? You okay?" he whispered.

Just as he suspected, she was asleep. He padded around her bed and knelt beside it.

Her face was crumpled in anguish. The small, feminine hand that hung off the edge of the bed twitched and clenched. He grasped it with his own. Softly. Gently. "Sshh, angel. I've got you."

Her hand stilled, clutched back. The strained sounds quieted. Her face relaxed. That his touch soothed her ignited a satisfied warmth throughout his chest. He wanted to bring her solace, happiness. He wanted to be the *only* one to ever again do that for her. It was why he'd been made in this form. Why she'd made him. Even if she didn't know it yet.

For long, quiet moments, he studied her peaceful countenance. She was lovely, beautiful even, her complexion mirroring the peaches and cream they'd shared. Blonde waves surrounded her face in a soft frame and tumbled down over her shoulder. He longed to brush the stray curls off her forehead, her cheek.

His need to touch her further meant it was time for him to return to his own makeshift bed. A man of his word, he would bide his time, to the extent he could, and let her come to the realization that she needed him. As much as he needed her.

He carefully untangled his hand from hers, watching her face to make sure he wasn't disturbing her. Missing her touch instantly, he retreated. But as he reached the bathroom door, she exhaled a low moan. His heart seized. He froze, pulled in two directions. When she did it again, he simply couldn't leave.

He'd stay. Facing the bed, he laid himself on the floor as close as he could. He reached up, gently reclaimed her hand, and repositioned her just enough for the mattress to support their hands' weight. Resting his head on his folded right arm, he shifted until he was as comfortable as possible.

She was quiet again, peaceful. He smiled and closed his eyes.

ജ∞ന

Megan blinked into consciousness, luxuriating in some of the best sleep she'd had in ages. God, what a difference it made. She yawned, then rolled onto her back as a stretch gripped her muscles. Something warm and heavy restrained her hand. Megan looked down and gaped.

Stunned, she yanked her arm out from under the big masculine hand that could only belong to one person. She shifted to the bed's edge and peered over, knowing what she'd see but not understanding it. Owen. Stretched out along the whole length of her bed. Her eyes raked over his body, drinking in his tousled black hair, miles of bare skin and cut muscles, the black trail of curls that led down to his pajama bottoms, which had settled low on his hips. Dangerously low.

Damn. She couldn't have built a better model if she'd tried. Even in the dim pre-morning light, his physical perfection was obvious.

Movement drew her gaze back to his face and she blushed. Dark eyes blazed up at her. Totally busted.

"Morning." His sleepy voice was pure gravel.

"Morning. Um, what are you doing down there?"

"Don't be mad." He tugged his hair out of his face. "You were crying in your sleep, having a bad dream, I guess. But when I held your hand, you stopped."

Her heart expanded in her chest. He'd laid there all night? Just to ward off her nightmares? She wasn't sure how that made her feel, but certainly not mad. "I'm not mad, but how long have you been laying there?"

He eased up onto one elbow. "Came in around two."

"Owen!" She pushed into a sitting position. "You're been on the floor for hours? You must be freezing." Her brain finally moved past his beautiful near-nakedness to the realization that nothing separated his bare skin from the cold, hard wood or the unheated air. He didn't even have a pillow.

He rose to his feet, yanked at his hair again. "I'm sorry. I'll just..." He thumbed over his shoulder.

"No. I told you, I'm not mad. I just can't believe you slept on the floor all night. For me."

"You needed me."

Three simple words. She sucked in a breath. So much meaning, so much potential. She'd been alone so long. Her heart pounded against her chest, as if trying to get to him. As he stood, shuffling his feet and looking anxious, her world wobbled, then full-out tilted on its axis. She *did* need him. She knew it was crazy, that she could never explain it to someone who hadn't been here, but despite only knowing him for twelve hours, they had a connection. She felt it. And his words told her he did too.

She debated only for a moment. "I'm sure the fire's out by now, so get in. It'll be too cold out there."

He gaped. Rubbed his hand over his chest. "Uh—"

"We're adults. We can handle sleeping in the same bed." She yanked back the covers and patted the far side of the mattress.

He eyed the bed, then glanced back to her. "You're sure?" She nodded and he rounded the foot of the wide bed. The lean muscles of his abdomen and back rippled as he moved. He slid into the bed with such grace and ease of movement. Reaching down, he grasped the thin white sheet and pulled it to mid-chest.

"Don't want the blankets?"

"Nah, this is perfect." Lying on his side, he smiled and burrowed into his pillow. "Thank you."

"You're welcome," Megan murmured as she resettled on her side. facing him. She had to restrain herself from thinking of where Owen lay as "John's side." Damnit. She wasn't betraying him, was she? No. Her mother was right. John would want her to be happy. Megan knew that was true. She huffed out a breath. For God's sake, they were only sleeping together for a few hours, not walking down the aisle.

Sharing her bed—feeling the dip of the mattress that said you weren't alone, hearing the soft sound of another's breath, knowing you could reach out and find the warmth and companionship of another person—it was all oddly nice. That it was *this* person, Owen, well, that was nice, too. She allowed her gaze to cross the bed. Good God, that one lonely bare shoulder was a monument to masculinity. The fist tucked under his chin brought the image of Michelangelo's *David* to mind, with his big strong hand curled at his side. Who knew a man's hands could be so appealing?

"What?" he asked.

Her eyes flashed up to his. "Nothing."

Sleepy humor played at his lips. It was so damn sexy. "Okay." She shook her head against her pillow and closed her eyes.

"Hey, Megan?"

She peeked one lid open. "Hmm?"

"Can we have ice cream for breakfast?"

Her mouth curved into a grin. She couldn't think of anyone, save maybe Kate, who could draw a smile from her so quickly. But he was just unexpectedly adorable. "Maybe. If you're a good boy." She cringed. Why the hell did she say that? Was she...flirting with him? Restraining a grimace, she chanced a look at him.

His dark gaze shifted from playful to scorching. "And what would that entail?"

Heat shot through her body, and unfamiliar desire pooled in her belly. Flustered, she kicked off the top cover. "Not asking questions like that, to start. Now go back to sleep. It's too damn early to be awake." She heaved a deep breath to calm her racing heart.

"If you say so." Even with his eyes closed, a smile continued to play around his lips.

Once again, Megan had a hard time falling asleep. She longed for the deep, restorative sleep she'd had earlier in the night, but it eluded her. Then she suspected why. She debated. Chided herself. Minutes passed, her body stubbornly awake. Could it be so wrong to want a bit of comfort? Besides, she really needed to get more sleep if she was going to be able to sort all this out in the morning.

Slowly, so as not to shake the bed, she scooted closer, closer, until she could grasp Owen's hand where it stuck out from underneath the pillow. She rolled onto her stomach so she didn't have to get *too* close, but found herself in the middle of the mattress before she could comfortably touch him again. She settled her palm over his palm, laced her thumb around his.

His eyes flashed open. The same heat and intensity blazed out of them. He squeezed her hand, winked at her, then closed his now-satisfied eyes again.

His acceptance of her touch and obvious enjoyment of it settled over her like the warmth of a freshly stoked fire after being out in the snow, all comforting and tantalizing where it soaked into cool skin. More than anything, his touch soothed her, grounded her. She slid off into an unusually restful sleep.

She did dream, but this time not of Christmas night accidents that turned her life upside down. This time she dreamed of Owen. Running through a snowy field, his legs fast and agile despite the deep wind-blown drifts. His completely delighted face as he collapsed into the snow while she pummeled him with snow balls. Him building an igloo in her front yard. Them sitting together eating big bowls of dessert inside the ice-block house.

Then, in that screwy way dreams veer off course, the mystery voice returned. *Good idea*, it said, inserting itself into her dream. *Owen needs the snow. You must take care of him. You must choose him. Before the snow melts.*

CHAPTER SEVEN

Megan awoke content and energized. God, sleep was a wonder drug. When had she last felt so good, so clear-headed, so light in her own skin?

"Morning, again."

Her gaze flashed across the bed to find Owen staring at her. A blush stole across her cheeks, the heat of it all the more pronounced in the chilly air. "Morning. For real, this time."

In the light of day, she drank him in, first noticing the warm brown eye peeking out from where he was still buried in the pillow. Megan yearned to comb his hair off his face, to push back the shiny, black disarray of long, layered strands covering his forehead. The urge made her distinctly aware her hand remained curled around his. She didn't want to release him, though, because she liked the feeling of being touched, of touching.

She thought back to yesterday, of waking up to the utter aloneness of Christmas morning. Never could she have imagined how different this morning would be.

"Is this a dream?" The words spilled from her mouth.

Owen's grip on her hand tightened, that lone dark eye trapped her with its serious intensity. "Waking up across from you is the stuff of which dreams are made. But, no."

Her heart skipped, took off at a sprint. She half expected a playful grin, an amused response. Instead, his solemnity brought her back to last night's conversation. Owen wasn't playing; her gut told her he was being honest. She held her breath and let it out with a question of equal earnestness. "Are you real?"

"Yes."

Megan's respiration joined her heart in the race. She swallowed thickly. "Am I going crazy?"

"Of course not." Concern shadowed his expression. "The situation is a little unusual, but you're in your right mind."

She licked her lips. "And, what's 'the situation'?"

"You and me."

Red lips curled around the words, drawing her gaze. Her mouth went dry. The urge to taste that full bottom lip ripped through her. "You and me," she managed. She hoped he didn't notice the breathy tremble of her voice.

He nodded against his pillow. "You and me."

She chuffed out a laugh. "Still the master of the vague."

Owen shrugged a shoulder. Defined muscles bulged with the movement. "You really want me to spell it out?"

Megan gulped. Did she? *Was* she ready to fully understand what was going on? Holding her breath, she said, "Yes."

"I'm here for you, Megan. Because of you. You need me —"

"You don't even know me."

His dark gaze bored into her. "Don't I?"

Tiny hairs raised all across her body. Owen had known her

name, about her rough times. What else did he know? And how? Who was this mutual friend?

Before she had a chance to think through a response, he spoke again. "I need you, too."

Pinpricks tingled across her scalp. "Why?" she whispered.

"Because you're the one who brought me here, who made me real. After a very long time."

Electricity sizzled in the air. She gasped for breath, sat up, and hugged her knees to stop the room from spinning. Her hand felt uncomfortably cold without the warmth of his grasp. "I don't…I…" She shook her head.

"I know." He sat up next to her. "Hey, guess what time it is?"

"What?" She chanced a glance his way.

Owen smiled. "It's time for more ice cream."

One beat passed. Then another. Finally, Megan chuckled. Ice cream. Tried. True. Real. Tangible. Not at all confusing or weird. She nodded, despite her brain's inability to understand what the heck was happening. "Yeah, okay. Let's have ice cream."

Without waiting for him to respond, she slipped out of bed, needing a break from the mystery. And from the lure of his lips, and that damned shoulder.

When she shut the bathroom doors, she found herself in darkness. In the sunny morning brightness of the bedroom, she'd forgotten about the power outage. Her first job after getting dressed would be hand-to-hand combat with the generator. Why they hadn't bought a push-button-start unit, she still didn't understand. The hand-pull unit had been fifty dollars cheaper, and John wanted the full manly-man experience while they were up in the mountains. That'd been fine when he'd been here. Now, she had to fight the hand-pull, which was so much trouble she almost never bothered unless the need for power became urgent. It was. They wouldn't have heat, lights, running water, or hot food without it.

She wished the power would just come back on.

In the meantime, she needed a flashlight by which to do her bathroom business. She felt her way to the door handle. Found it. When she pulled the door open, the lights were on.

The Christmas tree. The recessed lighting in the kitchen, over the fireplace, in the foyer. The Mission-style lamp on the side table. The fridge rattled to life. A low hum precipitated the return of the heat, and she grinned as warmth blew against her back from the bathroom register.

Unreasonable happiness gripped her as she returned to the bathroom. Could this day get any better? Positivity coursed through her, made her believe she could climb a mountain. The feeling was all the stronger for how long it had been since she'd last experienced anything like it.

Still, she had good reason for a little cheer, a little positivity. The storm had passed. The sun shone brightly. The power returned in time to save her from wrenching her shoulder on the generator. She'd shared her bed with a beautiful man.

She paused with the toothbrush halfway to her mouth. Three parts of her psyche played internal tug-o-war. The woman in her *wanted*. Knew that beautiful man would give her anything she asked. He was here *for her*, after all. Whatever that meant. The wife in her wanted to flee. She'd loved John. Some part of her would always love him. The widow in her struggled to make sense of it all, to wade through the need the woman's feelings created, to stem the wife's guilt and fear of betrayal.

"Any words of wisdom this morning?" she asked the room,

waited, then rolled her eyes. "Course not." She popped the toothbrush in her mouth and finished freshening up, glad for the return of the hot water. She fussed at her hair, trying to get errant curls back in line. No way was she letting herself think about the fact she was putting considerably more time into her appearance than she had yesterday. The frostnip blared out from her cheek, still dark red and now scabbing. She groaned. Resisted scratching at it. Wished it would go away.

Back in the bedroom, she found the bed empty. She stepped into slippers and her soft pink robe, then shuffled out to the kitchen. Owen was leaning against the counter, arms folded across his chest, waiting for her.

Megan almost pouted at the reappearance of the black T-shirt covering his body, but a chuckle bubbled out at the sight of two bowls, two spoons, and four half gallons of ice cream lined up on the kitchen counter. "What do you want for breakfast?" she deadpanned.

His brow furrowed. He looked from her to the ice cream and back. "I thought…"

She patted his arm. All solid muscle. "Just teasing. Dig in." God, he had the most amazing buoying effect on her emotions, her disposition.

Owen's expression brightened. He rubbed his hands together and ripped the lids off each carton.

She chuckled at his enthusiasm and prepared some coffee. "Want some?"

"Hmm?" He turned to look at what she was doing. "Oh. No. Thanks."

"I can't wake up without coffee." She set out a coffee mug, then leaned against the counter near him. "You having some of each again?"

"Nope." He scooped, then scooped again.

Curious, she peered over his arm into the bowl. Mint chocolate chip and peach today. She smiled up at him.

Sucking a bit of ice cream off one finger, he asked, "What?"

Her breathing stuttered at the thought of tasting the sweet cream off his skin. "Nothing."

"No, tell me." He stepped closer.

She shook her head. "Why mint and peach?"

He quirked a crooked smile. "Mint for fresh breath, peach because it's breakfast. You know, fruit."

"I don't think peach ice cream counts as fruit."

"What's that right there?" He pointed to the hunks of frozen orange buried in the mounds of ice cream overflowing his bowl.

"Peach, but—"

"Nuh uh. No but. It's peach. Case closed." He lifted the bowl and took a big bite.

When he started with the little moans again, she had to turn away.

"What flavor can I get you?" he asked between bites.

She glanced over her shoulder. Met his playful, satisfied gaze. His dark eyes peeked out between strands of black hair, waiting, expectant. She turned back to pouring a cup of coffee. "Peach. It's breakfast, after all."

"Now you're talking."

With a steamy cup of warmth in hand, she turned and found him holding a bowl out to her, the peach ice cream mounded up over the top. "Owen!"

"What?" His face was all innocence.

"I'll never eat all that."

He grinned. "Sure you will."

"It's breakfast." She accepted the bowl, peered down into it. Four scoops!

"I know. Most important meal of the day, isn't that what they say?" He spooned some mint into his mouth and nudged her shoulder with his arm.

"Ice cream's not a meal."

He swallowed. "Says who? Tastes like a meal to me." A bit of mint cream clung to his bottom lip.

"You're impossible."

"I'm here, aren't I? Totally possible."

Butterflies took flight in her stomach. She wouldn't win this. Didn't want to, really. She rounded the counter and perched on a stool at the breakfast bar. He followed her lead and joined her.

They gorged themselves on ice cream in relative silence. Well, she was silent. His small rapturous moans and groans echoed around the room. Jeez, if he took this much pleasure from a bowl of Edy's, what kind of sounds would he make in bed?

The hand holding her spoon froze halfway to her mouth and her cheeks went hot at the thought. Lost in her imagining and totally shocked by her body's ability to leap there, she jumped when Owen's fingers brushed her flaming cheekbone.

ဆဩ

Owen stroked her uninjured cheek once, twice, then dropped his hand. "What caused this? It's lovely." Gods, her skin was so soft. He wanted to explore every inch of it.

She squirmed under his gaze, shifted on her stool, stirred her ice cream. Fascinating. As he ate, he drank in each of her small movements, tried to decipher them. Her silence made him smile.

With two final spoonfuls, his bowl emptied. He hummed in satisfaction as he pushed it away. Thought about how soon they might be able to have more. Turning in his chair, he surveyed the sky through the large front windows. "Looks like the storm passed."

"Yeah."

The fresh, clean snowfall called to him. "Want to go for a walk after breakfast?"

She pushed her bowl away and swiveled toward him. "Sure, although I don't know how much walking we'll be able to do. Probably three feet of snow out there."

"Mmhmm." He could take care of that. Grabbing his bowl, he rose and rounded the counter. "Any chance you have more clothes I could borrow? Maybe some boots, a coat?" The jeans he'd shown up in last night were still wet, and though he didn't really need the layers, she'd expect him to wear *something*.

"Well, yeah, but what are you—"

"You get showered and dressed, and I'll shovel a path. We'll take it from there."

"You don't have to do that."

"I like to shovel snow, actually. I'm at home in the snow."

"All right." She hopped off the stool and stowed her empty bowl in the sink.

Pleasure rippled through him at the thought she'd eaten the huge serving he'd prepared, that her mouth was filled with the same flavor as his own.

"Come with me. I'll show you what I have, and you can pick whatever you think will fit." She led him back to the bedroom.

He fell in love with the thin knit of her pink robe. Tied

tight around her waist, it hugged her bottom. Her swaying hips held his gaze, taunted him. Everything about her appealed to him. Yet, his attraction was so much more than physical. In her grief and loneliness, Owen saw himself. Somehow, knowing she understood—no matter how much he hated her pain and ached to ease it—made his own easier to bear.

He was so glad he'd been asked to come to her. So glad he'd agreed. The idea it might've been someone else sparked a ripple of dark power that shuddered down his spine. A lone gust of wind whipped around the house. He shook his head and focused on how right it felt to be with her. She was his. At least, he hoped she would be.

In the bedroom, Megan yanked open the folding closet doors. Hesitated.

Her awkward, halting movements concerned him, and he grappled with what to say. He hadn't thought about her feelings when he'd asked to borrow more of John's clothes.

"Well"—she fingered over the hanging flannels, button-downs, and pants—"there's plenty of long-sleeved shirts. Some jeans and sweatpants. Couple of different boots you can try." She pointed at the floor, where four pairs of snow and hiking boots sat in a neat line. "And then"—she trailed across the room to the long, low dresser—"this drawer has T-shirts, and this drawer has socks and some longjohns." She turned to him, but didn't meet his gaze. "Coats are out in the front closet. Use whatever you want."

He stepped to her. His hands rose of their own volition to rub her arms. "I can just stick with what you've already given me. It's okay."

Her gaze flashed up to his. She shrugged. Looked away again. "Nobody's using them. You might as well."

His heart clenched at her eyes' glassiness. "Thank you."

She waved him off. "Well, I'm gonna grab a shower."

"Take your time."

She collected some clothes and disappeared into the bathroom.

He turned to the closet. All the pants would be too short, so he grabbed the first thing his hands landed on, a pair of black flannel-lined snow pants. He would be hot in them, but he decided to keep up appearances. For now. Soon he was dressed and out the front door.

Cold air blasted him when he stepped onto the porch. He held his arms out, tilted his head back, and sucked the winter wind into his lungs, one deep breath after another. It smelled like home, fortified his body with its frostiness. Made all these layers bearable.

He grabbed the shovel from its perch against the front of the cabin and cleared the drifted snow from the porch and steps. Hesitating, Owen looked over his shoulder. He had to be sure. He jogged up the steps, poked his head through the door, and listened. The whine of the plumbing told him she was still in the shower. He might be able to get away with this after all.

He set the shovel aside.

Standing on the bottom step, he reached out and touched the snow. On his command, a gust of white powder erupted, lifting itself from the stone path and scattering over the surrounding drifts.

The entire front walkway cleared before his eyes.

Chapter Eight

"Humanity agrees with you," came a deep voice.

Owen's eyes flared as he whirled toward the sound of the voice. "Boreas." He dropped to one knee, bowed his head before the Supreme God of Winter, the same god who had been the closest thing to a father he'd ever known.

A gust of wind ruffled his hair. "Rise, Owen."

Owen rose to his full height. Boreas hovered over the snow before him, agitation rolling off him in little wispy snowdevils.

Unease and confusion clenched in Owen's gut. He'd been with Megan less than a day, so why… "What brings you, my Lord?"

"I wanted to see how you fared with the female." Being the oldest of the four cardinal Anemoi showed in the white hair and beard that swirled against the robe of skins Boreas wore.

Owen crossed his arms. "Well enough, I think."

Boreas's silver eyes flashed and good humor momentarily shaped his face. "Good to hear." He frowned again. His enormous height seemed to float over the snow's surface until he paused next to the remains of Megan's snow woman. He heaved a sigh. "Chione has left Ular."

Owen grimaced at the mention of his long-ago fiancée, and mashed his lips together to keep from asking why he was supposed to care. Chione was Boreas' daughter, after all, and Owen owed the god his respect and civility. Still, he couldn't restrain the words, "For whom?"

Boreas' chuckle was without humor. The Supreme God's metallic gaze cut to him. "You know her well. Yes?" He turned away. "For Koli."

"Gods," Owen bit out. He had no love for the Norse snow god Ular, not after he'd warmed Chione's bed knowing that privilege should have been Owen's alone, but Ular didn't need another reason to feud with Koliada, the Russian solstice god. Their eons-old animosity was the stuff of legend. Few even knew the origins of it. "Well, I'd say Ular just met karma."

"Hmm. Indeed."

Now Owen was more confused than he'd been when Boreas first appeared. Did his once future father-in-law think he'd care about the machinations of his daughter after everything she'd put Owen through? He asked even though he really didn't want to know. "Why do you tell me this?"

Boreas skimmed over the snow toward Owen, his silver eyes flaring with an anger Owen didn't understand. The younger man wasn't used to feeling small, but between Boreas' immense physicality and barely harnessed powers, it could hardly be avoided. "You do not have much time," he growled.

"What?" Owen frowned, held out his arms, gesturing to the blanket of snow that spread as far as the eye could see. "How can that be? This snow will last for weeks—"

"It should have. It was a good snow. But Zephyros ran into Hy at the solstice celebration, and that set him off. Again. This time, he's unleashed a powerful West Wind, one that will drive a warm front through before week's end. This is why I've come. To warn you."

The news lanced through Owen. Week's end. It was already Monday morning. Not enough time. He couldn't expect Megan's feelings to bloom for him so quickly. Gods. "Can you stall it?"

"I will try. But you know of my brother's growing power," Boreas groused. Every year Zeph tried to bring the warmth and green of spring sooner. It was a power struggle the gods of winter had been steadily losing a bit at a time for the last half century. And Zephyros' generations-long foul mood made it impossible to reason with him. But this was something else. Nothing enraged the Supreme God of Spring into unleashing savage weather like a run-in with his ex-lover.

Owen tugged at his hair. Damn Zeph. Greedy son of a goddess. In any other circumstances, Owen would've been sympathetic. If anyone understood the kind of betrayal Owen had suffered, it was Zephyros. Several times over. So Owen usually empathized with rather than resented those moments when he let loose bursts of his enormous power to vent his turmoil. But, this time, Owen's chance at happiness had gotten caught in the crossfire. "Can Chrysander help?"

Boreas flashed a wry grin. The Supreme God of the Summer was the youngest and most jovial of the Anemoi and had a knack for disarming feuds between them. "It is summer in Rio, Owen."

"Right." Boreas' brevity on the subject was shorthand for 'Chrys is enjoying his fill of Brazil's nude sun worshippers, which you should know.' Owen rolled his eyes and looked away.

Well, there went his last hope. Gods knew Eurus, Boreas' final brother, was off the table as an ally. Owen couldn't recall the last civil conversation that had taken place between Eurus and the rest of his brothers.

So be it. All it meant was he had no time to stand around complaining about the games of gods. He needed to concentrate on Megan, on making her fall in love with him. He bowed to his god. "Thank you." Owen waited for Boreas to dismiss him before standing straight. He gasped when he felt Boreas's hand on his head, a true, rare honor. "My Lord?"

"I did you a great disservice, Owen."

Owen stilled. For the life of him, he couldn't think of a response to such an unexpected admission.

Boreas continued, "I should have warned you about Chione. Instead, I helped her make you think you were her first suitor, her first pairing. There were others. Before you. She'd kept them secret." He sighed, a tired sound full of regret. "When you have a child, you cannot help but give her the benefit of the doubt. Protect and safeguard her. But Chione has proven herself incapable of commitment. Her heart is ice. She was different with you, though, and your powers were so strong. You held your own against her, met her as an equal. So I gave in to her pleas to hide her past after I'd learned of it."

Eyes still downcast, Owen seethed. A cutting wind whipped around the house. Whiteout conditions surrounded the pair of gods. Owen's rage. Betrayed. Again. By the god he'd served with faith and loyalty, to whom he'd devoted his existence, considered as a father. His fists clenched.

"I was in the wrong. But you are better off. Here. Now. With this female. If John Snow's memories are any guide, she is worthy of you. It is why I summoned you back to answer John's appeal. If anyone could understand the pain of loneliness, it is the two of you."

Owen's gaze flashed to Boreas' face. For a moment the older god appeared haggard, deep creases carved into his timeless countenance. It took the sharpest edges off Owen's outrage.

Now he understood why Boreas called him back from his long self-exile when John begged for assistance. Now Boreas' care and interest made sense. It truly was atonement. Not just for Chione. But for himself, for his own role in Owen's betrayal and subsequent long absence from the Realm of Gods. And he'd admitted wrongdoing. The major gods rarely deigned to do so.

"Thank you for your honesty," Owen managed.

"It was long overdue. I want you to have this chance, Owen, which is why I'd like to give my brother a good thrashing right now."

Owen nodded once, let his black hair cover his eyes. The competitive posturing between the Anemoi often struck him as entertaining good sport, but not today. Not at his expense.

"Go to her. Win her heart. I will help you as I can. But you must not delay."

"Yes," he said, waiting. He could not turn his back on Boreas, or dismiss himself from the god's presence.

All at once, the wind and snow calmed. The sun-kissed sky returned, clear and bright. Boreas had sucked the energy out of Owen's storm upon his silent departure.

Owen paced the length of the stone walk, covered over again from the whirlwind he'd whipped up.

Boreas' revelations resurrected memories better left forgotten. Owen rolled his neck, seeking calm, wanting to return to the excitement he'd felt before over Megan. The golden curls, the pink cheeks, the uplifting sound of her too-rare laughter. He wanted to concentrate on her, think of her. Not the past. He'd wasted too much time wallowing there already.

What should've been weeks of time courting Megan, winning her affection—*earning* it—was now four days. Four days.

Disappointment and longing squeezed in Owen's chest. Megan could make him happy. No, she *did* make him happy. Already, her companionship, her warmth and kindness, eased him. Her own pain called to the protector in him, gave him purpose—easing *her*. He could make her happy in return.

But, unlike Megan, Owen had the advantage of time and forethought. John's memories of her were now his own. In the days before he'd become corporeal, as he'd prepared the snow that made his presence here possible, he'd observed her, learned for himself what a beautiful, intriguing creature she was. Now, having met her, touched her, held her in his arms, he knew. He wanted her *for her*, not just for the possibility of happiness and companionship she'd represented as he'd stood before the panel of gods and agreed to help John Snow.

Four days, then. There was still a chance. And that was more than he'd had in a very long time.

Resolve grew in Owen's gut. The need to see her, to be in her presence again, panged against his heart. He released a long, calming breath.

With a wave of his hand, he swept the thin, trampled covering of snow from the stone walkway. The crystals swirled and shimmered in the morning sunlight. He was ready. He'd give her the world today, his world.

CHAPTER NINE

"What did you do?"

Owen whirled at the sound of Megan's voice. "Hey. Uh, I'm done."

"I see that." She took slow, halting steps across the porch, down the steps. She tugged her zipper up in almost slow motion as she gaped at the sidewalk.

He breathed in her vanilla scent as she scooted around him. He thought of ice cream and bit back a groan. The sun illuminated her golden waves, secured back from her face with a rectangular gold clip. Stray curls framed her face, blew across her cheeks. Her eyes were bright, skin still pinked from the heat of the shower. She could've been the famed Snow Maiden, brought to life once again. The stress of Boreas' revelations ebbed in her presence.

"But how did you get so much cleared already?"

"Told you I liked to shovel."

"Uh huh." She looked back and forth, once, twice, her eyes

wide. "But, how did you get it *so* clear?"

Damn. From steps to driveway, there wasn't more than a dusting of snow left. Hadn't given that enough thought. Clearly. He tugged a hand through his hair. "It's all in the wrist."

She eyed him, her gaze skeptical and amused. "You're so full of shit. You even did in front of the garage doors. How the hell long was I in the shower?"

He leaned around her. Apparently, he'd put a little too much force into his command. "I, uh, I don't know." He kicked at the edged wall of snow along the sidewalk. A clump stuck to the toe of his boot.

"Well, thank you." The expression on her face flooded his chest with warmth. He adored her smiling. "Hey." She stepped closer. "Your eyes."

He looked down and his hair fell over his forehead, covered one eye. "Oh. Yeah." He wouldn't say anything more. She'd put it together for herself in her own time. That was the most likely way to obtain her belief, acceptance.

She brushed his hair back and studied him, wonder playing around her pink lips. "They're different colors. I didn't realize it 'til now."

The heat from her body radiated over him, she stood so close. Despite the gloves she wore, her touch blazed through his skin. He held himself still lest he reach out and collect her to him, like his body screamed for him to do.

"One brown, one blue," she mused. "So cool."

He remained still, not wanting to discourage her continued touch. So close. All he would have to do is lean down...

All at once, she dropped her hand.

Disappointment and need tore through him as she put a little distance between them. He turned his gaze away and looked out over the pristine landscape. "Beautiful country," he murmured.

"Mmm. Been coming up here since college. Actually met my husband at Wisp. The ski resort." She hugged herself.

His arms ached to embrace her, but he wanted her to share her story. Even though he knew a lot of it.

Megan stared off into the distance. "He died. Two years ago." Her gaze cut to him. "But then, you knew that, right?"

Owen's heart rate ticked up. He hesitated for only a moment, nodded.

Her baby blues held him in place. "Did you know it was my fault?"

The words struck him like a kick to the gut. Never. She could never be responsible for someone's death. And John's memories showed nothing of the sort. "No—"

"Well, it was." The iciness of her voice was so wrong, so unlike her.

"Megan—"

"It was Christmas night. I'd forgotten the eggnog. I acted like I wasn't disappointed, but John could read me so well. So he ran to the store for me. Three blocks from our house, a drunk driver ran a red light and broadsided him. He never had a chance." Her gaze swept back out over the snow. "He died, at the age of thirty-one. Because I wanted eggnog." One tear stole down over her injured cheek.

Between her words and her tears, Owen couldn't hold back. Grabbing the sleeve of her jacket, he tugged her into his arms. She held herself rigid for a long moment, then her body melted against his chest. At first she restrained the tears, but they finally broke through, soaking his turtleneck and from there, through to his bare skin.

He moaned and hugged her tighter, the life force of her tears jolting through him, seizing his heart, igniting a primal urge to protect her, defend her. Even from herself. "You listen to me, Megan," he said into her silky blonde waves, his voice gruff. "You wanting eggnog did *not* kill John." She shook her head, but didn't voice her protest. "No. John died because some other person made poor choices and demonstrated a lack of judgment. Got into a car he had no business driving in such an impaired state. That had nothing to do with you."

"He...wouldn't have...been there...if I hadn't asked him to go," she wailed. Her hands tugged at his shirt.

He sucked in a deep breath. "Trust me when I say this. Are you listening?"

She nodded against him.

"There is nothing, *nothing* that man wouldn't have done for you. You couldn't have stopped him from trying to make you happy. Am I right?"

"Yes."

"He doesn't blame you, Megan. He would never blame you."

Her shoulders shook within his arms' embrace. Her arms went around his back, held tight. She literally clung to him. He would've gloried in the sensation if her anguish hadn't been pouring into him through her tears.

"Sshh, angel. I've got you." He kissed her hair. His lips begged for more, for him to keep going, keep kissing, but he held back.

"How...how do you know?"

"Know what?"

"That he doesn't blame me. How can you know that?" She lifted her head and searched his eyes with her plaintive gaze.

"I know things."

She closed her red-rimmed, watery eyes and shook her head. "Mutual friend."

"Mutual friend." He offered a small smile when she peered up at him again.

"Master of the vague."

"At your service."

She smiled, even as her breathing still hitched, and it felt like the most handsome reward.

⚜

"I'm sorry." Megan halfheartedly wiped at the moisture and makeup on his white shirt.

She tried to pull back from his embrace, but he held tight. "I'm here for you. You don't have to hide your grief. I want to help."

"You did. Truly." In fact, though the tears hadn't yet dried on her face, her chest felt lighter, freer, than it had in a long, long while.

Because of Owen.

How many times had her mother, her sister, Kate—hell, even a therapist—tried to get her to open up, tried to reassure her John's death didn't lay at her feet? She hadn't been able to accept what happened, move on from it. But Owen's words resounded with a sincerity she couldn't deny. He knew things he shouldn't be able to know. She had proof of it. Could he really know, with the impassioned certainty he'd voiced, that John didn't blame her?

She heard Owen's voice again. *He could never blame you.* She sucked in a breath, covered her mouth with a shaking hand.

Oh, God. The truth of it exploded in her head and heart.

Big hands cupped Megan's trembling face. Owen thumbed away her tears. "Shhh, now."

She inhaled a calming breath and dropped her hand to his chest. "What you said. Thank you." As the revelation flowed through her, Megan's muscles tensed and relaxed. Shuddered. The guilt and despair she'd shouldered these past two years fractured. Pieces flew off, away from her, like snowflakes in the wind.

Owen nodded and his eyes flared, an odd light that lasted only a moment.

It passed so quickly Megan knew she'd imagined it. God, his eyes. So beautiful. So unusual. The blue was nearly navy it was so dark. As if he wasn't mysterious enough before.

She frowned. The strongest sensation of déjà vu flooded over her.

"Hey. I've got an idea," he said, pulling her from her thoughts. His hands dropped to her shoulders and squeezed.

Relieved for the distraction, she took a deep, cleansing breath. "Oh, yeah? Let's hear it."

"I'm gonna build you a house."

"Uh…" She smiled and pointed to the big wooden cabin beside them. "Think we got that covered."

The right side of his mouth lifted. "No. An igloo."

"Really?"

"Yep. And you're going to help me."

Why not? "Okay. I'm in. But, do you have any experience with igloo construction?"

His eyes flared again, that crooked grin turned into a smirk at the challenge. "Do I have any experience with igloo construction?" he murmured. He held out his arms, called out to the snowy field, "She wants to know if I have experience with igloos!" The laughter that spilled out of him was pure as bells and so joyous. She was enraptured watching him. "Yeah, I know a thing or two."

She adored how he drew her out, made her feel safe to be silly. Sometimes the label of "widow" weighed a thousand pounds with all the things you felt you shouldn't do. "All righty, then. You lead, I'll follow." There was no frickin' way they were going to actually build an igloo, but it would be fun trying. "What do we do?"

"I need a long, sharp knife, some cardboard and a handsaw. Got any of that lying around?"

"A knife, yes. The rest, probably. Let me go look in the garage."

"Okay. I'll clear a path out into the yard." Owen retrieved the shovel and dug right in, carving out a path from the sidewalk into the front yard. He didn't go all the way down to the grass, but instead left maybe a foot of snow as a pathway. Every so often he'd stomp it down to pack it tight.

Megan left to search for the saw. When she returned, empty box, saw, and knife in hand, Owen had shoveled a good fifteen feet and now worked on clearing a circle. The snow was deeper out in the yard, the wind having pushed it in drifts as it curled around the cabin and blew out over the flat plain of the great field in front.

"Come on out," he called.

She crunched across his path to the big circle. Her first step into it, she sank to mid-calf.

"That's what we need the cardboard for. We gotta pack this down real tight. Toss it here," he said, pointing to the box.

Megan laid the saw on top of the snow and chucked the box

to him. He unfolded and tore it in two, then handed a big, long piece to her.

"Like this," he said. He laid the strip of cardboard down and jumped all across its surface. His obvious pleasure brought out the boyishness in his face. "Easy." When he'd gone back and forth a few times, he moved the box piece a foot or two and repeated the process.

She could handle that. Cardboard underfoot, Megan began to jump. She felt ridiculous. Her hair flew around her face and her cheeks started to ache from smiling. But it was fun. So much fun. God, she needed that. She glanced up to Owen.

He'd stripped out of his coat. Every time he jumped, the bottom hem of his turtleneck rose up, exposing a sliver of ridged abdomen.

She stared a long moment, had to tear her gaze away. "Aren't you cold?" she asked as she continued to jump.

"No. I'm perfect."

Well, she couldn't disagree with that.

She jumped and jumped on the cardboard, worked up a sweat that almost had her considering shedding her coat, too. But it was damn cold out here. In the twenties at best. The sun was bright and high in the late-morning sky, but did little to abate the temperature. The air was crisp, biting even. She didn't know how Owen could stand it.

"Did you grow up where it snowed a lot?" she asked.

"Yep."

"Whereabouts?"

"Moved around a lot, but I've lived in Alaska, Canada, even Russia for a while."

Megan stopped jumping. "Russia. Wow. Why did you live there? For how long?"

"When I was younger. With my family."

"Do you speak Russian?"

Having made it across to her side of the circle, Owen stopped right in front of her. And launched into a totally incomprehensible Slavic-sounding monologue. She gaped at him. She had no idea what he was saying, but, damn, the way it rolled off his tongue. His eyes smoldered, upping the heat inside her already-warm layers.

She swallowed hard. "I'll take that as a yes."

He nodded. "It's a yes."

"Speak any others?"

"A few. I'm pretty good with languages."

"Good with languages," she murmured. With everything she learned about him, he got more and more interesting. Or more mysterious, depending on how you looked at it. "So, good with languages, shovels, and igloos. Anything else?"

The smug look he tossed at her was so wicked it shivered right down her spine. Walked right into that, hadn't she. She shook her head and, looking away to hide her blush, moved her cardboard forward one spot. Without doubt, he would be good at...other stuff. Jesus.

They resumed jumping together, like little kids, until they'd covered the entire circumference of the circle.

Breathing hard, Megan leaned forward and braced her palms on her knees. The exertion reminded her of building the snowmen the other day. She looked up. Pouted. "Aw, my snowmen." Only the crown of the snow kid peeked out through a drift. The woman still stood, though she was buried up to her waist, her scarf and gloved arms long lost. The snowman, though, was totally gone. Not a single trace remained. Maybe the wind had blown him over, the drifts covering his parts. His absence from the little family squeezed her heart. "My snowman must've fallen over." She glanced to Owen, who watched her with a strange look on his face, like he was waiting for something. "Was the snowman still standing when you borrowed his shirt?"

"Uh, I think I might've knocked him over," he said with a grimace. "Sorry."

She waved a hand. "No matter. It's not like he would've lasted forever."

Owen looked down at the ground. "You never know."

CHAPTER TEN

The presumed disappearance of the snowman had gone over better than Owen feared. For that, he was glad. While making the clearing, Megan had smiled freely, like a weight had lifted from her shoulders. He didn't want anything to chase that away.

He just hoped he wouldn't go the way of a real snowman. Owen shuddered at the thought of himself, puddled on her floor. The endless stretch of snow all around him should've provided solace. It should've protected him for a while. But it wasn't going to last, not if that West Wind came through.

Owen didn't want to go anywhere, damnit. Hopefully, not ever. But that would be up to Megan. And he had only four days to make her want him, too.

Her voice, so full of good humor, pulled him from his thoughts. "All right, Mr. Igloo Expert. What's next?"

Owen walked across the just-packed surface and grabbed the shovel. "Next, I'm gonna dig us a hole. Then, we'll cut out blocks." He booted the shovel into the snow, dug and scooped until he had about a two-foot diameter hole in which he could stand. Blades of frosty grass poked up through the snow under his feet. "Bring me the saw?"

"Sure." Megan retrieved the handsaw from where she'd placed it earlier. She gifted him with a big, open smile when she passed it to him. He'd build her a hundred igloos if it meant she'd keep looking at him that way.

"Thanks." He leaned down in the hole, basking in her happiness and in the fact maybe he had something to do with it, and sliced the saw horizontally into the snow. Cutting all around the bottom of the circle, just above the grassy surface, he freed what would become the bottoms of the blocks.

"You sure you know what you're doing?"

If she hadn't been watching, he could've thrown this together in the blink of an eye. But he wouldn't have traded her presence for all the world. "Yep."

Standing up again, Owen sank the saw into the top of the snow where they'd stomped and jumped. It was hard and dry, just what they needed. He made cuts on three sides, then carefully levered the block free. He caught it in his hands, then lifted it outside his small circle and set it off to the side.

"Whoa. That's awesome."

He melted a little at Megan's praise. Well, not literally. On the inside.

Soon, he had six blocks carved, roughly two-feet long by about a foot high and eight inches thick.

"Can I try?"

"Of course. Step on down."

Megan's smile widened as she joined him in the lower circle and took the saw. He adored how much she seemed to be enjoying herself.

Bracing her gloved hand against the surface, she pushed the saw's sharp tip into the snow. It went about four inches, then pushed back. "Shit. How did you do this?" With a grunt, she tried again. The blade sank another couple inches, then ground to a halt. She pouted up at him. "The snow doesn't like me."

Her ridiculous declaration made him want to drop to one knee and prove her wrong. "Want me to help?"

"No way. If you can do it, I can do it." She huffed and used both hands to push the saw forward.

It was no use. They'd packed it hard and tight. The lower layers were frozen through.

"Come on," she grunted.

Restraining a smile, Owen came around her and laid his hand on the snow's surface. With a silent command, he reworked the internal chemistry of the layers.

Megan nearly fell on her face when the saw sliced right through to the ground. She whooped out a cheer. "Woot! I did it! I did it! Take that, snow!"

Owen fell back against the snow wall and laughed. Gods, living felt so damn good. Filled his soul until he thought it surely couldn't be contained by this mortal body. "Good job. Might want to do the other two sides, though."

"Shut up, you. I'm getting there."

He held his hands up in surrender. "Sorry, sorry. At your leisure."

Her next cuts went much smoother, to her great joy and Owen's considerable amusement. He helped her lift the heavy block up onto the side. For the next half hour, they took turns cutting, lifting, and stacking more blocks, until Owen guessed they had enough. Block-making had opened up the small circle under foot to a six-foot diameter around which the igloo would stand.

Owen climbed out of the circle and grabbed the shovel, then carved a ramp-like path from the higher surface down into what would become the igloo's floor. "This will be where the door goes." He tossed the shovel aside. "Ready to build?"

Megan glanced at the stack of blocks. "Very. Can't wait to see how we're going to get those to stand up."

With a scoff, Owen grabbed the first block. "That's not doubt I'm hearing, is it?"

She pressed her lips together. It didn't hide her smile. "Maybe?"

He clutched his hands over his heart. "Aw. You wound me. I am injured. Most grievously."

She shoved his arm, making him stumble. "Oh, stop. You'll live. Now get to building me an igloo already."

"One igloo coming right up. And then you'll make me lunch and we'll have a picnic inside."

"Deal." She watched as he grabbed the first blocks and lay them in place.

As he worked, Owen felt her gaze as an almost physical touch. He wasn't used to being watched, observed. He'd spent so long in his unseeable elemental form. But her eyes on him made him feel real, present in the world. When was the last time he felt he was right where he belonged?

He threw himself into the construction to restrain the need building up inside him. Her joy, her playfulness, being out in the snow, in the cold—the whole experience set his body on fire.

The bottom layer of the igloo was the easiest. Standing on their longest sides, he laid the blocks along the edge of the raised snow wall around the pit they'd cut out. He worked the tail end of the first layer upwards, spiral-like, so the second layer grew increasingly taller as it progressed, leading naturally into the third layer, the one that started to tilt inwards in anticipation of the domed roof. Megan helped him brace blocks whenever needed, and he shaved shapes into the blocks with the saw to get the blocks to cooperate.

"The key is to pack them tight so the pressure of the blocks pushing against each other holds them in place. Makes the snow molecules bind together," he said as he worked another block into the wall.

"You really do know a lot about building igloos, don't you?"

He hoisted a block into place at shoulder height. "Just now believing me, eh?"

Face rosy from the cold and the exertion, Megan looked up and surveyed the growing walls. "Seeing is believing."

See me. Believe in me. He sighed. It was hard to be patient now that he had a deadline hanging over his head.

The fourth layer of blocks leaned forward at a forty-five-degree angle, so Owen took more care wedging them securely. The fifth layer left a hole in the center top of the roof. Grabbing another block and the saw, Owen cut out a shape slightly larger than the remaining space and carefully forced the last piece upwards into the gap. When the completed roof arched over them, he smoothed his hands all across the surface and willed the molecules to lock together. Just to be on the safe side.

He dropped his arms and looked expectantly at the beautiful woman standing beside him, her faced filled with amazement and joy.

"We did it!" she said and threw herself into his arms. "This is the coolest thing ever."

He wrapped her in his embrace. The warm satisfaction of triumph flooded through him. Not for finishing the igloo, but for earning this moment of happiness with her. Her breath caressed his neck, jolted down his spine, settled into the thick organ between his legs. "We did," he rasped.

With difficulty, he pulled away, not wanting his body's response to her enthusiasm to scare her off. "One last thing." He retrieved the knife and carefully poked a half-dozen holes into the sides of the igloo. "Ventilation. Otherwise, the ice traps carbon monoxide inside." He flipped the blade in his hand and turned to her. "So, what do you think?"

ಶೋಣಿ

"Wow." Megan turned in a circle, admiring the glittering ice walls that surrounded them. They'd really, truly done it. Thanks to Owen. "I think I know someone who earned some lunch."

Owen groaned, clutched his stomach. "Oh, please, tell me it's me. I could eat a polar bear right now."

"Not a polar bear." Megan grinned, loving his playfulness. "Why not?"

"For one, they're too cute. And two, they're an endangered species."

He smiled. "Good points. Well, I hope you have something else in mind."

Counting out on her fingers, she said, "I have the sandwich and salad fixings from last night. But I can also heat up some chili and cornbread. I have a pepperoni pizza I can bake. Oh, I have some very good chicken salad—"

"Chicken salad. Please. Sounds great."

Megan nodded, amused by how enthusiastic Owen was about, well, everything. "On a sandwich or a salad?"

"Surprise me." Saw in hand, he turned away from her and

knelt at the igloo's short doorway. "Hold on, let me make this a little taller so we can get in and out easier." He carved an arch into the bottom-most block, opening up a three-foot-tall doorway.

Megan's eyes quickly slipped from the saw's handiwork down Owen's bulging bicep, across the tight pull of his shirt over his muscular shoulders, over his strong lean back. The too-short shirt exposed a swath of fine, pale skin just above his firm ass. Oh, to sneak her hands through the fabric gap and burrow against him, wrap around him.

There was no denying it. It might be crazy, given how little she'd known him, but she liked Owen. *Really* liked him. His positivity, the tender way he offered concern and care, his ability to find joy in the smallest things. When was the last time she'd felt so carefree, so open to life? It was him. His influence. After so much time beating herself up and tearing herself down over what had happened to John, she actually liked who she was around Owen. It was so damn liberating.

Her eyes trailed lower, down from his very fine ass to the thick muscles of his thighs.

She didn't just like him, either. She wanted Owen. Craved him. Her body had been asleep these past two years, and he'd woken it up. With a vengeance. Looking at him, she felt like a starving woman at a feast. Warm as she was from hours of exertion, not all the moisture inside her clothes was from sweat.

"You okay?" Owen asked.

The blush was immediate. Megan's gaze flew from his ass to his laughing eyes. Jeez, she was out of practice. Busted. Again. She sucked in a deep breath and exhaled it on a chuckle. "Yeah, I'm great."

"Mmm, good." He flashed an infuriating but admittedly

sexy smug smile. "Food. Now," he called as he crawled through the door, good humor infusing his tone.

On hands and knees, Megan followed, her stomach growling for sustenance. "Come on inside. Take a break. Get warmed up while I pull things together."

He hesitated, his eyes shifting between the snow and the cabin. "Uh, okay."

Megan trailed across the snowy path to the cleared sidewalk. She stomped across the front porch, then dropped boots, coat, gloves, and scarf into a pile just inside the door. The temperature differential suffocated her. She ripped off the fleece Henley, stripping down to a thin short-sleeved T-shirt she had at the bottom of all those layers. "Phew. Much better." She tugged her hair into a pony tail and fanned her neck. She turned to Owen, who stood with his back against the closed door.

His face was bright red, sweat dotted his forehead and temple. The quick rise and fall of his chest revealed his accelerated respiration.

Megan rushed over to him, cupped his jaw in her hands. He felt cool to the touch, but sweat poured off him. "Owen? What's the matter?"

His swallowed hard. "Can I have a drink, a very cold drink?" he rasped.

She ran to the fridge and returned in an instant with a large glass of cold water and crushed ice. "Here."

He grabbed the glass from her hand and tilted it to his lips, chugged the whole thing back in one desperate swallow, ice and all. He blew out a breath and wiped his mouth with the back of his hand. "Better." The cup shook in his hand.

Megan frowned, wished she knew what had happened. "Why don't you sit down?"

"Yeah." He shuffled to the breakfast bar and dragged himself onto a stool, not at all the energetic powerhouse he'd been for the last three hours. "Mind if I take my shirt off? I don't do well with heat. Need a minute to adjust to the air in here."

Megan gulped. Mind? Not in the least. "No, course not." She rounded the counter to the kitchen side.

He ripped the turtleneck off with one hand and tossed it on the counter in front of him. Spreading his arms against the cold granite surface, he leaned forward so his chest pressed into it.

An idea popped into her mind and Megan whipped a clean dish towel from a drawer. She soaked it in cold water right from the tap, then twisted the excess water out. Turning back to Owen, she found him draped over the counter, forehead resting on the backs of his hands.

She debated for only a minute, then walked around to him and laid the cold towel over his upper back.

He groaned, a sound so full of primal satisfaction that the nerves in her lower abdomen twitched and fluttered. Quite simply, she loved taking care of him. Loved knowing that her hands brought him comfort, eased his distress, provided him sustenance. Made him happy. She got a second cloth, wet it, returned and switched out the first, which had already absorbed Owen's body heat.

"Thank you," he said when the second cold towel fell across his bare skin. He lifted his head and eyed her warily. "Sorry."

"Don't be." She grabbed his empty glass and refilled it. Worried he'd feel uncomfortable if she kept fussing, she busied herself with pulling out the fixings for lunch.

The chicken salad was chunky and hearty, with coarse chopped celery, onions, and some diced grapes for a splash of sweetness. Her mouth watered. She opted to make sandwiches, thinking they'd be easier to eat outside. One for her, two for him, on big crusty Kaiser rolls. She plated them, then added potato chips and salted tomato slices.

"Looks good." Owen sat upright again and looked more himself now. "Thanks."

"You're welcome. You sure you're okay?"

"Yeah. Sorry I worried you. Just"—he lifted one big shoulder—"I've lived most of my life in cold places, so I get along better when it's cool. It's what I'm used to, I guess."

It struck her as unusual, but Megan nodded. "No apologies necessary. Just glad you're feeling better." She grabbed a couple of bottled waters from the fridge. "You know what? I have an idea."

In stocking feet, she skittered across the great room to the thermostat and reset the program. The digital display read seventy degrees, but her adjustments would lower it to sixty within a few short hours. Easier for her to bundle up than for him to strip down. Though, now that she thought about it... Hmm, yes, all that sculptured back muscle argued in favor of the stripping down. The way he'd turned in his stool to watch her popped his corded lat muscle out all down his left side. Megan licked her lips. Tried but failed to ignore the desire to taste that lean length of skin.

As she crossed back to the kitchen, an old childhood memory came to mind. She instantly knew he would love it. "I have a treat for you," she said. "But it's going to be a surprise."

"No fair."

"I'll make it worth it, I promise."

"No doubt." He slid off his stool. "I'll help carry all this out, but mind if I grab a dry shirt?"

"Help yourself."

He retreated into the bedroom. Her gaze followed him until he disappeared through the door. She quickly gathered two big plastic cups, two spoons, a bottle of strawberry Gatorade and the bottle of Hershey's chocolate syrup from the fridge door. A separate plastic grocery bag hid the surprise from Owen when he returned.

Megan layered back up, while Owen stuck to a single long-sleeved T-shirt. They collected the supplies for their lunch and headed for the door. At the last minute, Owen swooped over to one couch and grabbed a blanket.

Back in the igloo, he spread the blanket over the floor and they laid everything out on top. She sat cross-legged in the middle to be close to Owen, who leaned with his back against the block wall. He was entirely himself again, teasing, moaning and exclaiming over the food, making her crazy with his little sounds and big heart. She finished her sandwich just as he finished his second.

The minute his plate was clear, he asked, "Okay, what's my surprise?"

"Eager, much?"

His multicolored eyes flashed from under long strands of black. "Always."

"Stay here." She pointed at him, waggled a finger. "I mean it."

"Yes, ma'am."

Scooping up her plastic bag, she crawled to the entrance, glanced back. "And no peeking."

"Cross my heart," he said, mimicking his words with his hand.

Excitement simmered under the surface of Megan's skin, this kind of frenetic energy unlike anything she'd experienced in so long. She chose a spot that hadn't been disturbed by their earlier digging and brushed away the very top layer, then used spoons to partway fill the cups with fresh, clean, icy snow. She poured strawberry Gatorade over the crystals and squeezed chocolate sauce on top of that. Two more layers of snow, strawberry and chocolate topped off the big, tall cups. Her heart fluttered in anticipation and the strangest sensation of them having done this before washed over her, but that was impossible. She shook it off. She wanted to please him. Wanted to see his eyes light up and hear his satisfied—and ridiculously hot—sounds.

"Close your eyes," she called as she knelt at the door.

"Closed."

"Keep 'em closed."

"I am, I am," he groused. "Hurry up already."

Megan settled right in front of Owen, a cup in each hand, her knees just inside his spread, drawn-up legs. A thrill rippled through her stomach, in the best possible way.

"Okay," she said, her voice higher, lighter. "Open your eyes."

CHAPTER ELEVEN

At first, Owen could only focus on the brilliant happiness shining from every inch of Megan's face. The apples of her cheeks so rosy and shiny. Bright blue eyes sparkling with excitement and anticipation.

Something smelled fantastic. His gaze dropped to the enormous plastic cups in her hands. Mounds of icy red and thick chocolate piled over the cups' edges.

He sucked in a breath. "You made us snow cones?" His mind reeled. She didn't realize the significance of what she'd done. Couldn't have known.

She smiled and nodded. "I made super-duper deluxe chocolate-strawberry snow cones, to be exact."

"Gimme." He snatched the cup from her hand. Lighthearted laughter spilled from her pink lips, lighting him up inside. He spooned in a helping of chocolaty snow. "Oh my gods," he mumbled before he'd even swallowed. The weight of her gaze fell on his mouth, pulling his stare back to her. "You put chocolate on snow."

"I know, right? It's fantastic."

"It's"—he gobbled another bite—"genius. Inspired."

And beyond the gooey, icy sweetness of the treat—in itself a revelation—the snow infused his system with a nearly electrical charge of energy, vitality. He shuddered. Goosebumps broke out across his skin. Between his legs, he hardened, forcing him to shift to accommodate the tightness. Each scoop hit him like a jolt of B12, caffeine, and Prozac in one. He couldn't get enough.

And she'd been the one to make him feel this way.

Megan Snow was perfect for him.

She sat watching him, so full of life. Her cup remained untouched.

"Why aren't you eating?"

She lifted her spoon. "Oh, I was just—"

"Here." He held out his spoon without thinking about it, but then his need for her to eat from his hands exploded in his chest.

Her eyes went wide and her mouth dropped open. Those baby blues flashed up at him, setting off a twisting heat low in his gut. She leaned forward. Wrapped her lips around his spoon.

Aw, hell. His hard-on throbbed. His breathing tripped and his heart took off at a sprint. He scooped another portion into his own mouth, watched her swallow hers. *More.* Holding out the spoon, he made the offer again and again. Over and over, she accepted. He leaned toward her, and she scooted on her knees closer, and a little closer again, until one knee finally kissed the back of his thigh.

He groaned and continued to feed her, nearly panting now. She held his eyes while she ate, her breathing audible between them, her chest rising and falling under her coat. In his gut, the snow morphed into raw power, ignited his veins, tingled through his muscles, setting off involuntary twitches here and there that felt like being tickled.

His spoon hit the bottom of the cup, scraped loudly in the confined space of the igloo against the empty plastic.

Megan didn't miss a beat. A spoonful of her dessert appeared at his lips. "My turn," she whispered, her voice breathy and low.

Tossing his cup and spoon aside, he devoured what she offered, savored the cold sweetness, drank it down into his belly. She was right there ready with more, then took some for herself. In her haste, red crystals spilled from the spoon down over her chin. A thin line of chocolate edged over her lip.

In a flash, he was on her, powerless to resist any longer. His big hands cupped the back of her neck, tangled in soft curls. Pulled her in. His mouth zeroed in on the flavored snow on her skin, a taste far more heady than the snow alone, all creamy vanilla and soft-scented woman. He kissed and sucked up her chin to the corner of her mouth, her warm exhalation tingling across his cheek. And then his lips found hers.

The moan she unleashed into his mouth flared in his gut. He dug his fingers into that beautiful mass of silky blond, held her to him. Urgent, open-mouthed kisses sought her lips, implored her to want him back. When her tongue sneaked forward, flicked his bottom lip, he groaned in triumph.

For a moment, he let her lead. He wanted her to be the one to breach the physical gap between their bodies. To come to him. Finally, the tip of her tongue curled around his, explored his mouth in the most tentative way.

It was all he needed.

He sucked her in, savored the echo of the strawberry-chocolate coldness that graced her mouth. Her shy exploration turned bolder, caught on to his urgency, gave it right back.

Megan's weight fell against his chest, the snow cone wedged between them. He pulled back, snatched the spoon from her shaking hand, and held a scoopful to her mouth. Their faces were close enough that her breath ghosted across his lips. "Take it," he rasped. "But don't swallow."

She sucked the treat in as Owen set the cup and spoon aside. Then, slowly, he leaned in, his eyes trained on hers even as their lips met. She opened to him when his lips and tongue demanded entrance. The sweet snow in her mouth made him dizzy. They both swallowed roughly, not letting go, sharing the dessert between them.

Megan ran her hands through his hair, pushed it back off the sides of his face. She held as tightly to him as his gentle hands did to her. Her grasp bordered on painful, but he wouldn't have traded the intensity of it for all the Arctic. When she scooted closer, until her knees burrowed under his thighs, he released her hair, scooped his hands under her bottom, and hauled her onto his lap so she straddled him.

She gasped. He groaned and pressed up into the cleft between her thighs, unable to heed the receding part of his mind that urged caution. He didn't want to scare her, push her, but the sensations this body was capable of creating owned him, took over his conscious mind, disabled all rational thought. Yet, she was about more than the physical pleasure firing through his synapses and pulsing between his legs. He needed her like he'd never needed anything in his very long, very lonely, very cold existence.

"Gods, Megan, you taste so good."

He swallowed her whimper and wrapped himself around her, his arms strapping her to his chest, his thighs pushing her forward into him. Her soft moans rang out with approval. Her hands held tight in return, clutching, stroking. Every kiss she gave him, every touch, every needy sound, filled him with the same magical strength as the snow. She'd made him. She'd called him. Now, finally, she was claiming him. And only through her claim would he become real, permanently corporeal and human. Only through her choice could he escape the transience of the North Wind, of the frost, of the snow.

He'd never wanted that before. Never really cared. But he clearly didn't know what he'd been missing. Now that he'd had a taste of the wonderful riot of sensation and warmth that was life, he wanted more, wanted as much as he could have. But only with her.

Through his kisses, he willed her desire. With each groan that rumbled from low in his throat, he begged for a chance. For warmth, for companionship, for love. It was there, between them, the Christmas miracle of his appearance. Now for her to see it, to grasp the silky ribbon of his life force and pull him to her.

The things he could give her if she would just let him…

೮೦೮೩

Even though Megan was on top, she felt completely possessed by Owen. His hands secured her against his broad chest. His mouth tugged her lips, stole her breath. Need shot out from him like static electricity—his dark gaze blazed and flashed, his lips sucked and pulled. Between her legs, his erection bucked and pressed. She opened her knees wider, slid forward, ground down against him in return. The friction they created heated her body, jolted her heartbeat. Her scalp prickled and the hair on her neck and arms raised. Her whole body jangled.

All that sensation pooled down low, right where she sat atop him. "Owen," she moaned. She ground and pressed and kissed and rocked against him until she was dizzy with lust and need.

"Oh, Megan." Big hands gripped her hips, steadied her rhythm against the long, hard ridge between them.

"Yes," she whimpered. Once he'd pulled her into his lap, her body declared there would be no going back. A primal, instinctual need to have him, to claim him, invaded her soul. It *had* been a long time, but this intense pull to him, the chemistry between them, was so far outside the ballpark of her experience that she couldn't confine it within reason or logic.

He bucked his hips against her pelvis just as his mouth devoured hers in a needy, urgent kiss. She unleashed a strangled moan around his exploring tongue, and all at once her body detonated between them. The forceful surprise stole her breath and blanked her mind. Electrical impulses rippled out from the clenching muscles of her core and suspended her body in a delicious stasis, head back, eyes unseeing, mouth open, her cries spilling out against the icy domed roof cocooning them.

She collapsed against his shoulder, face buried in his neck. His pulse raced against her lips, and she pressed a succession of little kisses there. As she panted, she breathed in his scent—all cool and fresh and male. Around her back, his arms comforted, warm and secure.

As she lay there, boneless and breathless—and completely stunned—she knew without question something inside her had shifted. While a small corner of her heart panged at the thought of John, her mind was at peace with what she'd just shared with Owen, what more she still wanted to share.

Just three months ago, she'd let Kate talk her into a double date to a Baltimore Orioles game. A Sunday afternoon in the sun, surrounded by crowds of people—it was supposed to be a low-pressure, low-risk reentry into the world of dating. Kate's friend had been nice, cute, the quintessential good guy. So much so that she'd felt bad at the idea of turning him down when he'd asked if he could give her a kiss at the end of the evening. The moment his lips touched hers she'd panicked, and icy regret had sloshed through her gut. That night, she sobbed herself to sleep.

It's time. You're ready now.

Her breath caught in her throat, eyes flew open. She wrenched back from Owen's shoulder, knowing he hadn't spoken those words, knowing she hadn't either.

She'd barely processed the return of the mysterious voice before another oddity assaulted her senses. All around them, it was flurrying. Tiny, gentle, perfectly formed snowflakes settled on Owen's black hair, his clothes, her eyelashes.

"It's snowing in here," she breathed, holding out a hand to catch the flakes.

Owen's utter stillness drew her attention away from the glittering crystals swirling in the indoor air. Her heart ticked up in her chest again when their eyes met. His…nearly glowed, like they were backlit. Gold and bronze flicked through his brown eye; teal and sky flashed through the navy. Beautiful. Impossible. Like the voice. Like the falling snow inside their igloo.

Like his appearance in the middle of one of the worst blizzards she'd ever experienced.

He blinked at her and the effect disappeared. But his expression told her she hadn't imagined it. He stifled a wince, twisted his lips. His eyes skimmed over her face, avoiding her direct gaze. The flurries still fell.

"What's happening?" Megan whispered.

He released a long breath. "Magic," he whispered back, looking at her again.

She half expected that response, but the word still unleashed a shiver through her body that had nothing to do with the temperature. "But…I don't believe in magic."

For being so big, his hands were soft and gentle when they curled around her neck. "You must." He swallowed hard and nodded.

What she was seeing, what he was saying—was totally crazy. Opened doors of possibility she'd never before considered. That just weren't real.

A snowflake tickled the end of her nose and she shook her head. The flurries were few and far between now, nearly gone. "It was snowing in here, right? I didn't imagine that? But, how?"

He watched her for a moment, then his lips lifted into a slow, tentative smile. "Sorry. You…affect me."

His tone skittered over the sensitive skin between her legs, made her realize he was still hard beneath her. Intriguing as his arousal was, and it damn well was, she had to focus or she'd never understand what was going on.

She looked up at the last of the tiny flakes, and then turned toward him. "So, you're saying, you…?" Her heart thrummed against her chest.

Watching her, he nodded.

Anticipation fluttered through her stomach. "And the voice?"

He shook his head, eyed her. "Not me."

"I know, but do you know—"

"Yes, and so do you."

Tears bloomed behind Megan's eyes, stinging but not falling.

"John?"

Owen stroked her jaw with his thumb. "Wants you to live, to be happy."

Her whole body shuddered, then wouldn't stop. The truth of his words settled somewhere deep, deep down into her psyche, until she knew it like a reflex, like breathing.

Still, she needed Owen to put the pieces into place. "You… know him? You've…met him?"

"Just the once, when he came to ask for help…for you." He spoke cautiously, his dark eyes scanning her face as if watching for her reactions to his words.

She released a shaky breath, her mind whirling to determine what he was saying without actually saying it. "So you're saying…what? Like, in heaven?" She peeked up at him, feeling stupid even as the words left her mouth.

His big hands surrounded her smaller ones, warm despite his lack of gloves. "There are many names for it."

Her eyes bulged with his tacit admission. "You're from heaven?" she squeaked.

His open expression was warm, gentle. "I spend a lot of time here, but, yes, I'm from elsewhere."

Her mind whirled. If that was really true… Panic seized Megan's gut. "But you said you were real."

"Shhh, angel. I am. You're making me real."

Megan dropped her face into her hands and groaned, the clattering of her teeth drawing out the muffled sound.

"Oh, for the love of Boreas." He rubbed his hands over her arms and muttered something that sounded self-chiding under his breath. "I'm sorry. You're freezing. Let's get you inside."

"Who's Boris?" she asked, a little dizzy from the orgasm and the revelations and the hard-left-turn change in topic.

He smiled. "Bor-e-as," he enunciated. "Long story."

She shook her head. Dropped her gaze to his stomach.

He dipped his head and caught her eyes from under his hair. "I know, I know. I'm being vague again, aren't I?"

She nodded, chewed her lip. Multiple topics fought for center stage, clung to the tip of her tongue. But cold permeated her body. She couldn't stop shaking. "You'll keep talking inside?"

"Of course." He lifted her off his lap. They each collected some of the lunch mess in their hands. Owen looked down into the consolidated frozen block that formed the remainder of the second snow cone. "Damn shame," he mumbled. "Thank you, by the way. It was magnificent."

"You're welcome." Megan nodded, met his gaze, then blushed. Her heart tripped over itself. The heat coming out of his mismatched eyes made it clear he wasn't thanking her for the dessert alone.

Jesus, he'd given her an orgasm without hardly touching her. And not just any orgasm. A scream-yourself-hoarse, feel-it-in-muscles-you-didn't-know-you-had orgasm.

In desperate need of a break from his intensity, Megan scrambled through the door of the igloo on shaky legs. Once out, she rose and stretched, sucked in a mouthful of clean winter air. Clouds had returned, dulling the morning's crisp blue sky into a milky white and dropping the temperature.

She glanced over her shoulder at Owen, now standing to his full height and inspecting the exterior of the igloo. He smoothed his hands over its domed roof. The action seemed filled with great care. His posture was relaxed, confident, full of the kind of easy grace a body exhibited when in its element.

Megan shivered. Wanting the warmth of the cabin, she crunched up the shoveled path. Thoughts—her own—whirled through her head:

Owen needs the snow.

Owen prefers the cold.

Owen's from 'somewhere else.'

Owen is magic.

The pieces of the puzzle shifted, tried to fit together. Her steps slowed as her mind drifted, focused on whatever it was she was missing. She stumbled a bit, caught herself.

When she reached the cleared sidewalk, she turned and waited for Owen, her mind still chugging…trying to…it was so close…

Owen looked up. His dark blue and brown eyes glinted playfully from under his black hair. Lips so red…

In a flash, she saw herself. Christmas Eve. The snowman. Sorting the buttons. Disappointed she didn't have a matching pair for the eyes. Deciding it didn't matter—the large navy and chocolate buttons were all she had…

Realization slammed into her.

She gasped and stumbled back against the wall of the porch, flailing away from what her mind had deduced. No, no. Impossible!

"Megan?" Owen shook his black hair off his face and frowned. "What's—"

"Oh my God. Ohmygodohmygod!" The black knit cap she'd pulled down over the snowman's head.

Oh, Jesus, the snowman was gone. Gone! Her eyes flashed from the man's empty place beside the family to Owen.

No, not gone. Not gone at all.

CHAPTER TWELVE

Dark spots flickered around the edges of Megan's vision, threatened to close in, swallow her up. She gasped for breath, the cold, cold gulps scorching on their way down into the tightened confines of her chest.

"Y…you…sn…snow…"

Owen's hands clutched at her biceps. "Shhh, angel. It's okay. Come on." He scooped her into his arms. The white of the sky hung above her, then the dense brown of the porch ceiling. Her body settled into soft leather-scented comfort, then he tugged her coat open, pulled off her gloves, and threaded the scarf from around her neck.

Breathe. Just breathe. Easier now. Easier. The halo around her vision faded. Her eyes focused on Owen's hovering form, looking down at her.

She pushed up into a sitting position, listed to the left for a moment until her equilibrium returned, then hauled herself off the couch. The impossibility of her realization set her heart crashing against her breastbone. "You're...you were...I mean... the snowman?"

His mismatched eyes were wary, his breathing on the verge of distressed. For just a moment he looked away, shook his head as if debating with himself. When his gaze cut back to her, determination framed his handsome face. His flushed, sweaty face. "Yes," he breathed.

Megan nodded, processing, pushing through her amazement to belief, and scanned her gaze over his body. His perfectly real, seemingly human, very male body.

His chest shuddered in a labored breath. Like before.

Oh, no.

What he was. Did it matter? He was standing before her. Hurting.

"What do you need?"

"I'll"—he swallowed hard enough she could hear it— "adjust in a minute."

"Sit." She pointed at the couch. He nodded and sat heavily against the leather cushions. Megan shed her coat and dashed into the kitchen to collect the things that had helped before. On the way back through, she opened the front door, letting the winter air pour in.

"You don't have to—"

"It's okay. Here."

Owen grasped the tall glass of ice water and chugged it down. Megan stood guard over him, his distress raising her protective instincts. Her mind insisted she was freaking crazy to believe he was her snowman come to life, but her deepest heart knew it was true. But how? When he finished, he wiped his mouth with the back of his hand.

"Take your shirt off," Megan ordered as she pulled the empty cup from his hand. Not hesitating, he yanked it over his head. He was gorgeous in all his raw, bare masculinity, but his discomfort was what most captured her attention. "Lay back." Megan draped the cold towel over his chest. He groaned and his eyelids fell closed. With a second, she mopped his forehead, wetting his hair as she pushed it back off his face. A healthy tone returned to his skin, the flush receding, his breathing easing. "Is this helping?"

He grabbed her wrist, unfolded her fingers from around the smaller cloth, which dropped to his stomach. Holding her gaze, he pressed a long soft kiss against her palm. "Yes, thank you," he finally said.

His gratitude was so palpable, Megan's stomach jumped and fluttered. "Are you going to be okay?"

"Yes, it's just the change from being outside. I'm kinda new at this. Have to remember to take it slower."

Megan nodded. "Yeah." She sucked in a breath, realizing he'd rushed in for her. She'd totally been on the verge of fainting. "Thank you for helping me."

He reached out a big hand and stroked her cheek with the backs of his fingers. "Anything," he whispered.

She kicked her boots off and shifted on the couch, pulled her knees up underneath her. "So…" Embarrassment and curiosity washed through her. Where to start?

"So."

A gust of wind shoved through the door, pushed Megan's curls forward to dance around her face. She shivered, wrapped her arms around herself.

Owen's gaze flicked over her shoulder. The door closed with a gentle click. Megan's pulse quickened again. She didn't need to ask if he'd done it. The raised hair on the back of her neck told her all she needed to know.

Owen stretched an arm out toward her. His gaze lingered on his fingers as they played with her curls. He released a deep breath. "The snowman was the easiest way to manifest. Your tears on the snow helped me take this form." He waved his free hand in front of his chest. "It's been a long time since I was last corporeal."

Megan heard the words, but felt foggy-headed, like she was watching the scene unfold from outside her body. "Corporeal. I don't understand. What are you?"

"A snow god, one of the gods of winter."

Her heart fluttered and skipped within her chest. "A snow god," she whispered, trying the words on for size. Megan dipped her head and caught his gaze. The moment their eyes met, she felt the truth of his admission. Restrained power rippled beneath his human façade, flashed behind the dark blue and brown. "Are there many of, uh, you…snow gods?"

He inhaled a deep breath. "Many gods rule over earthly affairs, Megan, though only some belong to the Realm of Winter."

Her mind reeled as Owen painted this new reality into existence. "So, what does this mean for, like, you know, *God*. And heaven," she added, thinking of John. Imagining him in a heavenly paradise had always offered a sliver of comfort.

"The spiritual and otherworldly elements of all the human religious traditions are based in some fact. My presence need not interfere with your beliefs in *God* and heaven and the angels. We co-exist quite peacefully." He smiled as if enjoying an inside joke.

Megan swallowed, sorted her myriad thoughts. "Is that how

you met John?" Her voice trembled, heart clenched, not out of grief or fear, but out of anticipation of learning what he'd experienced after dying. The idea of conscious existence after death thrilled her. It meant, somewhere, John was still out there. Solace and excitement filled her, shivered through her whole body until she could barely sit still.

"Yes. John was a special case, for me. Human, but a distant relative."

Megan gaped. "What? How?"

"John *Snow*," he said.

"Wait. Are you telling me—"

"The Snows were the product of a joining between a winter god and a human. Generations ago. He wasn't aware of it. In life."

"John was a god?" Boy, he must've gotten a kick out of that! "Don't let it go to your head, mister," she called out to the room. Megan's face warmed under Owen's adoring gaze.

"John wasn't a god. But his lineage caught the pantheon's attention. When his soul pleaded for assistance, we couldn't ignore blooded kin."

"And he wanted—"

"Happiness. For you. That's all he needs to find peace."

Megan gasped. Her eyes stung. *Oh, John.*

ဆာ‌ฆ

Owen squeezed her hand. "His memories of you were stunning—he saw you as full of life, beautiful, so kind. *Warm.* It had been so long since I'd last walked upon the earth as a human. I agreed to try to help you. And then you gave me your tears, and made me yours." He tossed the damp towels aside and turned toward her, then rested his head next to hers on the back of the couch. He looked at her a long moment. "And now I'm here for you, Megan. I am enchanted, as surely as if you were the goddess and I the mortal."

Megan blinked, shook her head, opened and closed her mouth. Her gaze pleaded with him. "I don't even know where to begin to respond."

Owen found her effort to even try to understand so brave, so appealing. Millennia of observing humans taught him they often rejected the supernatural out of hand, or ran screaming in the other direction. Such reactions were understandable, of course, which was exactly what made Megan's calm introspection so remarkable. "I know."

"Um, could he have"—her eyes flickered to his, then dropped—"well, come back himself?"

Owen swatted away the jealousy that wanted to spring forward. He couldn't hold the question against her. After all, she'd loved John. And their love was what brought John to request his assistance. "John's soul was mortal. Returning to life wasn't his path. He understood that and made peace with it."

She nodded. "If he couldn't come here, then how am I hearing him?"

"Mmm, yes. Well, you're hearing him because I'm here. He's interloping on my power."

Megan frowned. "But I heard the voice before you showed up. The day before."

Owen shook his head. "I was already here. Since the Solstice. The veil between our worlds is thinnest then."

"The twenty-second? But...you didn't show up until Christmas."

"I needed to lay some groundwork. Give this time to work."

He flicked his finger back and forth between them. "The snowstorm," he offered in explanation.

"That was you?"

"Snow god, remember?"

She sagged into the sofa back. "Right." She released a shaky breath. "So, what does it mean to be a snow god, exactly?"

"I'm one of winter's guardians on earth. In my world, they call us the Anemoi, the masters of wind, the guardians of seasons. Humans call us by many names. Makers of the White. Defenders of the North Wind. Bringers of Winter—"

"Winter." She smirked. "Owen Winters?"

Her good humor warmed him with hope. "Owen is my true name."

She bit down on her bottom lip. "Owen, God of Snow, Bringer of Winter…" She dropped her gaze to their intertwined hands, traced her fingers along his.

He groaned. Her incantation rocked through him, invoked him to respond regardless of her intent. Struggling to resist, Owen ground his teeth together, but the urge was too strong and he launched forward, captured her face in his hands, her lips with his.

His body roared back to life, remembered its earlier arousal. Demanded satiation. Megan moaned into his mouth, pawed and grasped at his bare chest. His tongue begged for entrance, which she granted. Gods, he could still taste the strawberry and chocolate on her—flavors that, for him, would forever be tied to her most intimate scent. In the confined space of the igloo, her enticing wetness had bloomed around him, exploded through his senses as she'd released. Her euphoria had seemed such a magnificent triumph that his power had flared, burst from him in a moment of unguarded weakness. It had snowed.

Hand in her hair, he pressed against her, laid her back onto the soft skin of the sofa. He settled atop her, his hips cradled between her thighs, his big body embraced by feminine curves. Small hands clutched at his shoulders and neck, made him feel claimed, wanted. Needed. He never knew how fulfilling humanity could be, but human connection offered such sweet satisfaction. Now that he had it, he couldn't imagine going without.

Small moans and whimpers rose up from Megan's throat. The sounds ricocheted through Owen's body, made him hard and impatient where he rocked against her. Her hands locked behind his neck, she held her breath, clenched her eyes shut.

She was still kissing him, but something felt off.

Owen pulled back to find tears streaming from her eyes. His heart dropped into his stomach. "Have I hurt you?"

She slapped a hand over her mouth, shook her head. Watery blue eyes peered up at him. Full of grief.

Mind reeling with concern and confusion, he stroked her cheek. The need to ease her rocked through him. "Please, Megan."

"Too good to be true. Knew it," she rushed in a tear-strained voice.

Owen frowned, tried but failed to follow her logic. "I don't—"

She dropped her hand, wiped at the tears on one side. "If you're a god, you can't stay. You'll have to go. Sometime. And I'll—"

He shook his head. "I want to stay, Megan." Perhaps the biggest understatement he'd ever uttered. Not only did he want her, he wanted what a life with her could offer—loving companionship, a satisfying conclusion to the empty endlessness of immortality. Not even the loss of his powers outweighed the myriad benefits of humanity.

She pushed against him, but he held fast. "Please don't. Don't make promises you can't keep. I couldn't—"

He cupped her face, leaned right over her, and forced her eyes to meet his. "You need only choose me, Megan, and I will stay forever."

She frowned, batted away more tears. "Choose you. How?"

He had the benefit of John's memories, days of studying her, an eternity of aloneness that she'd cured with her compassion and playfulness and kindness. He loved her already. Though the possibility existed she might never feel that way, Owen took a deep breath and asked for the same in return. "Want me. Need me. *Love* me. Your love can hold me here, with you. Forever."

CHAPTER THIRTEEN

Megan reached up and stroked the hard line of Owen's jaw. The desire reshaping his darkly beautiful face stole her breath.

Want him. No problem. How she'd missed the warm weight of a man atop her, and Owen's body was more perfect and tempting than any she'd ever seen.

Need him. God, she really did. Her body wept for him—and not because of his body alone. She found his kind words and caring nature just as attractive. The way he made her feel—light and buoyant, like she could handle anything—was utterly appealing.

Love him. Her heart stuttered, then pounded against her chest. The room spun around her. Despite their short acquaintance, there was no denying her deep affection for Owen Winters. But love? They'd only just met.

More than that, there had been a time she thought she'd never love again. How could she? John's death, her guilt, had shattered her ability to trust love. Once, she'd given her whole self over to loving, and the loss of it had shattered *her*.

But now?

The men in her life wanted her to be happy, wanted her to let go of the pain. Wanted her to embrace life. To live.

John couldn't. But she could.

Owen's mouth dropped open when she dragged her exploring fingers across the deep red of his bottom lip. So soft.

For now, she'd start with what she knew. "I do want you, Owen. And I need you." She swallowed. "So much."

A deep sound of satisfaction rumbled low in his throat and ricocheted down her body. Those soft lips found hers, already open, waiting for his touch. With his kiss, he possessed her. His scent—winter spice and male—filled her senses. His body covered her. She could live on the cool, sweet taste of his tongue. And, God, his little moans and grunts reverberated right down to the wet heat between her legs.

He trailed open-mouthed kisses over her cheek to her ear, sucked her lobe between his lips and flicked it with his tongue. She gasped as goose bumps erupted everywhere and she offered her neck to his exploration.

"I want you, Megan. Be mine. *Gods.*"

He licked and sucked down her neck. She shivered and grabbed onto the firmness of his sculpted biceps. He nipped at the tendon where neck met shoulder. A moan exploded from her, loud and wanton, but couldn't be helped. She threaded her fingers into his silky black hair and held him to her. "Again," she rasped. He teased her with his teeth, then his tongue and lips. "God, Owen."

She chuckled even as she whimpered at the spine-tingling nips and bites.

"What's so funny?" His warm breath caressed her bare skin.

"Sorry, it's just..." She covered her mouth with her hand, humor-induced tears now gathering at the corners of her eyes.

He pulled her hand away. "Never hide your smile from me." He pressed kisses to her knuckles, then pinned her wrist beside her shoulder.

She finally reined in her amusement. "I'm sorry. It's just, I said, 'God, Owen,' and then"—the chuckles threatened again— "it hit me that, you know, you really are a god, and all."

A playful smirk framed Owen's face. "Are you amused by my godhood?"

She nodded. He thrust his hips into hers, rocking the ridge of his impressive erection against her right where she craved him. Her lips dropped open as she sucked in a breath.

His mismatched eyes blazed. "Still amused?"

She nodded and pressed up against him. Wrapped one leg around his waist and dug her heel into his firm ass.

He grunted and ground down on her, just as she hoped he would. Then his mouth crushed against hers again, their tongue intertwining. He drew away with little kisses on the corner of her lips. "I like you amused. Smiling. Laughing. I want to make you feel that way."

His words wrapped around her heart, mending, binding. She cupped his cheek in her palm. "Sweet, sweet man." She took a deep breath and a leap of faith. "Make love to me."

"Gods, yes." In a flash, he'd pushed up from the couch, lifted her in his arms, and crossed the room.

Butterflies took flight in her stomach. His humor, his gentle kindness, his raw sexuality, his masculine beauty—he appealed to every part of her mind and body. And, maybe, just maybe, her heart.

He settled her on the edge of the bed so she sat facing his

bare, sculpted chest. Her mouth needed a taste. She leaned forward and rained kisses across the warm skin over his sternum, the light covering of chest hair tickling her lips. Grabbing the sides of his waist, she pulled him forward until he stood flush between her thighs. Her tongue curled around his nipple. His grunt and the grip of his big hand in her hair felt like triumph. She sucked the erect nub into her mouth, savored the needy sounds he uttered as she tormented him with her tongue, then her teeth.

Hands tugged at her fleece. She leaned back just long enough to let him remove it and the T-shirt beneath. She shivered, her body no longer familiar with a male's gaze upon her nakedness. God, all at once she was as nervous as a virgin. Scared to see his reaction, her gaze fell into her lap.

His fingers traced fire down the sky blue strap of her bra, over the curve of lace atop her breast. Her heart took off at a sprint, her mouth fell open to accommodate the rush of breaths. Tipping up her chin, he forced her to meet his gaze. "I have never stood before such beauty." He caressed her sore cheek with the back of his hand and his eyes flared, that mysterious light flashing behind the blue and brown.

Megan sucked in a breath. His words emboldened her. His magic enthralled her. She reached behind her back and unfastened the clasp, then dropped the blue lace to the floor. So much intensity flickered behind his eyes she wondered how she'd ever thought him just a man. He was glorious in his otherworldliness. Powerful. She took his hand and placed it on her right breast.

His other hand joined, cupped her left breast. His mouth dropped open as he massaged her, dragged teasing fingers over and under. Every time he touched her nipples, she felt it low in her stomach. A big hand pressed over her heart, pushing her to lie back on the unmade bed. Then he was on her.

Open-mouthed kisses fell over the curves of her breasts. He licked and sucked at her nipples, sending spikes of pleasure down her spine until she was writhing. Her hands tangled in his hair, holding, tugging. He made the same satisfied sounds as when he'd had the ice cream that first time. No, better—louder, more urgent.

While his mouth worshipped her, his hands found the button of her jeans. Dark eyes flashed up to her, questioning.

She nodded, whispered, "It's all right."

With her help, he tugged the denim over her hips and off. He rested his forehead against her belly and groaned, snapped the strap of her panties lightly against her hip. He mumbled against the ticklish skin of her middle.

She squirmed and stroked his hair. "Everything okay?" she whispered.

Without warning, he leaned down and laved his tongue from her panties to her breasts. Then he captured her mouth. The kiss was demanding, possessive. The room spun and she closed her eyes.

He spoke around the edges of their kiss. "Never. Better."

"Good," she snuck in when his lips allowed. "Though you…" She smiled as he came at her again and again. "Still have too…" His hands dug into her hair. God, the way he took control of a kiss.

He moved onto her neck, licking, sucking. "What's that you were saying?"

The smugness in his tone oddly aroused her, especially when it took a moment for the kiss-induced fog in her brain to clear. "Clothes. Too many clothes."

"Mmm. Couldn't agree more." Fingers threaded under her panties at both hips and pulled them off.

Megan gasped, drew her legs up and closed out of surprise. She pointed, pretending outrage. "You! Not me, you!"

His self-satisfied smirk told her he'd known just what she'd meant. "Let me look at you." Big hands stroked her knees.

She trembled, the result of her racing heart and shallow breaths. The adoration on his face gripped her, made her feel safe. Taking a deep, shaky breath, she relaxed her thighs, let them fall open.

His gaze followed her movements, alighted on her most private place like a physical caress. Her arousal spiked, coating the soft folds of her cleft.

Owen inhaled deeply, licked his lips.

His intense observation set her body on fire, had her wet, needy. After a time, she pouted. "Don't tease me."

He met her eyes. "Never," he said, as he tugged at the string tie of his pants.

Megan sucked in a breath. He was naked underneath. And huge. Her hips bucked at the sight. She couldn't tear her eyes away. He was long, thick, swollen with need, veined in ways that made her salivate. He gripped himself, stroked once, twice. Her mouth dropped open, fascinated. All at once, she understood why he'd looked at her so long.

≈≈≈

Owen crawled up onto the bed between her knees. His hands dug under her hips, pushed her diagonally across the mattress until her head landed on a pillow. Then he stretched out between her legs, kissed and licked up her right thigh. Her body became a live wire, squirming, wriggling. Her anticipation was palpable. And he didn't want to make her wait.

His gaze cut to hers, asking permission that she granted with a nod. When he dragged long, hard licks through her wetness, against the nerves at the top of her sex, she cried out, thrashed, rocked herself into his lips. He gripped her hips, held her in place.

Owen had never felt such power. He'd changed the seasons. Controlled the North Wind. Halted avalanches to save those who lived in mountains' shadows. None of those compared with being personally responsible for another's happiness, another's ecstasy. He'd never had a greater purpose. Never felt as if his existence had more meaning.

And, gods, without question, he'd never felt such pleasure. Everything about being with Megan set him ablaze. She smelled of the heady combination of vanilla and femininity. Under his mouth, her soft skin pulsed with life and vitality. Her hands ignited every nerve in his body.

He craved her. His body ached for her. Between his legs, his hard-on throbbed, his balls hung heavy and tight. He was a taut rope fraying in the middle.

"Angel, let go," he groaned against her wet, swollen lips, pulling her closer. She quivered and bucked beneath his mouth. He reached up, cupped and kneaded her breasts, sucked her clit in deep and hard.

Her body went rigid within his grasp and the muscles under his mouth quaked. "Owen!" His name ripped from her throat, morphed into a rasping moan. He wanted to roar in victory, but he was too busy devouring every bit of what her body gifted him.

Nails grasped at his shoulders. Her hand cupped under his

chin, pulling him away. She gasped and squirmed. "Need you, need you," she babbled. He crawled up her still-trembling body. She threaded her hands in his hair. "Incredible. Thank you," she murmured before pulling him down for a deep, exploring kiss.

Gods, the more she tugged at his hair the more he twitched and throbbed between his legs. Her grasp made him feel claimed, her aggressive kiss, with her essence all over him, in him, made him feel accepted. He reveled in every moment.

He lowered himself onto her, groaned deep in his chest as his bareness encountered hers. When his engorged tip brushed against her wet heat, he broke the kiss and gasped.

Instinct guided his body, drew him to her like a magnet. His whole frame shuddered with the need to bury himself in her, join himself to her for all time.

He reached down, grasped his length, his own touch almost painful. Before going further, he gave Megan one last chance to stop. Desire shaped her face, held her lips in an enticing oval. Affection warmed her eyes—he wasn't willing to call it more until she did so herself. She graced him with a small, soft smile.

It was all the encouragement he needed. He pushed forward, sank into her wet tightness inch by dizzying inch. His eyes closed at the soul-centering rightness of his body in hers. Gods, why did humans not spend every moment pleasing one another this way? When her body had accepted all of him, he paused, savored. He trembled with the effort to hold still.

She radiated beneath him. Cheeks flush, eyes open and inviting, their shared body heat wrapping them in a cocoon. She moaned and gripped his back, pulled him against her tighter. "Oh, move in me."

He groaned. Moved. Slowly at first. The deep, dragging strokes were pleasure and pain, but totally life giving. She locked her ankles around him, her heels digging into his ass. Driving him on. "Oh, angel, you are perfect."

She whimpered, rocked her hips, leaned up and kissed him. "You don't have to be gentle."

What had he ever done to deserve her, this? His chest filled with emotion until it was hard to breathe. "If I'm not gentle, I'll never last. You feel too good." It was true, he already felt on edge, the newness of such physical ecstasy more than he could resist. While he wasn't a virgin, it had been eons since he'd suffered Chione's betrayal and last been with a woman. And he'd never been with a human. Never shared a human's emotional warmth, guileless passion.

She thrust her hips again and pressed her heels, hard. "It's okay. Faster, Owen. Please."

His body answered her call. He thrust faster, harder. "Aw, good gods." The room blurred around him at the decadence of her hot, slick grip on his dick. He curled his arms under hers, gripped her shoulders for leverage.

Megan's breathy moans became his whole world. She threw her head back, rasped, "Yes, yes."

A tingling pressure formed low in his gut, pooled in his balls. His eyes rolled back in his head. Harder. Faster. Her body milked him, embraced him. She thrust and bucked under him. Fingers dug into his shoulders. The riot of sensation ricocheted down his spine, exploded.

"Fuck!" he roared. "Aw, gods. Aw, Megan." As he pulsed inside her, his thighs went rigid, his grip on her tightened. He thrust through it, his movements drawing out the ecstasy until he thought he could go mad from too much pleasure. His heart expanded. This feeling of completeness, togetherness—this was love, this was everything.

The sharp bite of her nails in the flesh of his back drew his attention. Under him, she gasped, panting hard. "Don't stop. Oh, please don't stop." She rocked and pressed herself against him.

He nearly growled. Primal satisfaction sent blood to his dick again. "Come on me." He ground his pelvis into the top of her sex, right where he'd earlier concentrated sucking kisses.

"Owen," she groaned. "Oh my God."

"Mmm, that's me." Remembering how much she liked it earlier, Owen nipped down her neck to her shoulder, all the while circling his hips against her.

"Yesyesyes," she ground out, then sucked in a breath. Held it.

Her slick walls tightened around him, dragging a rasped curse from his lips. Then her breath whooshed from her on a high-pitched moan. Her muscles clenched and pulsed. She dug her nails into his back. He relished the biting pain, knew it was the result of her pleasured loss of control. Would endure it for her over and over.

When at last her orgasm calmed, she shuddered and stilled beneath him. She cupped his face in her hands—a sweet, warm gesture he'd come to adore—and looked at him with the most hope-inducing affection. "That was…there's not even a word."

"Heaven on earth," he breathed. Even better. He'd never come close to feeling this kind of warmth, fulfillment, where he was from.

"Heaven on earth." She brushed her fingers over his lips. Then she frowned and chewed her bottom lip. She clenched her internal muscles around his length, still hard inside her.

He sucked a breath in through his teeth.

Megan's eyes went wide. "Are you…I mean, will you…" A blush bloomed on top of the flush that already colored her cheeks.

Owen thrust gently forward, watching her.

"Jesus," she breathed. She hesitated, then asked, "Could you...come again?"

He dropped a kiss to her forehead, already setting a rhythm within her. "I am a god, after all."

CHAPTER FOURTEEN

Owen was going to kill her. And she was going to love every minute of it.

The gray light of pre-dawn filtered through the curtained windows before they'd finally had their fill of each other. They'd only surfaced from the bed to get some dinner—if heaping bowls of ice cream counted—around midnight. Now, Megan wasn't sure she actually had any bones inside her body. Every joint felt loose and fluid, every muscle like Jell-O. She'd never been so tired, or sated, in her whole life.

Owen had proven himself such an attentive lover. Studying her every reaction, repeating those things that elicited her greatest pleasure. Talk about stamina. He could get hard again within mere minutes of coming. And, oh God, when he came. She'd never seen a more sexy image than his face at orgasm, strained with such open, honest pleasure. Not to mention the erotic soundtrack of his muttered encouragements and unrestrained groans.

Her body started responding to her thoughts. No, no. She had to sleep.

His hand squeezed her bare breast and he snuggled in closer behind her. He kissed her hair. "I can smell where your thoughts are heading," he murmured against her ear in an amused, tired voice. "Go to sleep. You need rest before I have you again."

Stupid, all-knowing god.

His low chuckles tickled her neck. "Sleep, angel."

Surrounded by his warmth, bathed in his scent, she finally drifted off.

When she woke, the room was dark, cold. She gasped, whirled over. Empty.

Oh no! She jerked to a seated position. Tears pricked behind her eyes. *It* was *a dream. Owen. Oh no, no.*

"Angel?" A dark form pushed through the bedroom door, perched on the edge of the bed.

"Owen." She launched herself at him, heart thundering in her chest. She patted her hands over him. Broad, bare chest. Muscled arms. That clean, woodsy scent that was all Owen. He was real.

"What's wrong?" His hand smoothed over her curls, brushed them back from her face.

"Couldn't find you," she whispered, afraid her voice would crack if she attempted a normal volume. He was here. Jesus. The last time she'd felt that kind of panic… No. She squashed that thought and buried her face against his chest.

"I'm sorry. I'm here. Right here." He threaded his hands under her arms and pulled her all the way onto his lap. "I was making dinner. Hungry?"

Megan swallowed the last of her panic. She nodded. "What time is it?"

"After seven."

"Oh my God, I can't believe I slept so long." And not a single dream, or nightmare. Now that her anxiety had passed, she could feel the benefit of all those hours of productive sleep. She stretched within Owen's embrace. God, she felt so alive.

Sore, but even that was proof of life, wasn't it?

"I think I wore you out." Even in the dark, his good humor shined through.

She slapped his chest. "And, I didn't wear you out, too?"

He kissed her hair, rubbed soothing circles on her back. "I only woke an hour before you."

Megan felt pleased to hear she'd affected him too. "Good." Her stomach growled.

"Ah, now, back to my question. Hungry?"

She nodded and kissed over his heart. "Ravenous."

He helped her stand. Laced his hands behind her neck, his thumbs caressing her jaw. The gesture made her feel so cared for. "Are you sure you're okay?"

She turned her head and kissed his palm. "I am now. I'll be right out."

"Okay."

Megan padded naked to the bathroom. She shivered and hugged herself—the temperature had dropped since she'd reset the thermostat. Her skin yearned for the refreshment of a warm shower, but she didn't want to keep Owen waiting, thought maybe she'd lure him in with her, after. She freshened up, then took the birth control pill she'd forgotten to take last night. Guess it was lucky she still took the pills after all. She and John weren't ready to start a family before he'd died. They'd wanted to save up more money. Buy a house first. Wait 'til John made partner at the law firm. They thought they had time. It was stupid, really, that she'd never stopped taking them. A total waste of money. When he died, she continued taking them out of habit, at first. Then, because not taking them would've been yet another admission he was gone.

Her mind returned to her panic upon waking and finding Owen gone. She frowned at her own reflection. The shock of John's death, his sudden absence from her life, had impressed a deep scar upon her psyche. A scar Owen's otherworldly origins clearly picked at. Would she ever be able to trust him not to abandon her? Not to leave? What did she have that would hold a *god* to her? And if she couldn't find her way to trusting, could she really give him her heart? Could she take that risk again?

The knock at the door made her jump. "You okay in there?"

She whipped her pajamas and a robe off the hook. "Yeah." When she'd dressed, she opened the door to the great room. "Sorry."

"No need to apologize. I was just checking on you."

"Thanks." She took his hand. "So, what'd you make me?"

He pulled her over to the rustic table that sat under a window by the kitchen. Two big bowls of salad and a pepperoni pizza covered the table.

Her stomach clenched in anticipation. The pizza smelled wonderful. The hunger that had built during hours of sex nearly convinced her she could eat the whole pie. "Oh, it looks so good. Thank you." She pushed up on tiptoe to kiss his cheek.

"Your nose is cold. Are you warm enough?"

Her flannel PJs and soft fleece robe helped, but it *was* cold in here. He needed it to be cold, though. "I'm okay."

Owen frowned. Grabbed a blanket off the back of the couch. "I'll not have you uncomfortable for me."

"I don't mind."

He draped the blanket around her shoulders like a cape. "Well, I do. Now"—he pulled a chair out for her—"the pizza might be a little cool. I didn't want to wake you."

She sat. "Pizza's better cold anyway."

He beamed and joined her at the table. They ate their salads over small talk. She answered all his questions about her life in Arlington. These days, there wasn't much to tell. She lived alone in the apartment she'd shared with John, worked in the city as an Admissions Counselor for American University, hung out with her best friend Kate, and often had Sunday dinner at her parents' house in Fairfax. Dull as it was to her, Owen hung on every detail and asked question after question.

"What is your life like?" she asked.

Owen pushed his plate away, having finished his whole salad and four slices of pizza. He sat back in his chair. "I've spent much of my existence as a force of nature, and very little as a corporeal being. I didn't mind, mostly. Though the last few days made it clear I simply didn't know what I was missing."

Megan gave a small smile, warmed by his last words but aware of the loneliness that resonated from what came before. "How long has your 'existence' been?"

"Eons? I don't know. Time has less meaning where I'm from. We don't account for it the way you do."

"Eons. Like, hundreds of years? Thousands?" The thought was nearly dizzying.

He simply nodded. "It never meant anything to me. Until now."

The words filled her chest. Still, she wanted more. "But, when you were corporeal, I mean, did you hang out with other gods, the other Anemoi? Did you have a house, or a place where you lived? The other day you said you had a family you lived with when you were young."

"I was originally from what is now Northern Ireland, but my parents died before I was old enough to know them, so I lived with Boreas, the Supreme God of Winter. I would have ended up with him anyway, when I was older, as he calls the most gifted children of the lesser northern deities into his service, develops their powers, and teaches them how to use them in the service of Winter. His main citadel is in the Kingdom of Hyperborea, beyond the North Wind, in the Realm of Gods, though he maintains residences all throughout the world's colder climes. I lived where he lived, most of the time, at least when I was not elemental. Boreas became like a father, included me in his family, trained me in my godhood."

Megan tried to picture the existence he described. Failed. Then another thought came to mind. "And, all that time, were you…well, alone?"

He shifted in his seat. Rolled his shoulders. Unease niggled in Megan's stomach, unsettled the big dinner she'd just enjoyed. "There was one woman."

"Another god?" She swallowed.

"A goddess."

"A goddess. Right." An ugly feeling crawled down her spine. A freaking goddess.

"Her name is Chione. She is a goddess of snow, and Boreas' daughter. We grew up together." Owen reached across the table and grasped Megan's hand. "Be settled. It has been over between us for a long, long time."

She swallowed, nodded. "Why? What happened? If you don't mind me asking."

"I don't." He tugged a hand through his hair. "She left me for another. Just months before our godhoods were to be joined."

Megan sucked in a breath and wrapped both hands around his on the table. "I'm sorry." How could anyone treat him so carelessly? The jealousy she'd felt a moment ago grew into outraged dislike of this Chione person, goddess, whatever. But then, now Owen was here, with her.

"I'm not. It brought me to you." Owen's eyes flashed, that magical light flaring behind them. How many times had she seen that effect last night? Now it made her stomach quiver.

"So, when that happened, you…left?"

He nodded. "I would not stay to watch her be joined with another. It was awkward enough watching Boreas try to balance supporting his daughter and tiptoeing around me. So I removed myself from the equation. It was Boreas who called for my return upon John's plea."

"Why?"

Owen rubbed his fingers over his mouth. "He said if there was a chance for happiness, he wanted me to be the one to have it, in recompense…"

Megan's breathing hitched. She launched herself from her chair and knelt next to his. "I can't believe that happened to you. I'm sorry." Her throat tightened. Owen needed happiness, too. She never would've imagined they could have that in common. How long had he exiled himself from the company of the other gods? She hugged him and pressed her face into his bare chest. Thoughts of him lonely and alone squeezed her heart.

"Your compassion warms me, Megan Snow."

She remembered how he'd held her when she broke down after admitting her guilt about John's death. "You do the same for me."

"Come now." He helped her stand. Then he kissed her,

once, twice. Lingering kisses full of thanks and quiet need. "I'll clean this up."

"I'll do it. You cooked."

"Let's do it together."

"Yeah."

When they were done, Owen tugged her into a warm embrace. "I would have you again." He pressed his growing erection against her belly. "But I know you are sore. I see it in the way you move."

Megan's cheeks heated. "Just a little. I'm not complaining." She really wasn't. The pleasure he'd given her over and over had far outstripped any discomfort she'd had.

"I'm glad," Owen said. "Why don't I run a bath? Would that soothe you?"

The tub at the cabin was heaven, extra long and with a sculpted back perfect for resting against. Ooh, taking a bath with him would be wonderful. "Yes, that sounds great."

He kissed her again. "Okay."

They made their way into the bathroom together, touching, kissing. While Owen got the water started, she brushed her teeth.

"See if this is the right temperature for you," he said.

Megan reached her hand into the warm stream under the faucet. "Just about perfect." She inched the nozzle to make the water a bit hotter. When the tub was halfway full, she shed her robe and stepped in.

Behind her, Owen groaned.

She wiggled her bare bottom at him before sinking down into the steaming water. When she looked up, his eyes flared again. She smiled. "Well, come on."

He frowned, winced.

"You're going to join me, aren't you?"

He knelt down next to the tub and rested his arms on the edge. "I can't."

She scooted closer, the water carrying her weight to where he was. "Why?" Then it hit her. "It's too warm for you."

He nodded. "Yes, for now. It's cold showers for me." He winked.

His attempt to be playful touched her, but didn't alleviate her concerns. "What would happen if you got in?"

"Really want to know?"

"Yes."

Owen reached out toward the warm stream still flooding into the tub from the faucet. Megan's heart took off at a gallop, fear for him prickled her scalp. He stuck the four fingers of his right hand into the water.

They disappeared. Simply melted into the water.

CHAPTER FIFTEEN

"No!" Megan moaned. She wrenched his wrist back from the flow. "Oh my God." Her mouth dropped open as, before her eyes, his fingers reappeared. Filmy at first, then solidified. She grabbed his miraculously restored hand and hugged it to her chest. "Don't you ever, ever do that again!"

With his other hand, Owen stroked her cheek. "I'm sorry. I didn't mean to scare you."

"What if...damn it, Owen. What if you hadn't come back?"

"I did."

"Yeah, but what if you couldn't. Oh my God! How did you get the pizza into and out of the oven?"

He blushed. He actually frickin' blushed. "Uh, well—"

"Did this same thing happen then, too?"

He twisted his lips, looked up at her through his hair. "I am strong, Megan. I can weather short exposures to heat."

She gripped his hand harder. Needed to know he was okay. Solid. She shook her head, refusing to cry again. Her tear ducts had gotten enough of a workout these past few days. But wasn't this exactly what scared her? That something bad would happen to him while he was helping her?

"Wait. You said 'for now.' You had to take cold showers, for now. What does that mean?" Her stomach clenched.

He laid his head on his arms, his expression earnest but guarded. "If you decide to choose me, if you could love me, I'll be freed from the limitations of my current form."

She knew he'd say that, on some level she knew everything hinged on her loving him.

It seemed something of a circular problem, though. She was afraid to love him, in case he'd disappear. Yet, keeping him here seemed to depend on her loving him. Trying to piece together *that* puzzle would take more brainpower than she had at the moment.

"Does that mean you'll become human? If…" The rest of the sentence stuck in her throat.

"Yes, that's exactly what it means."

"Oh, Owen, I do care for you, but I—"

Fingers pressed against her lips, quieted her apology. "I understand. It's been very little time. I do not mean to pressure you. Now, relax, settle back. Enjoy your bath. I'll keep you company, if that's okay?"

"Of course it's okay. More than okay." She kissed his fingers, one small peck on the pad of each finger, then released him and floated back through the now-deeper water. Reclining against the carved back of the tub, Megan blew out a deep breath in an effort to release pent-up stress.

Sometimes they spoke softly, sharing stories about their lives, asking questions to get to know the other better. Sometimes they sat in comfortable silence. Either way, Owen was such wonderful company. How Megan had missed that. And now, at long last, she'd found it again. Warm, pleasant pressure filled her chest.

After a while, the water cooled and Megan's skin pruned. She pulled the plug with her toes, earning one of his playful grins.

"Hand me a towel?"

He rose, grabbed a thick length of chocolate brown terry cloth. "Must I?"

She rolled her eyes. "Yes. It's chilly when I'm all wet."

He waggled his eyebrows. "I could warm you."

"I'm sure you could. But first, towel." He handed it over with a big show of reluctance. She yanked it from his hands, adoring the way he made even the simplest things so much fun.

She wrapped the towel around her hair, then sweet-talked him into a second one for her body. He held her hand as she stepped out over the tall edge.

Pouting, he stuck a finger between her cleavage and tugged at the terry, peeking down into the gap. She hugged him.

"Megan?"

"Hmm?"

"There's something I've wanted to do since I first saw you."

෨෨෪

Owen smiled down at Megan, hair and body wrapped up in brown towels. Skin all pink and warm and fragrant. A myriad of expressions played out on her face. Her openness and acceptance unleashed a safe, comforting warmth within his chest.

He was dying to take care of something for her, and now

seemed the perfect time. What good were his powers if he couldn't help her?

"Uh, okay? What is it you wanted to do?"

"Go sit on the bed. I'll be right there."

She braced her hands on her hips. "What you've wanted to do involves the bed?"

He laughed, a wonderfully satisfying sensation in its own right. "Well, yes. Now that I've had you I can safely say I'll always want you, bed or not. But I suggested the bed because I thought it would be a comfortable place to wait for a moment. I need to do something first."

"Uh huh." She bit down on her bottom lip, tried to restrain a grin.

"Good to see where your mind is, though." He tugged her into a hug as she scoffed. "Go on, I'll be right there."

"Fine," she huffed.

He smacked her bottom as she strutted past him.

"Hey!"

Owen chuckled, watched her hips shimmy under the short length of towel. Mmm. He adjusted himself in his borrowed pants. At some point he would need clothes of his own, or at least to wash the jeans he'd arrived in. He dashed from the bathroom, more comfortable out of the steamy air, and made for the front door.

Sockless and shirtless, he stepped onto the porch. The night air fortified him. He drank in deep gulps of it. Eager to finish his task and get back to Megan, he jogged down the steps and dug cupped hands into the snow. He brought icy handfuls to his mouth, again and again. Oh, gods. The frozen crystals filled him with renewed power, strength, eased away the draining impact of the oven, the bathwater, the steam.

Now he would be able to do what he'd been yearning to do.

He scooped up one more handful, taking the refreshing coldness of the winter elements into himself. His body hummed with nature's energy.

He stilled his body and extended his mind. Issued the request for an audience. Head bowed, he waited.

An electric ripple and whirl of wind announced Boreas' arrival. "Owen."

"My Lord, thank you for coming." The wind grazed Owen's hair. He lifted his head.

Boreas nodded. "All you ever have to do is ask. I only hope you know this."

The sentiment made Owen stand taller. "Yes."

"You want to know about Zephyros."

Owen met the Supreme God's serious metallic gaze. "Any change?"

Boreas tugged at his beard. "No. He's ignoring me, completely refusing to recognize my summons."

Owen blew out a breath and looked up at the star-brightened sky. "Three days, then."

"Yes, no more, and maybe less. I'm sorry, son."

The older god's affection bolstered him. "I appreciate that, Boreas, but this is no fault of yours." Owen managed a small smile. Even though there wasn't much else he could do, Boreas' support made him feel like he wasn't in this all alone. First Megan, now his god. How he'd missed this sense of belonging and connectedness he'd suddenly found after so very long. "Well, I suppose I best get back inside."

Boreas gave a wry smile. "Good luck."

The wind caressed Owen's hair, kicked up around him, and left him standing alone in front of the cabin.

Owen refused to let the news steal even a bit of the joy he'd found in the last two days. He'd simply had to show her, make her see, which reminded him she awaited his return.

Just inside the door, Owen paused, letting his body acclimate to the indoor temperature. Thirty seconds. A minute. He closed the door behind him. Waited. He didn't want to go to Megan distressed. But it was better this time. The snow gave his body reserves of power from which to draw.

Finally, he strode into the bedroom.

"Hey, there you are. I was beginning to worry about you," she said with a warm smile. She was sitting against the headboard, book in hand, the towel from her hair discarded and the blonde curls mostly dry.

"Sorry. Didn't mean to take so long." He climbed up on the bed. She reached out to him as he moved to her. He crawled over her covered legs and straddled her thighs, then plucked the book from her hands and set it aside face down, preserving her page. "Now. May I kiss you?"

"At this point, you really don't have to ask. Consider it a standing invitation."

His heart stuttered. He liked the sound of that. Tilting her chin up with his fingers, he leaned in.

She gasped. Grabbed his hands in hers and pulled them away. "Holy crap! Your hands are like ice! Were you outside?"

"Yes. Sorry." He brought his hands to his mouth and blew. They warmed on command.

"Are you okay? I mean, did you need the cold?"

Her concern eased the tension he carried over the impending change in weather and added another layer to his affection for her. He could count the number of beings who truly cared for him on one hand. And not even use all the fingers. His hands found her face again. "I'm okay, now. Better?"

She nodded. "Perfect." She gripped his wrist and squeezed, stroked his skin with her thumb. "Now, some god around here promised me a kiss."

"That would be me." He found her sweet, full lips. Wonderful as they were, though, her lips weren't his destination. He traced little kisses full of adoration up her left cheek to her cheekbone until he encountered the scabbed-over frostnip.

Power flared in his chest. He opened his mouth, swiped his tongue over the full length of the wound. Absorbed her pain into him.

∞∞∞

Megan gasped. Dizziness and confusion descended.

Something…something was happening. She gripped onto Owen's biceps, struggling against the loss of equilibrium. Pleasure surged, too, where his lips trailed fire over her skin, but then he'd licked her, and… She didn't even know how to describe it. Pins and needles. Zero gravity. Déjà vu. All of the above together, and more.

Owen pulled back from the kiss heavy-lidded, wearing a look of total satisfaction. His gaze, full of that unnatural light, skimmed from her cheek to her eyes. Words spilled from his lips that Megan didn't understand, a foreign language she'd never before heard. He spoke with a quiet passion.

Megan's heart thundered within her chest. She panted. Her equilibrium restored and the room righted itself once again. "What just happened?" she whispered.

"I've been dying to make it better," he said in a quiet, reverent tone.

With a shaky hand, Megan palmed her cheekbone. She dragged fingers over the skin there, the smooth, scab-less skin. She pushed against Owen's chest, wriggled her legs underneath him. "Let me up. Please. Owen?"

She had to be imagining this, right?

Owen swung his leg off and frowned, watching her.

Her shivers had as much to do with the palpable magic of the moment as with the cold air and minimalist towel covering she still wore. She skidded into the bathroom and flicked on the light.

CHAPTER SIXTEEN

Healed. The frostnip was healed.

Megan gaped into the mirror, leaned in. Instead of the crusty scab, the skin was healthy, free of the blemish created when she'd laid crying on the snowman. On Owen.

She whirled away from the mirror, found him leaning cross-armed against the doorjamb to the bathroom, head down. "How?" she whispered.

He shrugged one muscled shoulder. "You got that creating me. I wanted to make it better."

Megan's heart seized in her chest. She flew at him and wrapped her arms around his big body. "That is…I can't believe… Thank you," she managed around the lump in her throat.

Owen's arms surrounded her. He kissed her hair, laid his face against the crown of her head. "I would do anything for you," he said in a quiet voice.

Their eyes met in the mirror. Megan drank in their image.

Owen was tall and dark, eyes blazing and brimming with emotion. And, jeez, she wasn't sure she'd ever looked better than all folded within his embrace. A part of her bristled at the thought, cried disloyalty on behalf of John. But, then, he'd sent Owen to her, hadn't he? He'd wanted her to be happy. Was it so wrong of her to accept what John wanted her to have?

She turned her head to nuzzle into Owen's chest. From the corner of her eye, she was sure she'd seen something glint in the light. She pressed a kiss to Owen's bare chest and pulled away, stepped back to the mirror again. Leaning over the sink, she smoothed her fingers over her cheek and inspected the area.

There! She gasped.

"Oh, my God." Her eyes flashed to Owen in the mirror. He shifted feet and crossed and uncrossed his arms.

Heart racing, her gaze returned to her own reflection, this time easily finding what had caught her attention. At the back of her cheekbone, at the edge of where the scab had extended, was a little white mark, no bigger than the tip of a pencil's eraser. In the shape of a snowflake. Her fingers couldn't tell it was there, but she could just make out its six pointed arms stretching out from an intricate central star. When the light caught the marked skin just right, it glimmered.

"Owen?" she whispered. Dragging her eyes away from the impossible little mark, she turned to face him, sagged back against the counter. So many reactions competed for center stage, her brain nearly froze.

He came to her, grasped her hands. "I'm sorry. Healing is not my normal…area of expertise. The frostnip was going to scar. When I realized I couldn't remove the wound in its entirety, that it would leave a mark, I thought… Gods, I'm sorry." He tugged at his hair with both hands, stepped away.

Instead of an ugly scratch of a scar, he'd given her a beautiful piece of himself. A snowflake. Small and discreet, noticeable if you knew to look, but otherwise really just for her. A gift.

"Don't be sorry." She stretched up on tiptoes and kissed him, her clutching hands forcing him to bend down to her height. "I don't mind," she said around the edge of a kiss. "I love it, in fact." The power he demonstrated healing her, marking her—she was dazzled. Her heart and stomach fluttered.

All of a sudden, something occurred to her.

She looked up into Owen's heated gaze. "Did you have to go outside to be able to do that, heal my cheek?"

He nodded. "The snow intensifies my power. So, it helped."

Megan frowned. "Did it hurt you to do it?"

"Gods, Megan." His voice sounded almost choked up. He pressed a long kiss to her forehead.

"What? Did I say something wrong?"

"No, you said everything right."

She spread her fingers out on his strong, broad chest, skimmed them up around his neck. "Then what is it? You seem upset."

He shook his head. "I'm not. It's just... I've been alone a long time. Your concern, it's..." He shook his head again, stumbled over the words.

All at once she understood. She thought of him being orphaned, losing the only family he'd known to train as a god, of Chione's betrayal, of leaving the other gods to make it less awkward for everyone. Who did Owen have to express concern? To worry over him, for him? Megan feared she knew the answer, and didn't like what she suspected one bit.

Maybe she could be that person for him.

The idea was as appealing as it was terrifying. She'd had

someone to care for once, and he'd been ripped away in the dark of night, leaving a gaping hole in her life. Could she take that risk again, chance that kind of life-altering loss? She shuddered.

Owen rubbed his hands up and down her back, long soothing strokes from towel to bare skin. With his touch, he took care of *her*, calmed *her*.

She inhaled a deep breath and resolved to take care of him right now. Nodding her head toward the bedroom door, she said, "Come with me." Holding hands, they walked back into the bedroom. When they stood at the bedside, she cupped his face in one hand. "Thank you for helping me."

"You're welcome."

With her free hand, she tugged the thick terrycloth away from her body and let it drop to the floor. "I want you," she said.

Flaring eyes raked down her body. He licked his lips and kissed her cheek over the snowflake. "I'm glad you love this." He kissed it again, let his tongue caress the skin there. "Because I find you wearing my mark so fucking sexy."

Megan gasped, sagged into him. The possessiveness in his tone readied her between her thighs. Being marked by him thrilled her in ways she didn't fully understand. But she didn't think on it long. Instead, she grasped the waistband of his sweatpants and shoved them over his hips. Together, they worked them off.

Already hard, his erection jutted out against her, igniting flames under her skin whenever they touched. Her mouth watered. Kissing his neck and jaw, she said, "I'm gonna take care of you now, Owen." Then she dropped to her knees and licked his hard length from base to tip.

Owen groaned deep in his throat.

Under her eyelashes, she peeked up at him. That magical

light flashed behind his mismatched gaze. She swirled her tongue around his swollen head, savored the taste of him. Evidence of his arousal leaked onto her tongue. She closed her lips around him and sucked him in a little at a time, reveling in his taste, in how much she affected him.

His grunts and muttered exclamations echoed down to the nerves between her legs until her own moisture slicked up her thighs. She wrapped her hands behind the backs of his legs, loving the way his muscles clenched, and used the leverage to suck him harder, faster. To pull him deeper into her mouth.

Groaning, he threaded his fingers into her hair, exerted pressure. Just a little.

She moaned around him, thrilled at every bit of control he lost. Shaking with desire, she dragged her hands up the backs of his thighs until she could grab his ass. She pulled him tight, sucked him down deep.

He cried out loud enough that the sound echoed in the room. He thrust once, then exploded. Within her intimate grip, all six-plus feet of his huge body trembled and shuddered. His hold tightened in her hair.

Megan drank him down, his taste spicy and male. Pleasing him made her feel victorious. Her chest filled with a satisfied warmth.

When he calmed, she rose on shaky legs. The moisture between her thighs was even more noticeable standing. She clenched her muscles, igniting sparks from her center that radiated into her legs and stomach. His cock rebounded against her hip.

He gripped her waist and chucked her onto the mattress. She gasped and screamed out laughter even as her body bounced on impact.

Then he mounted her, pinning her wrists to the bed. He kissed her, long and deep, his tongue exploring her mouth. She groaned, totally enthralled that he didn't seem to mind the taste of himself in her.

They kissed and writhed together until Megan found herself about to beg for him to take her. She ached for the fullness only he could give. A thought sprung to mind and, before she lost her nerve, she gripped his shoulders and shoved, hard.

Owen fell to the side, mouth open, eyebrow arched. His quizzical expression spurred her on. She pushed him until he was prone, and then she straddled him. Hands braced on his shoulders, she dragged her wetness against his length, his pleasured groan and desperate grip on her hips urging her to draw out their anticipation.

When she could wait no longer to possess him, she met his gaze. His erection throbbed in her hand. She sank down on him, took him into her body without hesitation or reservation. He unleashed a guttural moan, wrenched his head back into the pillow. God, this felt so right—he filled her body like he'd been made for her; every moment together, he breached the grief-fortified walls around her heart.

She pulled his hands from her hips and placed them on her breasts, urged him to grip and massage her. "Just feel," she whispered. He nodded and licked his lips, his heavy-lidded gaze darting from one part of her to another.

Rising and lowering again and again, she rode him, their gazes locked, their labored breaths resounding in the night-darkened room. The bathroom light cast a triangle of diffused gold over them. He was so beautiful, *so* darkly beautiful. A warm pressure fluttered in her stomach. She gasped, fell forward over him, her nipples dragging against his chest. He pulled her down for a long, deep kiss, and she was lost in him. He was all she could see, all she could smell, all she could feel. His pleasured grunts and murmurings thrilled her as they always did.

Her Owen. Always so enthusiastic.

Her Owen.

How easy would it be to just leap. Her heart was getting there, was finding it easier and easier every moment to imagine the jump, the free fall, landing in that soft place of togetherness and partnership. But her head...her head couldn't stop with the "what ifs." Like she stood utterly still, her feet cemented. Grief disproved the old "better to have loved and lost" adage. And she didn't think she'd survive it a second time.

Fingers brushed her jawline. "Hey."

She blinked out of her thoughts and found Owen's concerned expression, brows furrowed over dark eyes. In that moment, she hated having worried him. This was supposed to be about him, about taking care of him. "I'm sorry," she whispered, then kissed him. "I'm here."

He dug his big hands into her hair and pushed it back off her face. "You okay?"

"Better than okay. I'm perfect. You're perfect."

"You're heaven," he murmured. From her hair, his hands skimmed down her back to her ass. He squeezed, and thrust to meet her downward strokes. "Oh, Megan, please come on me."

She groaned. The words ignited the nerves between her thighs, set her body to jangling. Their strokes quickened, shortened, became more frantic. Their bodies met right where she needed. Her stomach clenched. Sensation pooled, tightened, detonated like a hundred brilliant fireworks.

"Owen," she screamed, then went limp on his chest as her muscles continued to quiver.

No matter. He lifted her hips in his strong grasp, his muscled thighs continuing their dance, drawing out every last bit of ecstasy her body would provide.

Instead of leaving her sated, the intensity of her orgasm left her feeling frenzied. She pushed up on shaky arms and rode him at a hot, hard pace. Holding his gaze, she begged him with her eyes until the words spilled out. "Come, Owen. Come. I want to feel it. I want to see it. Come."

He gritted his teeth, jaw ticking. Eyes flaring, he thrust faster, faster. Inside her, he swelled. She clenched her muscles, using her body to encourage his release. He groaned from deep down in his gut, and then his body seized and bucked. "For you. Foryouforyou," he murmured over and over. Strong arms strapped her to his chest as his body pitched beneath hers. "Aw, angel," he whispered reverently when he calmed. He pressed kisses everywhere his lips could reach.

After a long, quiet moment, Megan scooted down his body enough that her hips settled between his thighs and she could rest her chin on his chest and look at him.

Utter adoration shone from his gaze. He gave her a small, affectionate smile, caressed her hair, her face, her shoulders. "That was magic," he whispered.

I love you, she thought. She nearly choked on the strong impulse to give voice to the emotion. Her heart beat out a staccato rhythm against his abdomen, and she was glad their recent activity would mask the real reason for its current pounding sprint. Could it be true? Or was the intense pressure desperate to spring forth from the thrumming organ in her chest the product of her postcoital bliss? It would be so easy to write it off as such.

The very thought of denying her true feelings soured her

stomach, made it hard to breathe. But, then, she couldn't share them with him either. Not yet.

God, why did this have to be so hard? Why couldn't she just be normal? Woman meets man. Woman likes man. Woman and man fall in love and live happily ever after, the end. Was that really too much to ask?

Fingers smoothed over her forehead. "Penny for your thoughts?"

She turned her head and kissed his wrist, then pulled his hand down and kissed his palm. "Just thinking about you," she admitted.

One side of his lips quirked up in a sexy grin. "Is that right?"

Still holding his hand, she nodded, her chin rocking on his chest. "Yeah."

Dark eyes blazed. "Anything good?"

"Everything good." It was true. Loving him was good. She knew it was good. Knew it *could* be good. Great, even.

Owen stared at her a long moment, his eyes brimming with emotion. Then he rolled them, settling himself over her. Lingering kisses rained down over her heart, making it stutter and thrum anew. Words spilled from his lips in that odd language again.

Megan didn't interrupt his hushed, ardent speech, not because she wasn't curious to understand, but because the tone of it sounded so much like a prayer. So she remained quiet, laced her fingers through the layered strands of his black hair. Finally, he laid his head on her chest over her heart. She held him and stroked his hair until the soft, shallow breathing against her left breast told her he'd fallen asleep.

Then, she lay there, cradling a god in her arms. Choked up with the emotions she felt but was too afraid to admit.

CHAPTER SEVENTEEN

A persistent mechanical growl pulled Megan from sleep the next morning. The sound was so foreign, she bolted upright, listened.

The fog lifted from her brain. Mr. Johansson, here to dig her out.

"What's going on?" came Owen's groggy voice.

She pecked him on the cheek, slid out from under him. "The man who takes care of my driveway when it snows." Her skin erupted in goose bumps, the morning air so cool against her nakedness. "Usually he calls…" She tugged on clothes, then dashed to the bathroom, realizing as she did so she hadn't heard from anybody in days. Odd.

When she returned to the bedroom, Owen was sitting on the edge of the bed, sheet draped across his lap but otherwise bare. She wedged herself between his thighs and threaded her arms around his neck. His kisses tempted her to stay, to push him back onto the mattress, but Mr. Johansson was a talker. He'd be knocking at the door sooner or later if she didn't come out on her own. "Sorry. Be back in a bit. Go back to sleep if you want."

"Nah. It's no problem."

She ducked in for one last kiss, then left him with a lightness in her step.

Opening the door, she was pleasantly surprised by the milder temperature. Granted, it was still cold, but it wasn't biting like the day they built the igloo. The morning sun made everything glitter and shine. Winter's beauty buoyed her spirits even more.

From the steps of the porch, she waved a hand over her head. Mr. Johansson signaled back from his perch on the big yellow tractor, perhaps a hundred yards down the long curved drive from the cabin. Mounds of snow lined both sides where he'd already plowed.

Since it would take him a while to get to the top of the driveway, she went back inside and made twice as much coffee as she normally would, knowing the older man would appreciate a cup. While the coffeemaker chugged and gurgled, Megan flipped open her cell phone to find a black screen. Out of battery. Of course it was. Why hadn't she thought about it sooner?

Shuffled footsteps caught her attention. "Hey," Owen said. She took in the sight of him, dressed in a new borrowed outfit—a long-sleeved navy T-shirt and a pair of khakis that had been too long on John. The shirt highlighted the difference in his eyes.

Well, okay, there was the reason she hadn't been thinking about the real world.

"Hey," she said. She hooked up her phone charger and plugged it into the phone. After a minute, the cellular provider's logo flashed across the screen with a musical jingle. While she waited for it to start up, she lifted the cordless receiver on the landline. Nothing. Her cell beeped incoming messages. "Oh, shit."

"What's the matter?" Owen wrapped his arms around her, kissed her cheek, peered over her shoulder.

Megan leaned back into his embrace and worked the buttons on her phone. Five text messages. Ten missed calls. Oh, shit. "Missed a bunch of calls." She turned in his arms, offered him a kiss. "Mind if I take a minute and listen to these messages? I'd better return some."

"Course not. Go ahead. You hungry?"

Megan nodded as she read the first of the text messages. "Starved," she said, then she frowned. The texts were from Kate, snarky at first, worried by the end. She pecked out a quick reassurance and apology, then with a grimace started in on the voice mails. Her mom, her dad. Kate, three times. Her parents again. Those were just the ones from Christmas night.

She dialed her parents' number.

"Oh, thank God," came her mother's voice. "Are you okay? Why didn't you answer your cell phone? The cabin number just gives a busy signal." The words spilled out in a rush.

"I'm sorry, Mom. I, uh, lost power. And I guess I didn't realize my cell battery died." Megan tugged her hand through her hair as she paced back and forth in front of the breakfast bar. Guilt for worrying everyone squeezed her gut.

"So, the power's back on now?"

"Yeah." She winced at the half-truth. The power had been back on for two days.

"Oh"—her mother sighed, a sound full of relief—"that's good. So, everything okay? How are you?"

"I'm fine, Mom. Good, actually." She glanced up at Owen, his shoulders taut under the dark shirt as he stretched to pull down some bowls.

"Good?" The hope in her mother's voice made tears prick at the back of Megan's eyes.

"Yeah," she said. Awe colored her voice and for a moment stole her breath. It was true. She *was* good. When was the last time she had said that and meant it?

"Sorry to interrupt," Owen stage-whispered. "Which do you want?" In one hand, he held a box of Special K, with the other, he shook a box of Lucky Charms at her. He waggled his eyebrows and nodded sideways at the cartoon leprechaun.

She shook her head at his antics. Right there. He was the reason she could say that and mean it. She muffled the receiver with her hand. "Surprise me."

"Is someone there?"

"Oh, uh, yeah. A friend."

Her mother paused, and Megan could imagine the expression she made when something didn't make sense — arched eyebrow, narrowed gaze, lips quirked to one side. "Anyone I know?"

As Owen poured Lucky Charms into their bowls, he popped an occasional colored marshmallow into his mouth. His eyebrows flew up every time as if he were surprised by the flavor. Megan suppressed a chuckle. "No. A new friend."

"A man."

She rolled her eyes. "Yes, mother." A beep interrupted the call. Then another. Kate, she guessed.

"Megan, what's going on?" Suppressed excitement undergirded the question.

Butterflies let loose in her stomach. She inhaled a deep breath and prayed her mother wouldn't freak out. "I, um, met someone?" Also not exactly true, but she wasn't broaching the whole he's-an-ancient-god-who-came-to-life-through-my-snowman conversation. Not yet, anyway. Maybe not ever.

A long pause stretched out. "Oh, Megan," her mother finally croaked.

Megan fought back a kneejerk reaction to downplay the situation, but given her realization last night, she couldn't bring herself to do it. At a loss for what to say instead, she cleared her throat. "I'm really sorry I worried you. I just wanted to let you know I'm okay up here."

"I'm so glad." Her mother's unsaid words hung heavy on the line. "Okay, dear, well, I'll see you in a few days, right? You'll be back for Sunday dinner?"

Shit, Megan hadn't thought that far ahead. Her gaze flashed to Owen, now sitting on a stool watching her. How did this whole thing with him work? "Um, is it okay if I get back to you?"

"Sure. I love you, Megan."

"I love you, too," she said, looking away from Owen. Her heart gripped in her chest.

Overall, the call with her mom left her feeling cautiously hopeful, lighter. She pulled up the text messages that had come in. They were from Kate, as she'd expected. Her best friend's usual snarkiness did little to hide how badly she'd been worried. Megan fired off another apology.

"Everything all right?" Owen asked as she slid onto her stool.

"Yeah. Everything's fine now. Thanks for making breakfast."

Colorful marshmallow charms dotted the cereal in her bowl. "Good choice," she said. The milk was cold, the cereal sweet. Her stomach rumbled as she ate. She'd better hurry, the volume of the plow told her Mr. Johansson would soon be done.

Owen scooped up a mound of cereal. "Box said they were magically delicious." He cleared his spoon with a big bite.

"Well, they're definitely delicious, but only you are both magical *and* delicious." She leaned over and pressed a sloppy kiss to his cheek. When she sat back, his eyes blazed at her. Holding his heated gaze, she put another spoonful of cereal in her mouth, then made a big show of slowly withdrawing the spoon from between her lips.

He groaned. "You know—"

A knock sounded at the door.

"Hold that thought." Eating one more heaping serving, she jumped off her seat and dashed to get the door. She'd been so engrossed in teasing Owen she hadn't realized the noise of the tractor had cut out. Cold air swirled in when she opened the door. "Hi, Mr. Johansson. Come on in."

They shook hands as he entered, then he stomped his boots on the slate entryway. "So good to see ya, Ms. Megan. Merry Christmas."

"Merry Christmas to you, too. How are things out there?"

Bushy salt-and-pepper eyebrows furrowed over kind blue eyes. "This is the durndest snowstorm I've seen in years. Down in town there's only maybe a foot or so, but up here on the mountain things are real bad. County just got the main roads cleared, that's why it took me a few days to get to ya. Tried to call, but a lot of the lines are down."

Megan waved off his explanation. "It's fine. Thanks for coming. I've got some fresh-brewed coffee."

"That would be just fine," Mr. Johansson said as he took off his parka. He finally noticed Owen. "Oh, I'm sorry. I didn't mean to interrupt."

"No worries. Mr. Johansson, this is my friend, Owen Winters. Owen, Carl Johansson." Megan stepped up to the coffeepot, then prepared a tall mug of black coffee, just as he liked it.

The men shook hands. Megan blushed a little as the older man's gaze flicked between them. Thank God they were dressed. She handed the mug across the breakfast bar to him.

"Why, thank ya, Ms. Megan."

The three of them sat and made small talk about roads and power outages, about how good ski conditions must be up at the resort. When Carl had asked about the igloo out front, he and Owen engaged in a whole discussion of how they'd made it. Megan admired Owen's easy manner with the older man. He listened with his full attention, asked questions, made jokes that brought Mr. Johansson's craggy face to life. When they got to the topic of the weather, Mr. Johansson found a kindred spirit in Owen, who could talk the weather like nobody's business. Naturally.

"Be warmer by this weekend, though," Mr. Johansson said after a while. "I reckon the warmer temps will help clean up all this mess."

Owen nodded his head, dropped his gaze. "I imagine you're right about that."

Megan frowned. She tried to catch Owen's eye, but Mr. Johansson prattled on and Owen gave the older man the respect of his attention.

"Spring seems to come earlier and earlier every year. Why, time was it wouldn't crack forty degrees round these parts 'til late January or early February. They're calling for fifty-five on Friday, providing them weather people know what they're talking about. Ya never know," he said. "Well, I best get back to it." He slid off his stool, extended a hand to Owen. "Good to meet you, son. Any friend of Ms. Megan's a friend of mine."

"Likewise, Mr. Johansson. Thanks for checking in on Megan."

The three of them chattered their way out onto the porch. Not having bothered with a coat, Megan hugged herself. The old man hoisted himself into the cab of the tractor. He waved, then the engine started up with a rumbling roar. As Carl drove back down her driveway, Owen wrapped himself around her from behind. His embracing body heat bolstered her against the chill.

Megan whirled in his arms, her stomach tossing around her sugary breakfast in an unpleasant way, and voiced the niggling concern the men's conversation had created. "Is the change in weather going to be a problem for you?"

CHAPTER EIGHTEEN

Owen gazed at Megan, her concern warming him even as he hesitated to broach this conversation. He felt the weight of his two remaining days, and didn't really want to devote any part of them to worrying about the passing time. And he certainly didn't want to worry her. "Let's cross that bridge when we come to it, okay?" When she opened her mouth to protest, Owen kissed her. He reveled in the cold air that embraced them, drew strength from it. Long, languid kisses later, he pulled back. "I have an idea."

She pouted. "You're changing the subject."

He pressed another kiss to her full lips. "I am. So, do you want to hear my idea?"

She rolled her eyes, but couldn't totally restrain the threatening grin. "Let's hear it."

"Let's go over to Wisp. You've never been skiing until you've skied with a snow god." He waggled his eyebrows.

She tried and failed to look unimpressed. "Is that so?"

"Definitely. What do you say?" He willed her to agree, wanting at least one more carefree day with her before the change in weather saddled them with the pressure of her decision.

The smile that broke over her face warmed him from the inside. He would never get enough of seeing her happy. "It's a really good idea, actually. I'd love to."

Owen was so pleased he lifted her up and spun her around, earning a lovely giggle from her and a tight embrace as she held on. "Shall we get ready?"

Megan was a flurry of activity after that, dressing, gathering gear, packing some things into the Jeep Grand Cherokee parked in the garage. After the Jeep's engine had a few minutes to warm up, they piled in and Megan backed out. "Er, this is going to be interesting," she murmured.

"What's that?"

"Well, Mr. Johansson usually plows me a turnaround on his way out, but I guess with us talking and all, he forgot."

"At your service," he said. He hopped out and walked around her side of the Jeep. Eyes on her, he reached down and palmed the snow's surface, willed it up and away. Snow whirled in a glittery cloud and scattered itself over the surrounding drifts, opening a rectangular clearing off the far side of the driveway.

Megan gaped at him through her window. Her lips formed his name.

Heart racing, power surging through him, he jogged back around and resumed his seat next to her. "Problem solved."

"You just…" She glanced from him to the cleared space, and back.

He nodded, reveled in the wonder playing out over her beautiful face.

She sucked in a breath, her eyes focusing somewhere over his shoulder. "You didn't shovel my sidewalk the other day did you?"

"Er, no." She was cute when she was exasperated—eyes flashing, cheeks flushing. "Didn't want to freak you out." Being able to admit and share this part of himself filled his chest with a warm satisfaction.

She twisted her lips. "How does it work?"

He grasped her hand, folded it in his. "I can manipulate the chemistry of snow and ice, call the clouds, guide the wind. I am part of the elements, and they are part of me." Megan shivered within his grip. He smoothed circles over the back of her hand with his thumb.

"I...wow," she said. "You're amazing, Owen." She shook her head.

Her praise jolted through him as much as consuming the snow had, built him up. His heart soared. He leaned across the console. With his hand, he pulled her face closer. Trailed kisses from her temple over the apple of her cheek to the corner of her mouth. Gods, he wanted her. Wanted her to want him. "Megan, Megan, Megan," he sighed, loving the feeling of her lips curving up.

"You start kissing me and we're not gonna end up using that nifty turnaround you just made."

Laughter spilled from him, the sensation so enlivening. He fell back into his seat. "Right you are."

Megan backed the Jeep into the turnaround. Their position put the igloo right in front of them, across the yard. Even though it was a little warmer, the cold continued to maintain it well. Megan glanced at Owen, then followed his gaze. "We need to have another picnic," she said as she pulled out onto the driveway.

"Yeah." He loved that she'd echoed his own thoughts.

The trip to Wisp didn't take long, although partially cleared roads slowed their progress in a few places. Owen enjoyed Megan playing tour guide, pointing out landmarks that meant something to her and sharing stories. He also admired her competence driving on the snowy, icy roads. She never once panicked when the Jeep's rear fishtailed, her instincts and reactions exactly what they should be. The way her little pink tongue flickered out over her bottom lip when she concentrated was nice, too.

The resort was busy, the new snow having lured winter sports enthusiasts out to take advantage of the fresh powder. Where they parked, they had a good view of a number of slopes and lifts. Megan had her own equipment, which Owen lifted out for her. Holding hands, they crossed the parking lot in the direction of the lodge. The atmosphere was festive—everyone wore bright-colored snow gear, kids declared in loud voices their impatience to get to the tubing runs and the unique mountain coaster, laughter rang out as people planned their days.

Excitement rushed through Owen. He couldn't have been more pleased Megan agreed to share this with him.

Groups streamed toward the main building, making Owen realize he needed to do something before they got in line to purchase tickets. He tugged Megan over to a secluded spot along a fence, propped her skis against it, and knelt down. Glancing up at her, he debated for a moment, then beckoned her to join him with a sideways nod of his head.

"What are you doing?" she asked.

"You'll see." With a deep breath, Owen scooped a ball of snow into his palms and closed his eyes. He visualized the private chamber he maintained at Hyperborea. Saw the ornate chest sitting on a long table. Imagined disengaging the locks and removing what he needed. Transformed the ancient coin to make it useful here, now.

Megan gasped.

Owen's eyelids flew open. The snow was gone. In its place lay a stack of hundred dollar bills. He smiled, pleased it had worked. It wasn't often he found himself in need of human currency.

"Holy shit," Megan rasped, eyes bugging at the bills in his hands. She looked all around behind them, over her shoulders, but no one paid them any mind. "You just made money out of snow. Holy shit!"

Owen grinned, folded the bills in half, and tucked them deep into a pocket. "Well, I could hardly ask you to pay when this was my idea. And I have resources I rarely have occasion to use."

Megan's eyes danced with excitement and amusement. "Wow." She shook her head. "Well. All righty, then."

Needing to kiss her, Owen leaned in and tasted the amazement straight from Megan's lips. She fell into the kiss, into him, and he held her tight. He pulled them to their feet and collected the gear he'd dropped. "The snow awaits."

Soon, he bought their tickets and rented his equipment. Together, they suited up. Standing at the bottom of the mountain, they had several slope and lift options in front of them. "What's your pleasure, madam?"

Megan unfolded the resort map. "I can handle the intermediate slopes. This one's particularly good," she said, pointing at the map. "A couple really fun turns."

Owen nodded. "You lead, I'll follow." Gods, how true that

was.

Chair Lift 3 took them where they needed to the top of the mountain, and Owen loved how Megan snuggled into the side of his body, their thighs pressed tight together. He gazed down at her. "Beautiful up here," he murmured as the unnoticed resort glided by beneath them.

"Yeah." She turned away from his chest and took in the view, then glanced up to see him staring at her. A blush bloomed over her cheeks, discernible even under her ski goggles and beanie. She leaned back against him. He squeezed her in with his arm around her shoulders. At the end of the lift ride, they jumped off together and she guided them to the trail she wanted to try.

"Okay, promise me you won't cheat."

"Cheat? What do you mean?"

"None of that snow god voodoo," she said.

Owen's whole body shook with amusement.

"I mean it," Megan said, humor coloring her voice.

He steadied himself using his poles. "No voodoo. Got it."

"Good. Okay, then. Wait here a second, I want to show you something."

He nodded. "All right."

Megan slowly skied away from him. "Stay right there, now," she called over her shoulder. Just as he started to frown at how far she'd gone, she threw him a mischievous look, dug her poles in, and shoved off. "Catch me if you can!"

Owen gaped. "That little…And she told *me* not to cheat." He didn't think on it long, though, because he was after her in a flash. He knew why she made him promise not to use his powers. She was good. Surefooted and centered. Handled the turns with ease and zigzagged on the straightaways to pick up speed. Gods, her competence on the snow had him hardening in his pants.

He whooped out a cheer of pure exhilaration. The cold air whipped at his hair—he wore neither hat nor goggles, not needing them. He filled his lungs with the wind, fed off it. Tightening his stance, he gained on her, but never caught up. Man, was he going to make her pay.

At the bottom, they twisted to a stop, their downhill skis carving into the snow and sending up sprays of powder. Owen glided toward her.

"Sorry, sorry," she giggled out with a hand over her mouth.

Owen grabbed it and pulled it away, wrapped it around his back. "I told you, never hide your smiles from me." He kissed her cold lips. "Naughty, naughty girl."

She nodded. "Yep. Ready to go again?"

He smacked her bottom, though her insulated snow pants kept his bare hand from having the effect he really wanted. "You better believe it."

The rest of the morning, they sampled the numerous intermediate slopes together, sometimes skiing alongside each other, sometimes racing. All the joy was because of her.

Having worked up an appetite, they found a quaint café in the mountaintop village and feasted on stacked sandwiches. Owen discovered the wonders of Nutty Buddy ice cream cones and went back for seconds. He almost got a third to keep Megan in such good cheer.

By the time they'd flown down the mountain on inner tubes and taken their third ride on the mountain coaster that was part Alpine Slide and part roller coaster, Owen knew, unequivocally.

He was totally in love with Megan Snow.

Everything about her drew him in. She was fun-loving and adventurous. Athletic and competitive. Breathtakingly

beautiful, especially with the pink windburn on her face, her
blonde curls tousled around her shoulders, his mark on her
cheek. The way she touched him filled him with hope and need.
The interest she demonstrated in his life, his most basic thoughts
and opinions. She knew him as much as anyone ever had. More.
When they were together, her attention and concern made him
feel like the center of her universe. He might've been a god, but
he'd never before felt so important.

Their tickets were good through nine p.m., so they continued
playing long past sunset. The mountain took on a mystical
quality in the dark—the trees turned black, the snow glowed
under the profuse lights. He couldn't resist pulling her into the
shadows to taste her, feel her.

As they kissed and embraced, the urge to share all of himself
nearly overwhelmed him. "Come with me," he said, tugging her
hand toward a darkened trail.

"I think that one's closed, Owen." She pointed to a sign.

"Yes, I know. Come on." He led them just far enough down
the slope to be hidden from view, then pulled her over to the
tree line. Excitement shuddered through him, sent adrenaline
pounding into his muscles.

She chuckled, the sound nervous and curious at the same
time. "What are we doing?"

Using his poles, he pushed the levers behind his boots and
freed himself from his skis. He helped her do the same.

"You won't need these," he said, carefully lifting the goggles
off her head and removing her bulkiest outerwear. The less
he had to deal with, the better. He laid all their shed gear into
a hidden pile under a tree. Digging his hand into her hair, he
kissed her lips, once, twice, forcing her head back so he could
possess her completely.

Megan moaned and grasped onto his biceps.

With all that he was, he willed her to agree, then pulled back from the kiss and bored his gaze into hers. "Do you trust me, Megan?"

Chapter Nineteen

His flaring eyes stole Megan's breath. Already, the air around them sizzled. Something was happening.

Did she trust him?

"Yes," she heard herself say. Her answer was instinctual. She didn't need to think about it to know.

His heated, brilliant smile eased the nervous energy rushing through her veins. This day with him at Wisp had been unequivocally the best she'd had in two years. She had loved every minute of it.

Her body felt awake and powerful. Her heart, full and warm. She was *alive*. He'd brought her back to life.

"I want to share myself with you, Megan. I want to share everything," he whispered, his voice nearly that same reverent intonation as when he'd murmured those foreign words against her heart.

"Yes," she said again.

"It's going to feel odd to you, like a tingling weightlessness.

But it won't hurt and I'll bring you back the very instant you desire. If you want to say something to me, just think it. And I promise I won't let you go." He bent down and scooped a handful of snow, packed it into a loose ball.

Owen's words did little to staunch the anxious excitement bubbling up inside her. Every nerve and muscle on edge, she could barely stand still. But she yearned to know what he wanted to show her. Something told her she was about to have a once-in-a-lifetime experience. "You lead, I'll follow," she said, echoing his earlier words.

The flare behind his eyes intensified. He dropped the snow into her bare palm. "Here, eat this, please."

Megan brought the snow to her mouth with a shaking hand. The way he dragged his tongue back and forth against his bottom lip made what they were doing feel like foreplay. As soon as she'd closed her lips around the last bite, his mouth was on her, kissing, probing. Then, he pulled back, laced his hands around her neck and leaned his forehead against hers.

"Megan Snow, I love you."

Megan gasped at his declaration. Her brain scrambled, tried to figure out how to respond.

Before she could, she ceased to be corporeal.

Owen! she screamed in her mind.

I'm here angel, and I've got you. Just feel. Take it all in.

I'm scared. Though she was no more than consciousness adrift, she would've sworn she felt his lips and hands caress her. The impossible sensation squelched the fear, left only a mystical thrill in its place.

I would never let anything happen to you, Megan. On my honor. On my life.

I believe you. What's happening? The world glided under

her, around her, like she was a bird soaring on the ebbs and flows of air currents.

We are the wind.

Her soul shuddered in freedom and ecstasy. They dipped and swirled and threaded with ease and grace through the trees, down the mountain, and up again. Up, up, until the darkness swallowed the forest in one black mass and left only the blazing white lines of the illuminated trails. Up, up they went, until the starlit night surrounded them, made her feel she could almost reach out with her mind and touch a star, take it inside her. She thought of the stars on her bedroom ceiling, and imagined herself part of that brilliant symphony of matter.

Is this real?

He managed to project a chuckle. *As real as I am.*

Are you real?

As real as you want me to be. Desire and intensity imbued the disembodied thoughts.

Her soul shuddered, consciousness rippled. The wind moaned, or maybe that was her.

Shhh, angel, Owen soothed, calmed.

Will I remember this, Owen? I never want to forget being with you this way.

Gods, Megan. Yes.

Time had no meaning as they soared on the wind, with the wind. Megan thought she had the smallest understanding of what he meant when he'd said the elements were part of him. Because she felt more connected to the world around her than she'd ever been in her whole life.

As frightened as the odd situation had made her at first, now she reveled in the weightless, airy, nearly electrical sensations. She drank in the beauty of the nighttime world, let it fill her soul, ease those damaged parts of her psyche that kept her awake at night, that pressed guilt and regret on her shoulders like an iron anvil.

You're doing so well, Owen murmured from time to time. But otherwise they fell into a comfortable silence. They didn't need words to establish a connection between them. Soaring with him on the wind was as intense and intimate as sex—and as ecstatic. Like this, they were one, joined, inseparable.

When the distant edge of the horizon brightened, Megan felt the light touch the depths of her soul. She'd never seen anything more beautiful, more spiritual. They soared through the sunrise, flowed through the pinks and peaches and lavenders the rising sun cast over the awakening world.

We must return now, Owen said softly.

Knowing the wondrous experience was nearly over, Megan soaked in every sensation, every sight as they returned to earth, to their bodies. Peace filled every corner of her consciousness with a sleepy, fulfilled satisfaction.

You'll be disoriented for a while. I'll take care of you.

I trust you.

The network of freshly groomed white trails came into view. It was hours before the resort would open. Tranquility blanketed the mountain. They descended, narrowing Megan's sightlines from the whole resort, to a few trails, to the trail from which they'd ascended the night before.

And then she was flesh and blood again.

She sucked in a gasping, heaving breath, the air cold and raw in her throat. The world spun. Up was down and down was sideways. Orientation eluded her. Neither shape nor color had meaning. She clutched onto the warmth in front of her in an effort to anchor herself to the world.

A soft, wet sensation played at her lips. Megan moaned. Sought it out. Owen. Her hands clutched tighter, yanked him onto her. His weight pressed her down, reconnected her to the physical plane. The cold of the snow beneath her radiated through her clothes to her skin.

They kissed and writhed in a frenzy. Desire overwhelmed her. "In me. Get in me."

"Yes," Owen rasped.

Grunting and desperate, they tore at one another's clothes, the layers between them infuriating. Still disoriented, she was putty in Owen's hands. He moved her how he wanted, offered words of explanation she couldn't fully understand. All she knew was the wet ache between her thighs.

He turned her onto her stomach. She'd expected the snow, so the layers of puffy fabric under her body surprised her, took the edge off the surrounding cold.

"You'll be warmer this way," he ground out, then laid himself atop her back, totally covering her with his strong masculine frame. His thighs positioned outside of hers, his tip searched out her entrance.

Megan arched and thrust her rear up against him, opening herself to his welcome invasion. He filled her completely, and it was like air after being too long underwater, like drink after being lost in an endless desert.

₧₧

Owen pushed into her and roared in ecstasy. Mother of Gods, she was tight this way. Perfect. Everything.

He couldn't go slow, couldn't hold back. Neither could she, apparently, because she arched up and met his body thrust for thrust. Above her shoulders, their hands intertwined. The sides of their faces pressed together. They swallowed one another's rasping breaths.

His hips pistoned against her, driving them toward desperately needed releases. She was wet, so wet, and her walls clenched him in tight velvet. His heart threatened to explode with his body.

This woman. This woman who had shared the night wind with him in total trust, with godlike courage. She owned him. Completely and forever.

An ecstatic scream ripped from her throat. Her slick muscles squeezed and milked at his length inside her. Cupping her jaw, he devoured her cries with a consuming kiss. In turn, his body erupted, his release streaming into her again and again. He clutched onto her so tightly he feared bruising her, but he couldn't get his muscles to relent.

Long, semi-conscious moments passed with Owen still wrapped around Megan's panting, shuddering curves. But he couldn't risk her health anymore than he'd already done.

"Come on, angel, let's get you dressed."

"Okay," she mouthed, barely making any sound.

Owen stumbled as he helped her to her feet. He frowned, his muscles fighting back against every direction he gave them. His limbs felt heavy, like he was fully clothed under deep water. Drawing and holding a human in the elements so long had clearly cost him, but he could never regret it. His enraptured soul was still singing from sharing a fundamental part of himself. With her. He helped Megan dress, then rushed through dressing himself as quickly as his sluggish muscles would allow.

An arm around Megan, Owen glared at the sunny morning sky. Damn Zephyros. Despite the early hour, the temperature was noticeably warmer than it had been yesterday. A black pit of worry rooted in his gut. *Please, gods, don't let my time with her be up.*

Megan swayed. Her head hung limply. She shivered nonstop. Someone would likely think her drunk, her body was so fluid.

He leaned her back against a thick tree. "Put your hands against the tree, Megan. Hold yourself up for a moment."

She offered a small whimper of recognition.

Owen tied all of Megan's equipment and his poles into a bundle using her scarf, then stepped into his skis. Squatting onto his haunches, he plunged both hands wrist-deep into the snow and clenched his eyes in concentration. He commanded the snow to conform to his needs, then lifted Megan with an arm behind her knees and one around her upper back. The way she curled into his chest made his heart swell, and he pressed a lingering kiss to her forehead. He threaded the scarf holding her equipment onto his right forearm, then skied out onto the trail, away from the tree line.

The snow sensed Owen's weight, remembered his command. Slow at first, the top layer of powder immediately underfoot shifted, carrying them down the hill like a carpet lift, minus the rubber conveyor belt the real apparatus would've had. Despite the incline of the intermediate trail on which they found themselves, the magic carpet guided them down at a slow, steady rate, even circumnavigating the fallen tree that explained why the trail had been closed.

When his eyes weren't confirming the safety of their descent from the mountain, he studied Megan's beautiful face. The full, pink lips. The long lashes that fanned out above flushed cheeks.

He loved her. *Loved her.*

The words were inadequate to the feeling that consumed

him.

When she'd declared her trust, demonstrated it so freely by agreeing to let him share something with her that she had no chance of understanding beforehand, he hadn't been able to hold the declaration back. The words spilled forth, lightening the pressure within his chest. But he'd made sure to relieve her of the obligation of a response by transforming them into the North Wind that very moment.

And, *gods*, the absolute joy of sailing over the world with her. Even now, his soul vibrated with the glory of it.

The trail bottomed out beyond the edge of the parking lot, which was good. It meant they wouldn't have to pass by the main grouping of buildings around the resort lodge to get to Megan's Jeep. Sweating now, he willed the carpet effect to carry them to the edge of the macadam, then squatted with Megan in his arms so he could reach the release mechanisms on the skis. Hopefully someone from the resort would find the discarded equipment; he couldn't expend energy worrying about it. Not now. He shoveled handfuls of snow into his mouth, groaning as the cold crystals slowly—*too damn slowly*—restored his reserves of power and energy.

Glad he'd seen the pocket she'd zipped her car keys into, he fished the metallic ring free and unlocked the doors, settled Megan across the rear seat. She grumbled and frowned in her sleep, but finally curled into the back of the seat and calmed.

Against the protests of his muscles, Owen loaded her equipment into the trunk and dragged himself in behind the wheel.

His body weighed a thousand pounds. With sluggish, imprecise movements, he turned the ignition and backed the Jeep out of the space.

No way he was going to be able to drive like this. He threw the truck into park and shoved his shoulder against the door. It swung open.

Owen's body tumbled out onto the snowy ground.

CHAPTER TWENTY

Owen jolted awake, disoriented at first, aware but confused after a moment. He knew the dark ceiling that hovered over him. His eyes drifted to the side. Weathered log beams formed a wall around a familiar door. Megan's cabin. He was at—

"You know, I am too fucking old to worry like this."

Owen's head whipped to the other side. Boreas stood where the snow edged the cleared sidewalk. Robes of white fur swirled around him. "What happened?"

"What happened," Boreas grumbled as he started pacing. "He wants to know what happened. He depleted the powers of his godhood until he collapsed and he wants to know what happened."

Owen rose to his feet, immediately noting his body's rejuvenation. Gone was the sluggishness, the bone-crushing exhaustion, the internal tightness that was almost like severe dehydration. He was himself again, mostly. But where was Megan?

The angles on Boreas' ancient face sharpened in his fury. His words roared out in their native tongue. "You are not in the Realm of Gods, Owen. You have not the full use of your powers. You cannot expect your body in its present state to shoulder the weight of a full night of a human's transformation into the wind, command the snow to your will in massive ways over and over, and weather forty-five-degree temperatures."

Thunder rumbled, rolled uneasily across the cloud-covered sky.

Owen fisted his hair back, bowed his head in the face of Boreas' anger and righteousness. He dropped to one knee. "I apologize, My Lord. I wasn't thinking."

Boreas chuffed out a laugh. "Oh, you were thinking, all right. Just with the wrong damn head."

Boreas wasn't too angry if he was cracking jokes.

"Get the hell up." He shook his head and crossed his fur-covered arms. "She's fine, by the way. The Snow woman. Asleep in her bed."

He couldn't help it. Owen narrowed his gaze at Boreas.

The older god rolled his silver eyes, amusement playing around his lips. "Jealousy, now? All these human emotions must be a bitch."

Owen struggled to clear his throat. "How did you know I was in trouble?"

"Your joy." Boreas shifted his stance. Owen sucked in a breath to question him, but Boreas cut him off. "When the two of you were of the wind. I felt your joy. It resonated through the Realm… But then you held her in it too long, so I kept an eye on you. Good thing."

Owen exhaled a long sigh. "Thank you."

"You have not much time now, Owen. Zeph fought back

against my efforts to restrain the warm front. It is upon you even now. I imbued you with some of my strength, but it will not endure another trial of this magnitude. There will not be a next time."

"I understand. Thank you."

Boreas' gaze cut to the door. "She wakes. Go." In a swirl of snow, the ancient god disappeared.

ॐ

Megan's eyelids fluttered against something cool and soft. She was comfortable, *so* comfortable, but for the life of her she swore she'd heard thunder. She never wanted to move again, wanted only to bask in the luxury of the cushy mattress and bundled covers around her exhausted body. Her eyes drifted closed.

Owen?

Her lids popped back open, the question firing a jolt of alertness through her. His side of the bed lay empty. She narrowed her gaze. When had she started thinking of it as Owen's?

She frowned and pushed up onto her hands and knees despite the body-wide protest the movement unleashed. She sat back on her heels and rubbed the grogginess from her eyes. How did they get home? When? The last thing she remembered was...the wind. No, after. Making love in the snow. Without question, the most intense, magical, spiritual night of her life. Assuming it had happened... Maybe she couldn't remember anything afterward because it had been a dream?

Her stomach soured and clenched in disappointment. Listless hands fell to her lap. She gasped. Nylon snow pants still covered her legs. She *had* gone to Wisp with Owen. Their night wasn't the product of her subconscious after all. Relief flooded every cell. Boneless and weary, her posture sagged.

She cleared her throat. "Owen?" Her mouth was dry, making her thirsty, hushing her voice. She swallowed and tried again. No answer. Maybe he was outside.

Shifting her legs out from under her, she slid down off the bed. Her equilibrium faltered and she swayed. She grabbed a handful of covers to keep from falling.

"Angel, what are you doing up?"

Megan sucked in a breath and looked over her shoulder. "There you are," she said in a scratchy voice. "I was coming to look for you." When he walked right to her, she threw herself around him.

"It's okay, I'm here." His arms curled around her, embracing, steadying.

She nuzzled her face against his chest. "How did we get home?"

He kissed her hair. "You were out of it, so I let you sleep in the backseat. Don't worry about it now. You should be resting."

She nodded, sighed. "Tired. Rest with me?"

"Gladly." He squeezed, then let her go.

Megan turned to the bed. "Oh. Wanna change first."

Owen wrapped himself around her again and blocked her. "Sit. Tell me what you want and I'll get it for you."

"I love that idea," she said, sleepiness making her mumble. "Any shirt and pants from the top right drawer."

"Top right drawer. Got it."

When Owen stepped away, Megan tugged at her clothes, removing her turtleneck and the silky long john top beneath, then fumbling with the fasteners on her snow pants.

Owen's hands brushed hers away. "Let me. Lay back."

Megan collapsed atop the fluffy comforter. Lifted her hips when he asked, pointed her feet when he needed. His soft touches made her feel cared for. And it had been so long since someone had done such small but meaningful things for her…

Soon, Owen had redressed her in ultra-comfy flannel pants and a cotton shirt. Big hands helped scoot her toward the top of the bed, placed a pillow beneath her head. Her eyelids drooped, weighing five pounds more every time she forced them open again, but she wanted visual confirmation that he was in bed with her before she gave in to the urge to sleep. Standing near her side of the bed, Owen shed his clothes in a heap with hers. Something about the appearance of their laundry commingling on the floor… It was stupid, but she really liked it.

Sans clothing, Owen climbed over her and settled into the middle of the mattress. Like he was a magnet—or her North Star—Megan's body turned to press into the nook along the side of his tall frame. His bareness managed to be soft and hard at the same time—the skin soft and smooth, the muscles hard and ridged. She inhaled deeply, taking his crisp, clean scent into her, and let out a long exhale that relaxed her into him further. Now. Now she could be content to never move again.

When Megan woke up, the room was dark, meaning she'd slept the day away. Again.

"Sleep well?" came Owen's quiet voice, still right next to her.

She rested her head back against his shoulder so she could see his face. "Very." It was true. She'd slept better—if at odd times—these past few days than in many months. Her fingers traced shapes on Owen's bare chest for a long moment, then her stomach growled, the sound loud in the quiet between them. She covered her warming face with a hand.

"Seems like another need is going unmet, though."

Megan dropped her hand back to his chest, dragged the pads of her fingertips lightly down his abdomen, through the trail of dark hair and over the sculpted muscles.

His big hand clamped down on her wanderer. "If you find what I think you're looking for, it's going to be a long while before you get dinner."

"That wouldn't be so bad."

"No, it wouldn't." He rolled on top of her, rained open-mouthed kisses across her face and neck. "But food first." He sprang out of bed and offered his hand.

Megan pouted, but accepted his help and let him pull her from the warmth of the covers. She curled right back into his chest, nuzzled her nose against his neck.

He wrapped his arms around her body and kissed her hair. For a long moment they stood in the dark, embracing.

Megan's stomach growled again. The loud grumble sent them both into a fit of giggles.

"We better feed that beast, lest he get loose," Owen quipped.

Megan stood back, clutching her stomach. "I know. Jeez. I am totally starving."

Minutes later, they stood together at the open fridge door and surveyed their options. The way Owen ate, she was lower on groceries than she should've been. She didn't mind, but she'd need to make a run to the general store in the next day or two. The thought made her realize she'd already decided not to head back to Northern Virginia for family dinner on Sunday. She made a mental note to call her mom.

Nothing jumped out at her, so Megan turned to a drawer, plucked out a spoon, popped the half-gallon of chocolate chip from the freezer, and tore off the lid. Still standing in front of the fridge, she dug her spoon into the cream and ate a big bite. The sweet cold immediately eased her hunger. She took another bite.

"So, what looks good?" she mumbled around a spoonful. She looked up at Owen.

Mouth hanging open, eyes dilated, he stared at her while she held the carton with one hand, ate directly out of it with the other. He licked his lips.

"What?" She smiled. "Oh, want some?" She dug out some chocolate chip and held the spoon to him.

He leaned forward, mouth open.

At the last second, Megan yanked the spoon away and stuffed it in her mouth.

If she thought he'd been gaping before, it was nothing compared to his expression now. Amused outrage raised his eyebrows up to his hairline, then had him narrowing his eyes.

"Sorry, sorry," Megan said, covering her mouth as laughter spilled out of her.

Owen tugged her hand away and none too gently pushed her back into the fridge. "What did I tell you"—he kissed her, plundered her mouth with his tongue—"about hiding your smiles and laughter"—tongue flat, he licked ice cream off her bottom lip—"from me?"

He grabbed her wrist and forced her hand to spoon out another scoop from the carton trapped between their chests. Breathing hard from the forceful kiss, Megan pouted. He guided their joined hands to his mouth, sucked down the cold cream while boring his heated gaze into hers. His dominance, playful though it might've been, tingled low in her belly.

Warm, dizzying pressure filled her chest, making her feel

she could fly or take on the world. Or both. She sucked in a breath at the sudden appearance of the foreign sensation. A rectangular chunk of chocolate lodged in her throat, stuck there, refused to clear. Her eyes watered as she coughed, her hand covering her mouth.

In a flash, Owen's weight disappeared, as did the tub of ice cream. "Here," he said, thrusting a cup of water in front of her.

She nodded and grasped the glass, took a long pull of water. The cold soothed her throat, calmed her distress. She drank every drop.

"Okay?" Bending down to look in her eyes, he tucked a few stray curls behind her ear.

"Yeah," she croaked. "Went down the wrong hole. Sorry."

"Don't apologize."

She nodded and shuddered. Why couldn't she just embrace that feeling, give voice to it? But before she'd even finished the thought, she knew the answer. She was scared. Scared of how much she cared for Owen, and how fast it had happened. Scared that what she felt for Owen promised to exceed the intensity of what she'd felt for John. The comparison sat uneasy in her stomach, but that didn't make it any less true.

She'd loved John. Truly, deeply. During the two years of their courtship and four years of their marriage, he'd been her whole world. Had that horrible night two Christmases ago never happened, she would've lived a long, happy, perfectly satisfied life with him. But Owen made her think she hadn't known the full beauty of what love could be. Her heart beat for him; her body sang for him. His pleasure was her pleasure, in all things. John had been a wonderful partner, but Owen felt like her destiny.

Oh, John, are you still out there? Are you listening? What must you be thinking of all this? But he didn't answer, no voice responded. He'd been quiet for days. Maybe that meant his spirit had found peace? How she hoped.

Megan sagged back against the counter, weighed down by the sappy ridiculousness of her thoughts, and by the guilt and disloyalty her pre-Owen self foisted on her. Not to mention the whole, you know, ancient-god-from-the-other-side problem. She adored a...man?...and he wasn't even real. *As real as you want me to be.* That's what he'd said.

But the last two years had taught her that what she wanted and what was real were not always the same things. More often than not, they were about as different as could be.

CHAPTER TWENTY-ONE

Fingers stroking her cheek yanked her from her thoughts. "You're so far away," Owen whispered, standing right in front of her still.

"Sorry. I'm just a little out of sorts, I guess."

He nodded, pressed a chaste kiss to her lips. When he pulled back, concern darkened his gaze. "It was too much," he whispered. The tone chiding, he shook his head. Strands of black fell across his eyes.

Megan frowned, then, figuring his meaning, gasped. "No." She brushed his hair back and cupped his face in her hands. "No, don't say that. What you shared with me...God, Owen. I've never... I don't even have words. But I will remember it for the rest of my life, and cherish it beyond anything you can imagine." She kissed him, lingering over the kiss as she willed him to feel her awe and gratitude. "I never said, 'thank you,' so, thank you." She kissed him again.

He watched her face intently while she spoke, and soon

his expression eased, brightened. "It was my pleasure," he said quietly. "You're welcome."

The talk about their night as the wind resurrected in her memory what he'd said *before*. He loved her. She wanted to say it back, so bad. To embrace their love without fear or reservation. Her shoulders drooped. Every time she even thought the words, her fight or flight instinct kicked in, sending jolting tingles out her extremities. Clearly, her self-preservation instinct wasn't yet convinced of the wisdom of voicing her feelings, of putting her heart in harm's way again.

"I just feel a little off," she murmured, talking to herself as much as to him. She gave a small smile, hoped it didn't come off as a grimace. "It's not your fault. Maybe some food will help."

"Food. Done." He turned back to the fridge, still open all this time.

She hadn't really noticed the cold radiating out from behind her. Maybe he was wearing off on her, because she was starting to enjoy the cold. "I could go for something cold, I think," she said, knowing that would be his preference, too.

He kissed her cheek. "I knew there was a reason I liked you."

Dinner was quick and casual. Despite how long she'd slept, Megan was surprisingly tired again and eager to be back in Owen's arms. In bed, Owen settled on his back and Megan crawled on top of him, settled her hips between his thighs and her head on the broad plane of his bare chest. Her hands burrowed under his upper back and she squeezed him.

Under Megan's stomach, Owen hardened.

She smiled against his pec, sleep already luring her. "I'll take care of that in the morning," she whispered.

His body shook beneath her. "No pressure. I have no control

of that reaction when I'm around you." He hugged her into him and lightly tilted his hips up against her.

"I'm glad," she said, unable to resist wriggling her abdomen against him.

"Little snow devil." He kissed her hair. "Be still. Sleep."

∞C∞

Boreas had been right, Owen groused to himself the next morning. All these human emotions were a bitch. The intensity of his feelings for Megan could fuel a record-setting blizzard or preserve the polar ice cap. Surely this mortal body could not restrain such power. Anticipation made his gut jump and squeeze. Megan was coming to him, he was sure of it, could almost feel her choice of him bursting forth. But it was all so fast, and he understood her reluctance. Time operated differently in his native realm; the gods' immortality made them less conscious of time, made its passage less meaningful in their motivations and decisions. But that left him no less surprised by how quickly he'd fallen so hard.

And if those emotions weren't enough, anxiety unsettled him, tensed the muscles in his neck and shoulders. Today was his last day. Outside the house, a symphony of drips played out, had been playing for hours.

The West Wind had arrived. The melt was upon them.

And his body knew it. The sheets under him lay damp with sweat.

A crash clattered outside the bedroom window. Megan's head jerked off Owen's chest. Tiny impressions of his chest hair lined her cheek.

He traced a finger over the light marks. "Good morning."

Her eyes shined bright blue from the hours of sound sleep. "Mmm, very good." A low scraping sound preceded another crash. Megan frowned. "What is that?"

Owen sighed. "Snow, sliding off the roof."

"Oh. *Oh.* How warm is it out?"

He wanted to keep his focus on her, not the problematic weather. "Don't know. Don't care." He refused to use even a minute of his remaining time watching the sand pour through the hourglass. Doing so would not win her heart, would not earn his chance at humanity. Even if this didn't work out the way he wanted, he could leave here with the best memories of his existence. So, today…well, today was about making memories that could sustain him for eternity. In case.

He looked to the ceiling and sent up a fervent, silent prayer that memories not be all that would remain of this amazing week. He needed more. He needed everything.

He needed Megan.

Soft fingers stroked his cheek. "Hey." His gaze returned to hers. "You okay?"

He grabbed and kissed her fingers. "Never better." Her warmth and affection beckoned him. He slid down underneath her until he could claim her lips. "Been wanting you," he murmured around a kiss. Just to make the point, he rocked his waking hard-on into her lower abdomen.

She clutched his hair, dragged her legs to the outside of his hips so she could straddle him.

Owen's hands went right to her ass. He pressed her down, used the leverage to grind them together. Every moan and whimper that spilled from her throat reverberated straight to his cock. He needed her. Needed her with everything he was. Wanted to see her face painted with the ecstasy of release.

Again and again.

The urgency of the moment gripped him. He tugged at her flannel pants. "Get these off," he said against her neck. "Gods, I need you to come on me."

"Jesus," she bit out, already pushing the pants down and shimmying her hips and legs to kick them off.

He groaned as her actions tormented him with delicious friction. Tugging at her shirt, he bared all of her.

A rumbling groan sounded low in his throat. Without warning, he rolled on top of her, laying them both on the edge of the bed. The cool air tingled over his back, enlivening every sensation. With his hips between her thighs, he rocked his hard-on against the nerves at the top of her sex, wanting her frantic when he entered her. She clutched at his shoulders, her short nails scratching and biting against his skin in a way that drove him harder. He rested his body weight on her chest and reached both hands under her ass. The new position gave him more control over their movements. Her wetness coated him, made him slick against her—exactly what he wanted.

Megan's low moans turned to whimpered cries. Her heels crossed over his lower back. "Oh, Owen," she panted. Then she held her breath, wrenched her head into the mattress, and came.

"Yes," he hissed. "So good. How do you want me?" He kissed her lips, her cheek, her eyelids. "Hmm? What do you want?"

Even as she still shuddered, her skin heated under his lips.

He tasted the flush warmth with slow open-mouthed kisses. "Come on, Megan," he whispered. "Tell me what that blush is all about."

She met his gaze, her eyes intense and unsure.

"You can tell me anything, angel."

Her lips lifted to his ear. Pants and raspy words spilled out. "Bend me over the bed, Owen."

He flew off her and tugged her body just how he wanted it—how *she* wanted it—feet on the ground, upper body bent over the bed. Cock in one hand, he found her entrance and sank in to her very depths. Her muscles still quivered with the pulsing end of her orgasm.

Pleasured cries spilled from Megan's mouth. Her fingers tangled into the sheets. "Oh, God, Owen, you're so deep."

He bit out an ancient curse. She couldn't talk like that and expect him to make this last, not when he felt the weight of time's passage—no matter how much he pledged to ignore it. And not when she was so warm and so tight and so wet around him. But that didn't mean he didn't love the hell out of her muttered pleadings and encouragements.

Owen tugged her hips away from the edge of the mattress so he could reach around and stroke her. He dropped panting kisses onto her back. "Look at me," he rasped.

Megan pushed up on elbows and looked over her right shoulder. The blue of her eyes was deep with lust, so damn beautiful.

"I want to see you when you come again."

Megan groaned, her backward motion meeting him thrust for thrust now. Her lids sagged closed.

"Open your eyes, Megan. And come."

Her slick muscles tightened around his length. Her brow furrowed in concentration, anticipation.

"That's it." The circles Owen drew around her clit grew tighter, faster, harder.

A low whine rose up out of Megan's throat, then exploded in volume along with her body. Her walls milked him. Her knuckles went white around the fisted sheets.

Victory surged through Owen's veins, pooled in his balls. He gripped her hips harder, wrapped his chest over her back, his arms around her breasts.

I love you, he roared in his mind. The words seeped from his every pore, but he wouldn't let them out of his mouth, not right now. He didn't want to throw her out of the moment. He wanted her to focus on pleasure, on feeling good, on how good—how *great*—they were together. So he focused on showing her with his body.

Arms wrapped around Megan's chest, Owen slowly lifted her into a standing position. He bent his knees to hold the angle that most pleased her, that hit the spot deep inside that made her tighten and groan. His peripheral vision caught movement, and he glanced to the right. Gasped.

"Megan." He swallowed hard. "Look, angel."

She followed his voice and her gaze drifted to the right. "Oh, God."

The mirror over the dresser framed their lovemaking. Neither could tear their stare away from the erotic image reflected back to them. Megan's golden waves bounced with his every thrust. Owen's body curled around her, held her. The muscles from his ribs to his thighs corded as he moved against her. Their eyes met in the mirror.

And hers were absolutely alive with unspoken emotion.

Owen threw his head back and roared out his orgasm.

"Oh, yes," Megan whimpered. "Owen, I— So good."

Long moments passed as Owen shuddered and released himself deep within her beautiful body. When he calmed, he gently withdrew, then sat on the bed's edge and pulled Megan onto his lap. He cradled her, nuzzled her neck, so content in the amazing connection they'd just shared.

And then Megan burst into tears.

CHAPTER TWENTY-TWO

Megan's distress hit Owen like a punch to the gut. Had he hurt her? "Angel?" He ducked his head down to her level, tipped her chin up with his fingers.

Tears streamed from Megan's baby blues. She clapped a hand over her mouth, smothering her hitching breath and whimpered cries.

"Please tell me what's wrong." One arm supporting her back, he used his free hand to try to dry her face, but it was no use. The tears kept coming. So he let her cry, let her get out whatever she needed to release while he held her close.

After a while, she quieted, only occasionally shuddering.

"Can you tell me now? I'm worried about you. Did I…did I hurt you?" Owen remembered their half-joke the night he'd arrived—he would welcome her use of the iron poker on him should he ever cause her harm.

She shook her head. "No, baby," she managed in a high, strained voice.

The endearment ballooned within his heart, setting off the most pleasant warmth in his chest. "Then what—"

"Happy," she whispered. Softer tears fell with her pronouncement.

Owen frowned. Happy? It uplifted him to hear her say so, but then— "Then why do you cry, angel?"

"Little...over...whelmed," she said between hitches. She palmed away the wetness on both cheeks. "Don't know why I'm so emotional. Stupid."

"Megan Snow, you are a lot of things"—he pulled her hands to his mouth and kissed the back of each one—"but stupid you are not. You feel what you feel. But, can you explain—"

She kissed his cheek, just one small press of her lips, then combed her hands through both sides of his still-damp hair. "I don't know. It's just...being with you felt so good, so right. Everything was so intense. I realized I was happy, so happy, Owen, and then...this." She waved at her wet face. "I didn't mean to worry you."

Owen's smile was small at first, broader as she spoke. "It's okay. Being overwhelmed by happiness is a good thing. I'm glad I was a part of it."

She ducked her head into the crook of his neck. "You definitely were. Are."

Arms back around her again, Owen held her tight and basked in the memory of her words: *being with you felt so right. That's because it* is, *Megan. We are meant to be.*

"Are you hungry?" she murmured when she'd calmed completely.

He nodded. "I could eat."

"Me too," she agreed. "Wanna have a picnic in the igloo?"

Owen hesitated only a moment. The ice house should

protect him from the morning's increasing warmth. And he loved that she wanted to be there with him again. Maybe that little place meant as much to her as it did to him. "Absolutely," he finally said.

After dressing, they collected for their igloo picnic grapes, juice, yogurt, and two bowls of cereal—Lucky Charms, naturally—he would *never* forget the seductive set of her eyes when she'd called him "magical" *and* "delicious."

He hated how everything they experienced today felt like the last time it would happen.

Not if he could help it.

Megan opened the door and stepped out onto the porch. "Oh, it's really ni—oh no." She whirled around so abruptly, Owen nearly spilled the milk out of the cereal bowls. "You can't come out here. What was I thinking?"

Even in the thin, short-sleeved T-shirt and light track pants he'd borrowed, Owen was uncomfortably warm in the air flowing through the open door. But it would be better in the igloo, so he nodded her forward. "I'll be fine. Now, move it, woman. I've got some marshmallows to eat."

"I'm serious, Owen."

"So am I." Owen gave her a quick peck. "Really, it's okay. We don't have to stay out too long."

Megan narrowed her eyes, her gaze running over his face. "You promise?"

Her concern warmed him, in a good way this time. "I do."

"Okay." She turned and jogged down the steps, then made her way across the shoveled path.

Owen inhaled a deep breath, ducked his face, and stepped out into the sun. "Fucking Zephyros," he mumbled. Normally, the sun didn't bother him. When the mercury hit the thirties or below. But it was already fifty-five if it was anything, and it was only ten o'clock in the morning. He jogged over the path, not caring about spilled milk, and ducked into the igloo's doorway.

He handed Megan the bowls first, then crawled through the low arch. The embracing ice shaded him, eased his discomfort.

Megan's hand was suddenly right in front of him. "Here."

Owen lifted the snowball from her fingers, and lost an even bigger chunk of his heart to her thoughtfulness. "You're amazing, do you know that?"

"No, I'm worried. Please eat it?"

"I don't want to worry you," he said, taking a big bite in hopes of easing her. It certainly eased him, cooled him, relaxed the muscles that had tightened almost as if preparing for a fight.

"Can't help it," she sniffed as she laid out their breakfast feast on the blanket between them. They'd left it out there the other day. "I guess I'm a worrier." Suddenly, she froze. "Oh, hell, I've turned into my mother!"

Owen chuckled.

"It's not funny," she pouted, tossing the bag of grapes on the ground. Two green balls rolled away.

Which struck Owen as hilarious. One grape came to a stop against his boot. Laughter spilled out of him, felt miraculous as always. Then a four-leaf clover whacked him in the cheek, fell into his lap. He stilled.

With great gravitas, he reached down to his leg, picked up the green marshmallow, and popped it in his mouth.

Megan pressed her lips together, then burst out laughing.

Still chewing, Owen couldn't hold back his own smile, loving that he could make her feel that way. Her face and eyes were so alive when she laughed, so bright. What greater purpose could there be than the happiness of the one you loved? Owen couldn't imagine anything more fulfilling. He would devote his life to her joy, if only she would let him.

⁛

Megan adored Owen's ability to make her laugh and smile, both of which had been completely absent from her life for so long before the Christmas night miracle of his arrival.

Her laughter didn't mean she wasn't worried, though, because she was. When he'd ducked through the igloo door, his face bore the flush of exertion, despite the fact that during the three hours of constructing the thing he hadn't even broken a sweat. It *was* surprisingly warm for the week between Christmas and New Year's. The kind of warm that had you hoping you might just get away with your strappy little New Year's Eve dress without freezing the girls off.

Perfect for humans.

Not good if you were a snow god, apparently.

She sighed, determined not to ruin the fun they were having while they ate, but not totally able to sidetrack the insistent questions her brain raised about what would happen if it continued to heat up. So, she struck a middle ground and focused her words on their fun banter and her eyes on his face—watching for any signs of distress.

Her hunger made it easy to focus on the food. She'd skipped a number of meals lately—not unusual for her, really—but her body now seemed determined to make every one of them up. She didn't mind. It was nice to socialize over a meal, to not have someone constantly suggesting you try to eat a little something. So she relished every cold, crunchy bite of her Lucky Charms, every creamy spoonful of yogurt, and the way the sweet of the grapes burst on her tongue when she bit down.

Megan's ears insisted on catching every crash of falling snow, off the eves of the cabin, from the tree branches. The pitter-patter of melting icicles played all along the front sidewalk. Amazing that the igloo was holding up so nicely. It didn't seem to be melting at all…

Her spoon paused midway to her mouth.

She frowned at Owen. He leaned back against the igloo wall, cereal bowl cradled in his lap, one hand resting on the snow floor beside him. Despite suspecting the answer, she asked the question. "Why isn't the igloo melting?"

Owen swept his hair off his face. Scanned his gaze over the ceiling. "Just well built." His mouth lifted into that cocky grin.

Megan narrowed her eyes, her gut insisting he wasn't being straight with her. He'd been more than happy to show her his ability to clear out the turnaround yesterday, so why would he hide his power now? "What aren't you telling me?"

Cute as hell, his grin became totally sheepish. He ducked his head, silky black falling over his eyes. "Nothing. This is probably the last time we can use it, and I wanted to make the picnic nice. For you. So I…"

She pushed the remains of their breakfast aside and crawled over to him, settling on her knees between his thighs. Her hands cupped his cheeks and tilted his face up. "And I love that, but" — she debated how to phrase her question, decided to go with the most direct, even if it was also the most accusatory — "why wouldn't you just admit you were holding it together?"

Pink tinged his cheeks. "Sorry."

She shook her head. "Just make me understand."

"Didn't want you to worry." He turned his head and kissed her palm.

She frowned. "I know you can make the snow do stuff. Why would that make me—" Her head tilted when she paused, her thoughts spinning off in multiple directions. Out of nowhere, the memory of his voice filtered through the cacophony in her brain. *The snow intensifies my power.* He'd needed to go outside, to go into the cold, to build up enough power to heal her cheek. To build it up. Did that mean it could be depleted too?

She gasped. All of a sudden, she knew.

Her hands trembled where she still held his face. "Holding the igloo together." She swallowed. "It uses your power, right?"

He nodded within her grasp. "Yes."

"Uses your power," she murmured to herself, her mind chugging through something that seemed just out of reach. Her hands slapped against her thighs. "You think I'll worry because…" Snow crashed to the ground somewhere close. Her eyes flashed to his. "The heat…it's already…running you down?"

"I'm okay, Megan."

His assurance soured her stomach in a way a direct admission wouldn't have. She pushed herself away from him. "I didn't ask if you were okay, Owen. I asked if the heat was draining you, and whether holding the igloo together was making it even worse."

"Meg—"

She groaned. Turned and started jamming their breakfast mess into a bag. "You may be ancient, Owen, but I'm not a child. And I don't need you to treat me like one."

"That's not what I—"

"You promised, you promised you'd be okay, and yet you're—" Tightness in her throat choked off her words. Damn it, she didn't want to cry again, but she was so pissed he would endanger himself and then hide it. On hands and knees, she turned to the arched doorway.

Strong arms wrapped around her waist. "You're right. I wasn't thinking. Stay."

"I have to go." She needed some time to calm her thoughts. Between the anniversary, and Owen's appearance, and the impossibility of their whole situation...

"Megan, you can fix this, make these worries go away."

She sagged back against her heels, looked over her shoulder at him. His dark eyes blazed, pleaded. "What do you mean?"

Big hands cupped her face, drew her to him. He kissed her, once, twice, then looked into her eyes. "I love you, Megan."

Megan sucked in a breath. No, no. She couldn't face *this* conversation shaking with anger, when she felt like she was falling to pieces. "Owen—"

"Choose me, angel. Love me. And we'll have forever."

I promise to walk by your side today, tomorrow, and forever.

The memory of John's voice, saying their wedding vows, pledging her forever, sliced through her. "I can't—" She shook her head, unable to get further words out. Then she scrabbled out the door.

Running, slipping, she dashed to the cabin, burst through the front door. Not caring about the snowy footprints she tracked through, she grabbed her purse and keys off the kitchen counter. She just needed a little space. A break from the magic. From Owen's intensity. She loved it. She *did* love it, and love him, but she couldn't think, couldn't breathe. When she'd first grabbed her keys she had no plan in mind, but then an idea came to her: groceries. Real. Normal. Exactly what she needed. She'd go get more groceries. Calm down.

They could talk when she got back.

At the door, she slipped in the slick mess her boots had left. She grasped the door by its edge, groaned when she heard fabric ripping. When she was surefooted, she glanced down. Her coat pocket had caught on the doorknob, ripped along the seam. "Damn it. This was my favorite coat, too." She huffed and fumbled getting herself unhooked, then with a frustrated sigh, freed herself and stomped outside. The door slammed behind her, and in her state of mind she found it a satisfying sound.

Gray clouds had appeared in the few moments she'd gone inside and cast an odd light over her front yard. Owen leaned against the igloo, arms crossed over his chest. His gaze snapped up when she pounded down the front steps.

God, he was freaking gorgeous even when she was pissed at him. "Going to the store. I'll be back," she said without breaking her stride to the garage.

"Megan, don't go. Talk to me," he called.

"Go inside, Owen. I need a break." She punched the code into the pad at the side of the garage door. It eased up.

She tugged open the driver's door of the Jeep and froze.

CHAPTER TWENTY-THREE

Megan stood at the door of her Jeep, frowning, trying to make sense of the scene in front of her. The driver's seat was pushed and reclined so far from the steering wheel it was nearly in the backseat. How in the world could Owen have reached the pedals with the seat like that? He was tall, very tall, but *this* tall?

Odder, wisps of white fur covered the seat and clung to the short-napped carpet in front of the pedals. The breeze swirling through the garage picked up the fuzzy tendrils, blew them around the car's interior.

The passenger seat had also been adjusted—pushed back and the backrest also reclined, as if someone had laid there. Smudges of mud had dried here and there on the gray leather.

Her brain couldn't explain why the car looked like this... because she hadn't been awake the last time she'd used the car. The last time *they'd* used the car. But...Owen said she'd slept in the back, right? So then...Her eyes drifted to the front seats. Both had been moved. Used. She sucked in a breath.

"Owen Winters, who drove my car?" she yelled. Stomping out of the garage, she nearly slammed right into him just behind the Jeep. She pointed. "Who drove my car?"

"Megan—"

She glared at him, sure she would totally lose her shit if he didn't just tell her what was going on.

He nodded once, and his shoulders sagged. "Boreas."

Megan frowned. "Boreas. As in the Supreme God of Winter Boreas?"

"Yes."

"Why?"

Owen's lips pressed into a tight line and his jaw ticked. Once. Twice. "I couldn't drive."

She wasn't sure what she'd expected, but it wasn't that. "Why? When?" All this confusion and weirdness was why she *really* needed that trip to the store.

Owen blew out a breath. For a moment, he appeared older, ragged around the edges. She fought the urge to hug him, stroke her fingers through his soft hair.

"I was drained," he whispered.

Megan's eyebrows flew up. "Drained? Like…meaning…?"

He shifted on his feet. "I overextended my powers. Between the night in the wind and getting you down the mountain, and it was already warmer. I didn't realize…"

She stepped back. Her mind couldn't conjure an image of him where he wasn't tall and strong and exuding that sexy, masculine otherworldliness, certainly not one of him too weak to sit behind the wheel of a car and drive. Him being hurt for her—wasn't this precisely what she feared most? And what guarantee did she have if she chose him, made him human, some other vulnerability wouldn't befall him?

"How bad was it?" she said through a tight throat. He was fine now, obviously, but that didn't keep a belated panic from turning over the contents of her stomach.

He came closer and rubbed her arms. "Angel, I'm fi—"

She grabbed his T-shirt and tugged him to her. "Please. If you say you're fine I will lose my mind." Every moment he delayed his answer allowed her brain to construct worst-case scenarios. She recognized the queasy foreboding creeping up her neck and prickling her scalp. In her mind's eye, the image of opening their front door to find two uniformed policemen standing on the Christmas-light-brightened porch, illuminated by flashing blue and red, played in slow motion.

He nodded once. "I collapsed."

She gasped.

"Ma'am, we're sorry to disturb you on Christmas. Are you Mrs. John Snow?"

She whimpered. He was a god, and he'd collapsed. He was a god, and he hadn't been okay.

"Mrs. Snow, may we come in?"

She whirled and jumped into the driver's seat. A lever on the side adjusted the back and moved the seat forward, but at a ridiculously slow pace that made her grit her teeth. Her hand trembled against the little knob. A scream threatened to tear free to voice her frustration, anger, fear.

Owen's broad chest filled the door's opening, blocking her from closing it. "Megan, I'm sorry."

"Mrs. Snow, we're sorry to have to tell you…"

Finally, her feet could reach the pedals. She stabbed the key into the ignition and started the car.

"I didn't hide what happened from you on purpose. We slept all day, and then…I should've."

Trembling now, Megan patted his chest. "I understand. I can't talk about this right now." She hated the quiver in her voice. "I need some time to think. Okay? You go in." He didn't move, his expression so sad. She hated herself even more for that. "Please, Owen?"

"I don't like this. You shouldn't be driving when you're upset."

She shook her head. "I'll be fine." *Fine. Fine. Fine.* Focusing on the internal repetition, she bit back the threatening tears.

He groaned, but relented. Stepped back.

When he was clear of the door, Megan yanked it shut.

Megan!

Megan growled, shook her head, refused to look at Owen, refused to believe John's disembodied voice had decided to make a reappearance *now* of all times.

She forced all her concentration into backing out of the garage, turning around in the spot Owen had cleared. The melting snow left the driveway bumpy and uneven, so Megan took her time and went slow. Owen *was* right. She probably shouldn't be driving. But she had to get away. Just for a few hours. Then they could talk. She hit the gas and took off.

ಬಿﬗಣ

Owen roared in frustration, his emotions kicking up a whirl of wet snow. He'd fucked up. He knew he had. Her quivering bottom lip, the way her cheeks paled, the glassy sadness of her blue eyes—her hurt sliced into him, tore at his heart. Her disappointment shamed him, twisted his gut. His intent hadn't been to deceive her, but the effect had been the same.

In the distance, the Jeep fishtailed.

Owen frowned, stepped into the snow. Damn it all to Hades, she shouldn't be driving. He sank into a squat, plunged his hands deep into the snow. Head bowed, eyes closed in concentration. He sent the command out, far, far out, willing the snow and ice still covering the roadways to carry her safely to her destination. Long minutes passed as he extended the directive along the whole route to the general store, glad she'd pointed it out to him on the way to Wisp. Power bled from him into the distant snow.

He withdrew his arms and opened his eyes. For a moment, the world blurred and dizziness swamped him. Gasping, he swayed and fell back on his butt. Sprawled out on the driveway, the warmth of the too-early spring surrounded, suffocated. At least the cloud cover he'd called had tempered the sun's strength. Stumbling, he pushed to his feet, that heavy feeling sinking back into his limbs. Scooping up some snow, he ate as he clambered up the porch steps. This snow was wet, as much water as ice, and though it eased him, it didn't provide the immediate jolt of power it had before. Still, he ate it, taking whatever assistance he could get while he could get it. His internal gauges told him the temperature was flirting with sixty degrees.

Gripping the doorknob, he pushed. His shoulder crashed into the closed door. He rattled the knob. Locked.

He gaped, stumbled back from the barrier. Had she locked him out on purpose? But then, she'd told him to go in. The memory filled him with relief. His eyes scanned the porch— there weren't any hiding places for a key save one. He ran his fingers along the top molding over the door. Nothing.

Almighty gods, he was trapped outside.

He wiped his damp forehead with the back of his arm, assessed his options. Busting through the door would render it useless for her. An obvious last resort. Long rectangular windows surrounded the door's frame. He bent and glanced through the middle one. If he broke the pane, he could reach through and unlock the door. He preferred to avoid damaging the house, if possible. Recalling the door inside the garage, Owen dragged himself around the front of the house and in through the still-open garage door. His footsteps thumped against the plank steps. He reached out and twisted the knob. Locked again.

"Fuck." He knocked his head against the solid door. His sweat left a mark when he pulled away. He slumped down to the wooden steps and rested. Between the concrete pad and the lack of insulation, the garage offered a cool respite. He cursed again. Hadn't Boreas warned him he couldn't withstand another major expenditure of power? Between the weather and calling the clouds and the enormous command to shepherd Megan safely to the store… Yeah, he hadn't listened.

Truth be told, though, he would do it all again if it meant keeping Megan from harm. He wasn't used to the limitations his in-between status imposed on him, neither fully human nor fully god. But while he could tolerate the draining weight of physical deterioration, his soul would never survive a failure to protect her. No matter the cost, even to himself.

Owen sat stone still, conserving power and energy. For a while, his body eased. But the midday temperature heated the garage's interior enough that he became uncomfortable again. A trickle of sweat ran down the edge of his hairline. He stripped off his T-shirt and chucked it between his hands while he thought through his options.

He went out to the igloo, sheltered himself within the icy walls for a while. Using power to sustain the ice, however, seemed risky given how sluggish he felt. Drips rained down from the joints in the blocks, a few at first, then in a steady stream. He gave up. It couldn't be helped—he had to get into the house.

At the front door, Owen wrapped his right fist in the shirt, reared back, and let loose a punch. Glass exploded inwards from the sidelight. Jagged edges dug into his forearm. He knocked the remaining shards free on the door side of the window and reached in.

He blew out a relieved breath when the door unlocked. Pushing through, he stumbled into the great room and stopped. It *was* cooler, but it wasn't as cool as he wished. Still, it was better than nothing.

Owen washed the wounds on his arm and knotted the refolded T-shirt around them to catch the blood until they healed. His godhood would make quick work of healing the injuries. He retrieved the biggest pieces of glass from the floor and threw them away, then opened the freezer in search of some ice cream.

Of the four containers they'd originally had, only one remained. He pulled out the mint chocolate chip and yanked off the lid. His shoulders sagged. In the bottom corner of the tub sat maybe one scoop's worth of the cold dessert. Not bothering with a bowl this time, he ate the ice cream right out of the carton. Too soon, it was gone.

Warm air streamed through the broken window. Allowing spring an entry into the house was clearly a strategic mistake. He saw that now. He'd just avoid this room.

In the bathroom, he splashed cold water on his ruddy face, then staggered into the bedroom. Megan's scent lingered in the air, on the bedclothes. He trailed his fingers over her side of the bed and laid himself down atop the cool covers.

Please be okay, Megan. And hurry back to me.

He missed her. Her touch, her smile, her laughter, the sound of her voice. After eons of aloneness, the great joy of her companionship left him lonely without her.

Dampness pressed against his back. He groaned and sat up, the air drying the clinging sweat. He pushed off the bed, swayed, and lurched forward. Leaning against the doorway of her bedroom, Owen warily eyed the angled streams of sunshine pouring in through the wall of windows in the great room. The cold air of the refrigerator beckoned him, but to get to it he'd have to weather the sun and the spring breeze that together had noticeably raised the temperature of the cabin's central room. Maybe he'd just soak in a cold bath. He turned to retreat to the bedroom.

A rectangular box on the wall caught his attention. A jolt of triumph enlivened him. The thermostat.

Owen flipped the plastic box open and scanned the controls. He flicked the power level from "Heat" to "A/C" and lowered the temperature gauge to its coldest point. With a bit of a spring in his step, he returned to the bedroom and sat on the bed's edge, awaiting the first blast of conditioned air. Minutes passed. Nothing happened. He rechecked the controls. Then he realized he hadn't heard the heat blowing through the vents lately, either. Despite Megan lowering the setting, it still should've come on from time to time.

The gods were in the world, even if they weren't of it, so Owen knew enough to know the basics of how mechanical systems worked. And he suspected the most likely answer lay beneath several feet of melting snow. To check—and, if needed, fix—the condenser, Owen would have to go back outside.

It could be worth it, though, if it meant he'd be able shut

himself in their air conditioned bedroom until Megan got home. He froze. His gut clenched. Never in his long life—not even with Chione, and didn't that tell him something—had he thought of the place where he belonged in the plural. *Their bedroom*. It had the most intensely satisfying ring to it. And he wanted it to be reality more than he could express.

He wanted to belong to Megan.

Not bothering with a shirt, Owen sucked in a deep breath and crossed the sunlit room. The heat of it seared through his skin, drawing out a flush and soaking him with sweat almost immediately. Outside, he rounded the house and slogged through the deep snow until a mound behind the garage caught his attention. Tall, squarish, and ice-glazed, the metal of the unit revealed itself as Owen ripped away a heavy chunk of ice. Palming the slick surface, Owen closed his eyes and issued the command.

Under his hands, the ice rattled, dripped, held.

He glared at the frozen shell covering the unit. Outrage joined a shot of adrenaline barreling through his veins. Bending, Owen consumed mouthful after mouthful of snow, cooling himself from the inside out. That should do it.

He tried again. Tremors shook the ice. *Come on!* He grunted, the strain of the command taxing his muscles, stealing his breath. A crack sounded out, loud and glassy. On one side of the air handler, the ice fell away into the surrounding snow drift with a wet thud. Once freed, the other side followed suit.

Owen staggered, his weight falling against the box. He praised the gods that the sun's rays fell on the front side of the house in the afternoon. Every movement set his muscles to screaming. Not wanting to further test his powers, he removed the remaining snow from the unit's top with his hands and dug out a narrow trench around it, hoping doing so would allow the air to flow properly. Looking through the top metal grate revealed the ice-crusted fan blades that were surely the problem.

His fingers wouldn't fit through the grate, that much was clear. Tugging sweat-soaked hair back from his eyes, Owen surveyed the area around him. A broken icicle laying in a shallow indent in the snow caught his attention. He fought his knees' urge to buckle as he trudged the short distance to retrieve it, then, back at the unit, guided it through the narrow opening.

"Yes!" he cheered to himself when the icicle made contact with the ice-covered blade. Please gods let him have one last reserve of energy. He closed his eyes and sent the command to melt along the length of ice to the frozen mass inside.

Within a minute, the glorious sound of dripping commenced. The icicle disappeared from his fingers and joined the interior ice in turning to water. A few minutes later, a mechanical whirr sounded and the fan rotated. Slowly at first, then so fast the blades became indistinguishable. Triumph washed through him, gave him the jolt of adrenaline he needed to make his way back in.

Owen pushed off the unit and chose the shorter route around to the front door. Groggy, leaden, he fell in the wet snow again and again. The cold entombment would've been welcome if he'd been shielded from the sun, but the side of the house was completely engulfed in bright yellow light. So, he dragged himself back to his feet. By the time he made it to the sidewalk, he was hunched, staggering. He lurched up the front steps, clinging to the railing to remain upright. The sun blistered his back. Sweat ran down his spine, soaking the waistband of the black track pants he'd donned earlier. His breaths came in ragged, wheezing scrapes.

Yet hope abounded because he'd accomplished what he set out to do, and now everything would be all right.

He stumbled across the porch like a pinball, bouncing from one stabilizing object to another. But after he pushed the door shut, there was nothing immediately available against which to steady himself. He fell to his knees, so hard the floor shook and the nearest window rattled.

Needing to get out of the streaming sun before he let himself rest, he crawled on hands and knees across the wide great room. He caught sight of an air vent under a nearby window, and he stuck his hand out to feel the cold fruit of his labors. His outstretched fingers reached just to the vent's edge.

Hot.

The air was blowing, and it was hot.

"Nonono," he mumbled, his voice raspy. Had he not set the thermostat properly? In his mind's eye he could see the lever pointing to "A/C," but maybe his exhausted brain was playing tricks on him.

Grunting, he crawled toward the far wall where the thermostat hung just outside their bedroom door. Time and again, his sweat-slicked hands slipped, testing his already questionable balance.

When he slipped again, he went down on his right elbow, hard, the impact radiating into the depths of his bone. Willing his hands under him again, he gasped. He hadn't slipped in sweat—well, not sweat alone. Blood streamed down from under the knotted T-shirt.

His wounds weren't healing.

Nausea swamped him, rocking his body forward until he collapsed in a fetal heap. A long rectangle of brilliant afternoon sun framed his tortured body.

One by one, Owen's senses went offline. He stopped hearing the constant patter of the melt. Lost the feminine smell of Megan that permeated the cabin. In his mouth, the sour taste of the threatening bile faded away. The world went black, empty, just a moment before he lost all feeling.

And then he was nothing, not there, not anymore.

CHAPTER TWENTY-FOUR

Anticipation clawed at Megan's stomach, that tingling, unsettled feeling that made it hard to sit still. She bounced in her seat, impatiently tapped her fingers against the steering wheel, chewed at her lip.

Just when she was in a hurry to get back to Owen, of course she was stuck behind a plow. She hung back to avoid the spray of salt shooting out of the big truck's rear.

She inhaled a deep, steadying breath, not wanting to undo the calm she'd found while running her errands. Well, really, she'd found the peace afterward, in a most unlikely place. The busywork of shopping refocused her, gave her the shot of normalcy she needed. By the time she checked out, the fog had cleared from her brain and she could think clearly again.

So, after she loaded her bags into the car, instead of rushing right home, she drove to the only other shopping center in the immediate vicinity and hopped onto a stool at the Mountain Beanery coffee shop. Browsing groceries had made her hungry, so she ordered a bulging blueberry muffin and a cup of coffee, and sat and read the walls.

The Mountain Beanery's idea of décor amounted to wallpapering bumper stickers over every flat surface. "What if the Hokey Pokey *is* what it's all about?" read one. "I got kicked out of Cub Scouts for eating a Brownie" read another. She lost herself perusing them. "Mean People Suck" hung above "What if the whole world farted at once?" Megan's appetite returned with gusto as the sayings, some silly, some clever, some downright rude, had her smiling again.

Occasionally, though, one gave her pause. "Life is short: Break some rules." She knew only too well how short life could be. A runner, skiing enthusiast, successful attorney—John had been in the prime of his life. But so was she. With him gone, what kind of life had she been living? And how long was she going to tolerate living it this way?

On another sticker, Helen Keller declared, "Life is either a daring adventure or nothing." Wow. You couldn't really argue with Helen Keller. Was Megan honestly willing to give up the amazing adventure that was Owen Winters? Could she really be so cowardly as to allow her fear to leave her with nothing?

Her eyes scanned over the colorful array of words until another saying caught her eye: "Life's greatest happiness is to be convinced we are loved." She sucked in a breath. Oh. How many times had Owen told her he loved her and she hadn't said it back? Even now, he was at home, and he didn't know. He didn't know, because she hadn't told him. The muffin sat like a rock in her stomach.

Her eyes scanned for more kernels of wisdom. How ridiculous was that? Oh, jeez, the Dalai Lama now. "Take into account that great love and great achievements involve great risk."

She scrambled off the stool and tugged her coat on, not willing to wait another second to get home to Owen. The barista called out a thank you and she waved. Over his head, a sticker read, "Thoughts are Reality."

"Okay, okay, I get it," she mumbled to the universe.

As she made her way home, Owen dominated her thoughts. His playfulness, his enthusiasm for the smallest pleasures, his incredible skill at giving *other* pleasures, his dark beauty.

Since first waking in front of her fireplace on Christmas night, Owen Winters had showed her with every word, every action, that he was hers. She only had to claim him, to accept the gift he so clearly was. Owen's words came back to her. "*Want me. Need me. Love me. Your love will hold me here, with you. Forever,*" he'd said the first time they'd made love. Later, when they'd ridden on the night wind, he'd declared himself "*As real as you want me to be.*"

Realization came to her in a flash of clarity. It didn't matter that it had taken a wall full of pithy bumper stickers to screw her head on straight. All they'd done was reinforce what she already knew: loving Owen was worth the risk. Loving him would be the great adventure of her life. Loving him would make her life worth living.

The fear wasn't gone. But she wouldn't let it rule her. Not anymore.

Finally, she turned onto the rural route that led to her long driveway, thankful the plow hadn't come this way, too. When the cabin came into view, a million butterflies erupted in her stomach. She was nearly giddy. The scene played out in her head. She'd run to Owen, throw herself around him, declare her love over and over.

What happened next... well, she had no idea. But they'd figure it out, together.

At the top of her driveway, she came to a hard stop and threw the Jeep into park. In a quick succession of movements, she hopped out, swung around the back of the Jeep, and ran down the sidewalk.

"Owen?" she yelled as she thundered up the steps. "I'm home!"

As she reached out for the door handle, she skidded to a stop. The decorative window next to the door was broken. Her heart leapt into her throat.

"Owen?" She wrenched the door open and ran in. She gasped, the air inside nearly a physical wall of heat. Panic squeezed her gut. "Owen?"

She took off across the great room, nearly slipped and fell on a small trail of puddles across the wide plank floor. Then she lurched to a halt.

Her eyes saw what lay there, but her brain couldn't interpret it. A long, narrow oval puddle stretched out in front of her bedroom door. In it lay a pair of black pants and—

The agonized sound that ripped up Megan's throat was nearly inhuman.

She dove forward, careful to avoid the puddle, that dreadful keening spilling out of her. "Nooooo. Nonononooooo."

At the opposite end of the puddle lay a black knit cap. And two big buttons. One navy blue. One brown.

She reached out a hand, yanked it back. "Owen!" she screamed. "Owen, come back! I love you! Pleeeeease!" she wailed.

Her heart clenched until it was hard to breathe, until the room spun and black specks played at the edges of her vision.

This couldn't be happening. Not again. It couldn't.

She wouldn't let it.

The idea slammed into her brain so forcefully, she developed a headache, but she ignored the dizzying pressure and jolted from the floor. She flew out the open door, off the porch, into the snow. Her jeans quickly soaked through, but she ignored their dragging weight as she bent over and mounded the heavy, wet snow into a ball. Into three of them.

When she attempted to lift the two smaller balls atop the large, uneven base, her back screamed in protest. "Come on, come on, come on, please," she chanted, a desperate prayer, a litany. When she finally hefted the middle section into place, it cracked in two, one side crumbling. "No!" she moaned.

Her bare hands icy and red, Megan repacked the middle ball where it sat atop the base. This time, it stuck. She held her breath as she settled the head into place. A deep fissure ran down the side, and she quickly patched and pressed it until it stabilized.

"Owen, I'm here, baby, I'm here. And I love you!" She scanned the heavens, called out, "Do you hear me?" Was he even out there?

Stepping back, her eyes scoured the snowman in front of her. Not nearly as tall as last time, and misshapen and a little lopsided. But he'd do. She hoped. *Please let him do!*

She stared at the blank canvas, knew what he was missing, but didn't think for the life of her she could disturb the hat and buttons on the floor. A queasy shiver ran through her. She had to. They were part of what made him real before.

Fighting back nausea, she turned and ran back inside before she chickened out. The heat was suffocating. Why the hell was it so hot in here? Careful to step around Owen's remains—

the word curdled in her stomach, turning her saliva sour—she flipped the thermostat open. It was set to air conditioning.

She moaned. "Oh, Owen." The unit's freon leak; she'd known about it but not yet gotten it fixed because she hadn't needed the cold air. She slapped her hand over her mouth. But he had. Owen must've needed the cold air. Shaking her head in horrified disbelief, Megan switched the unit off.

John…John hadn't been her fault. But Owen…

She squeezed her eyes shut, ground her fists against them, and beat back the images that wanted to play on the insides of her eyelids. Owen, in distress. Face red, gasping for breath. Struggling, collapsing. Melting. "No," she whimpered, then she dropped to her knees.

Carefully, reverently, Megan lifted the sodden black cap from the puddle. It settled heavy and soaked into her lap, and she stroked it, her hand feeling his silky layers in place of the soft knit. "I'm sorry," she said, her stomach rolling as she gathered the buttons. She couldn't have felt worse if she were plundering a grave. She shuddered and shook her head. *Don't go there*, she warned. *Just. Don't.*

"Hold on, baby," she murmured, then pushed up from the floor. She willed herself out the door, down the steps, across the yard.

She stopped short. The snowman had collapsed. In its place stood a crumbled pile of wet, heavy snow.

She swayed, turned in a helpless circle, her arms flailing. Despair made it impossible to form a complete, logical thought.

The blue of the mid-afternoon sky was oppressive, weighed down heavily on her tired shoulders. She crumpled to the ground, hugged the cap and buttons to her chest. Rocking back and forth, the tears flowed. Her breathing hitched, her gaze lost focus.

By the time her eyes ran dry, it was getting dark. Bright pinks and oranges played along the western horizon, but they didn't hold any splendor for her. She didn't have her North Star. Without Owen, she was simply lost.

Everywhere her body touched the snow, she was thoroughly wet and numb. She shifted positions, unleashing a torrent of pins and needles all down her legs. The sensation was a welcome diversion from the alternating extremes of nothingness or devastation. When she shifted again, an odd shape in the snow caught her attention.

Megan reached out, felt its firmness. All at once, she knew what it was. The snow kid she'd made. However many inches melted today had uncovered his head and shoulders. Hope jolted through her.

Frantic, she dug the kid's form out of the drifted snow, careful to work around his body so he didn't fall over. When the whole front side stood clear before her, she stopped. On her knees, she crawled up to the smallest snowman. He was shorter and narrower than the day she'd made him, but otherwise in good shape. The little guy was her last chance.

Hands so numb she couldn't feel the fabric, Megan struggled to get the knit beanie on the kid's head. It mostly covered the small face, so she folded the edges up as best she could. Cupping the back of the head in her left hand, she pressed the eyes into place with her right. The brown on the right side, the blue on the left. Just like it was supposed to be.

Then she curled up against the snow kid's belly, the snowflake mark Owen gave her against the icy cold. The tears came unbidden, ran down her cheeks, dripped into the snow.

She lay there through the sunset, into the night. Time's

passage meant nothing, particularly as her body lost feeling. Her eyelids drooped, closed for short whiles, reopened, unseeing.

Some time later, she awoke. Groaning, she tried to move, but her body wouldn't cooperate. She sagged back into the snow, the reality of Owen's loss crashing over her anew. Nausea swamped her and she clenched her eyes shut.

When it passed, she stared up at the broad dome of the soaring nighttime sky above her. A thousand stars twinkled. The brilliant canopy made her think of John. She frowned then, shame heating her face and finally giving her some motivation. John wanted her to live, to be happy. He wouldn't want her out here wallowing. Neither would Owen. She was doing none of them any good falling apart like this.

Casting her gaze over the sky one last time, she caught the bright flash of a distant star—for just a moment, it had dazzled with a kaleidoscope of colors. "Okay, I hear ya," she whispered, taking the little display as a personal sign to her despite the fact it had originated thousands of light years ago.

With a grunt, she shoved herself into a sitting position. "Oh, not good," she moaned. Her body throbbed where it wasn't numb. Where it had numbed, her skin burned. Every movement she attempted radiated shooting pain in more directions than she could process. But she pushed through it, literally and figuratively, because she had to get inside, warmed up. At a minimum.

Taking baby steps to let various body parts have their turns to come back to life, she finally staggered onto her feet. She rose in small increments and breathed through the dizziness that threatened.

The door seemed a million miles away, but she was determined to get through it. She trudged forward, made a plodding progress at best. The snow was still so deep, and her legs were wasted. She stumbled, lost her balance. Hands out, she braced for impact.

Strong arms caught her, scooped her up. "I've got you" came a deep voice.

CHAPTER TWENTY-FIVE

A moan of utter relief rolled through Megan's body. It worked. It worked!

"Owen," she cried. She turned her face into his chest, inhaled deeply, wanting any part of him in her. "Owen, I love you. I love you," she said.

"Then why didn't you tell him? Why didn't you choose him?"

Her eyes snapped open. She dropped onto the sofa and gasped. A giant of a man towered over her, long white hair and beard and miles of fur robes swirling around his body despite the lack of breeze in the living room. Silver eyes flashed at her, demanded an answer.

She stared. "I…I—" She swallowed, gulped down some air. "Boreas?"

He nodded once, his stare piercing into her.

"Oh my God. *Oh my God.*" She flew forward in her seat so fast she slid off to her knees. "Owen. Is Owen…okay? I mean"—

she swallowed hard, gesturing with her hands—"obviously he's not okay, but is he—" *Alive? With the other gods? In the wind? Here?*

"He is convalescing." Boreas' eyes bored into her with an intense impassivity. Lines carved into his face, especially around the corners of his eyes, but somehow he looked younger than she'd expect given all that white hair.

Relief flooded her system so forcefully, she collapsed back against the edge of the soft leather. So tired, suddenly so very tired. Threatening tears choked her, and she clapped a hand over her mouth. "Oh, Owen. Oh, thank God," she moaned, glancing up at the inhumanly enormous man. "Can I see him?"

"Where he is, you cannot go." His eyes narrowed, turned steely cold. "Thanks to you, he lies unconscious in the Acheron. I know not how long he will require the healing waters to be restored."

Thanks to her? Megan gasped, wrapped her arms around her stomach. Through a tight throat, she asked, "What is the Acheron?" That tingly, surreal feeling blanketed her again.

Boreas ignored her. "Was it your intention to lock him out?"

"What? No. When?" Megan's breathing shallowed. She massaged her fingers into her temples. "Are you telling me Owen got locked out of the cabin?" Her gaze cut to the windows alongside the door, the pieces fitting together. "He broke a window to get in. Oh my God. I"—she shook her head, pleading for his belief—"I can't explain what happened. I didn't lock him out though. I would never do that. I told him to come in and wait for me." Oh, God, what had he been through while she'd been out sipping coffee? A low whimper rose up her throat.

He gave one sharp nod. "Then, back to my question."

"Which?" She stared up at him in confused awe.

"The only one that matters!" he bellowed. All around the great room, frost crackled over the interior window panes. The temperature dropped.

Trembling, Megan swallowed, then poured out her every truth. "I was scared. And I felt guilty. And disloyal." She staggered to her feet, stood on shaky legs. "With Owen, it was so good, too good, and I didn't trust it to last. And then he hurt himself, and he hid it, and I just couldn't…I just needed…" Her voice cracked. "I thought I had more time." She swayed.

In a flash, Boreas appeared beside her, steadied her. "Be well, child. Sit." He sighed, a long weary sound.

Still standing, she looked up at him. "I was coming back. I came back. To tell him. But I was too late." The sob pressed outward from her chest. She caved into Boreas' huge form, her head just hitting his chest, and threw her arms around him. "I'm so sorry, Boreas. I love him so much."

Boreas tensed under her grasp, then relaxed. One big hand patted her lower ribs. Settled there. Pressed. "Megan?"

She wrenched back and frowned at the big hand frozen in mid-air. Of course he was pushing her away. One minute he was yelling at her and the next she was crying on him. She bit back a groan. Wanting to escape his intense gaze, she shrugged out of her coat, and threw it over the back of the couch. "Sorry about that," she muttered.

"No, that's not—" He stepped toward her, stretched out his hand. Suddenly, kind silver eyes pleaded for something she didn't understand. She wasn't scared, only curious, yet the hairs still raised on the back of her neck. "May I?"

The tentativeness was so incongruous with his earlier commanding presence that she smiled. "Uh, I don't—" She shook her head.

Boreas bent down, pressed his hand to her lower stomach. His breath caught, flaring eyes flashed to hers. Reverent words in that same language Owen sometimes used spilled in hushed tones from his lips.

"Boreas?" Her quiet voice trembled. Something about the set of those mystical eyes sent her stomach aflutter.

His whole face brightened. "You carry life within you."

Megan frowned. She opened and closed her mouth. "Um"—she shook her head—"that's not possible." Was it? She mentally began counting dates. No. There was no way. She was on birth control.

He crossed his arms and waited.

Megan swallowed, her mind whirling. "No, Boreas. The only person I've been with is Owen"—she ignored the blush that bloomed across her cheeks—"and *if* I really was pregnant it would be too new to—"

"But there's something you forget." He drew himself up to his full height and smiled down at her.

Unease fluttered through her stomach. She *had* taken her pills late a few times since she'd been with Owen. And maybe him being a god negated her birth control somehow? The more she thought about it, the more she was afraid to hear what Boreas had to say. "What's that?"

"The child is a demigod. For all intents and purposes, my grandchild. I can feel him."

Demi...? Her breathing hitched and Megan swayed, moaned. She was...pregnant? With Owen's baby? And he was a...him? A demigod him?

Boreas clutched her elbow and settled her back into the embracing couch. He knelt on one knee next to her.

"Sorry," she whispered, dazed, her pounding pulse stealing her breath. She was pregnant? She was pregnant! "You can't tell Owen!" Boreas' face fell. "I mean, I want to be the one to tell him. Please?" *Oh, Owen, will this news make you happy?* God, she hoped so. Her stomach flip-flopped.

He nodded. "By all means."

"Oh jeez." She slapped a hand against her forehead, rubbed her fingers back and forth. "I'm going to be a mom." Her other hand curled over her abdomen.

"So it seems."

Awed by the very concept, she smiled up at him. "You're going to be a grampa."

He threw his head back and laughed. "Indeed. This pleases me," he said. His white teeth gleamed.

It pleased her, too. So much. Utter astonishment tingled over her skin. "Oh, my God."

"Literally."

She gaped. The Supreme God of Winter just joked about her having gotten knocked up! Shocked laughter spilled from her. But she reveled in it, glad someone was here to share her amazed happiness, even if it wasn't who she wanted most. Besides, Boreas' apparent acceptance and pleasure in the news gave her hope Owen would respond the same way.

Thoughts and questions and worries and plans tried to take up root in her mind, but there was no room for them amid her wonder and joy. Owen had filled her with love, brought her back to life, given her a family. His presence in her life, short though it might've been, was an absolute gift she would cherish forever. Her heart panged at his absence. Her soul yearned for its true partner to be here, standing at her side.

Megan sighed. "So, what happens now? Can he come back?

What can I do for him?"

His more reserved demeanor returned. He clasped his hands behind his back. "First, his injuries must heal, then his godhood must revitalize. The rest is up to him."

"Okay," she whispered, fear and hope and anticipation flaring in her gut. "Okay." She had faith in him, trusted in what he'd said, in what he'd shown her. She would be strong for him. And be right here waiting when he was ready to come back to her. For she could believe nothing else. Still, she begged of Boreas, "Will you tell him how badly I want him back? Please?"

Boreas offered a small nod. "I'll see what I can do."

Bleary-eyed and foggy-headed, she looked up at Boreas. She heaved a deep breath to calm her racing heart. The old god's presence helped. She found comfort in his paternal character.

"You should sleep, now. You are about as worn down as he was."

She nodded. He was right about sleeping, if not for herself, then for the baby. But she had to know. "Was it bad?"

His whole body sagged. "It wasn't good."

A shiver raced across her shoulders, down her spine. *I'm sorry, Owen.*

"Come now," he said, rising and offering a paw-sized hand.

She accepted his assistance. On her feet, she continued to lean on the arm he offered. "Thank you," she murmured as they walked in slow, halting steps—all she could manage. She directed them to the bathroom, pointedly avoiding the spot in front of her bedroom door. For all she knew the puddle had dried, but either way she couldn't stomach looking.

"For what?"

She heaved a deep breath. "For taking care of him. For coming here and taking care of me."

His lips quirked as he looked away. He appeared almost embarrassed. "You're welcome."

At the bathroom door, Megan leaned against the doorjamb. "Will you wait a moment?" She blushed at asking, but didn't want him to leave yet.

"All right." He crossed his arms and leaned against the wall.

Megan plodded through changing and spared energy only for the bare minimum of her nighttime routine. She padded out into her bedroom and climbed onto the big mattress, choosing the very spot where she'd laid on Owen's chest the night before. God, could that really have been *just* last night? So much had happened that it didn't seem possible. Yesterday seemed worlds away.

"Boreas?" she called.

His mammoth silhouette filled her bedroom doorway, hesitated just outside.

"Would you please sit with me? Until I fall asleep?"

He nodded, and had to duck and turn sideways to clear the door frame. The mattress tilted toward him when he sat on the bottom corner of the bed. Were his cheeks pink?

She sank into the pillows and buried herself under the covers. "When you're not being all godlike and intimidating, you're pretty good company," she murmured, then yawned into her pillow. Sleep pulled her down, as if she were anchored by lead weights.

"And you are amusing, for a human. Now, sleep."

"'kay. Night, Grampa."

෧෦෬

Megan woke up on Monday morning, her third full day without

Owen's presence. The cabin was too big, too empty, too quiet.

For each of the past two days, Megan had awakened hopeful that Owen would return. Each night, she'd gone to bed disappointed and lonely. She had to remind herself to be patient, have faith. Whatever time he needed to heal, she wanted him to have.

In the meantime, she busied herself with distractions. Stapling thick plastic over the broken window. Setting up repair appointments for the window and the condenser unit. Doing laundry. Calling everyone back home to explain her decision not to return for New Year's—reassuring them she was okay. And for once in a long, long time, she mostly meant it.

But here it was, a new week in an already unseasonably warm new year, and her body longed for Owen's touch, her soul yearned for his companionship. Pressure filled her heart with the need to voice the emotions that burned through her.

"I love you, Owen, with my heart and soul. Come back to me," she said out loud, in case he could hear her, in case he was listening. "And I love you, too," she whispered, smoothing her palms over her belly.

Three days later, and her mind still struggled to wrap itself around the idea of a baby, but the very thought of the life growing inside her cut the edge from her loneliness and filled her with nervous hope for the future.

Megan pushed out of bed, the air cool against her sleep-warmed skin. Wanting Owen to be comfortable when he returned, she'd reset the heat to its previous low setting. She made a pit-stop in the bathroom, then shuffled out to the kitchen. Her stomach growled, empty and clenching. She put on coffee and ate a blueberry Pop-Tart right out of the foil wrapper. She hadn't eaten them in years, but she'd bought two boxes at the store thinking Owen would adore them. He had such a sweet tooth. After she ate the first one the other night, her body craved the junk food and she gave in. The past two years had been hard on her body, and she could stand to gain a few pounds. And not just for her, now. Plus, having an appetite again felt so nice.

After breakfast, she dressed and sat on the front steps with a book. She read some, stared out across the broad expanse of her front yard some. With the temperature hovering in the fifties, more and more snow melted every day, to the point where grass now poked through in spots and her driveway was clear and dry. The sagging igloo struck her as sad, as did the collapse of the little snow kid. But she had her own now.

What would their baby be like? Look like? She hugged herself tight. If she was honest, she was intimidated by the idea he'd be a demigod—what did that mean? In what ways might he be different from other kids? Would she be equipped to give him everything he needed? She tried hard not to let herself get too spun up by these questions—Owen would help her figure everything out, right? When he came back. If he came back. Oh, God. She couldn't face the 'if.' She was clinging to 'when' with everything she had.

Megan never lasted long outside before she got a little too warm and sleepy. Long midday naps became an everyday indulgence. Dinner was a low-key affair, and then she'd watch a DVD or find another book. In the evenings, she found it difficult to resist peeking out the front windows. That first time, Owen had arrived in the evening, after all.

Late at night, she laid in bed, staring up at the low glow of the stars covering her ceiling and talking to John. He didn't answer back, of course, not without Owen here. But Megan still needed to say good-bye, was ready to do so, finally, and believed somehow he would be aware.

Tuesday and Wednesday brought more of the same routine, with the exception of the return of cold weather on Wednesday morning. But she enjoyed winter's return. In a weird way, it made her feel closer to Owen. So, before lunch, all bundled up in coat, scarf, and mittens, she took a walk to the end of her driveway and back. Fresh and crisp, the air tasted good and made her feel alive.

With each satisfying thump of her boots against the pavement, Megan stomped back the threatening worry Owen wasn't returning.

Five days had passed—each day it grew harder to wake up as hopeful and distract herself from the loneliness. Maybe, by not telling him she loved him before he went back to his own realm, she'd blown it. Maybe Boreas had let news of the baby slip and Owen didn't want it. This fear was the one that caused her stomach to plummet. The next thought lodged a thick ball of tension in her throat. Maybe he wasn't healing. Maybe Owen was—*No*.

Back in the house, Megan shed all her outer layers, sweat dampening her skin and underclothes. The shower's call sounded so delicious, she gave in to it, decided to eat after freshening up, no matter how much her stomach protested. Apparently, this baby had inherited Owen's appetite, because she was ravenous almost all of the time and craved ice cream above everything else. Another trip to the grocery store would be in order soon.

Megan washed herself quickly and then let the lukewarm spray beat down on her body, infusing relaxation into every cell. For a long moment, she just stood there, eyes closed, head down, back to the showerhead, and allowed the jets to knead all the worry and tension from her muscles. It was heaven. The thought was bittersweet. How many times had Owen said that about being with her? *Oh, Owen, where are you?*

Her stomach growled. "All right, all right." This baby was going to turn her into a house. The thought comforted her. "I'm movin' it." On a deep sigh, she straightened up and opened her eyes.

And found herself staring into the mismatched gaze of Owen Winters.

CHAPTER TWENTY-SIX

Megan screamed in surprise, her heart slamming in her chest. For a moment, the air sucked out of the room. He was here. And then she moaned, a long, low sound of desperate relief. Oh, God, he was really *here*.

Her hands yanked open the stall's glass door. Her feet were in motion before her brain ordered the movement, and then she had him. She had him in her arms. Her hands fluttered over him—stroking his silky black hair, massaging his big shoulders, feeling the strong, solid realness of him. Tightness closed off her throat and kept her from offering any more than that choked moan.

His arms wrapped around her slowly. Between them, the soft fabric of his shirt dampened from her body. The sensation delighted her, because if he was a figment of her imagination, he'd have been naked. The ridiculous thought opened her throat a bit. "Oh, Owen," she whispered. She pulled back, prepared to tell him everything.

His expression stole her words and her breath.

Stone faced, eyes distant, lips pressed into a line. His arms dropped away.

The emptiness in Megan's stomach felt like a rock. Dread snaked down her spine. "Hey." Her eyes scanned over his face, searching for some hint of the warmth and openness she associated with him. She couldn't find it. The wrongness of it… Goose bumps broke out across her damp skin and she shivered. "Um, sorry, can I just—" She reached toward her towel, hanging on a hook behind him.

He stepped back, allowing her access. She frowned when she thought of how he'd tried to keep the towel from her another time. A time that seemed so long ago now.

The soft terry made her feel less vulnerable, but did little to quell the growing ball of dread pressing outward from her chest. Finally, when there was nothing else to distract herself from his distance and coldness, she looked at him again. She took a deep breath and asked, "What's wrong, Owen? Are you okay?"

"I'm fine," he said quietly. His gaze dropped down her body, then flashed back to hers. "Perhaps you should dress."

Megan frowned. Since when did he ever want her to dress? Fear-induced adrenaline spiked through her veins, made her tremble. "Owen—"

"Please." The set of his shoulders mirrored the tense tone of his voice.

"Okay." She strode toward the bedroom door, then looked back over her shoulder. "Um, I'll be right out?"

He nodded once. "Yes."

Something was wrong. Very, very wrong. Megan's mind whirled through possibilities, but couldn't make anything stick. Anything except the one thing her brain refused to acknowledge and her heart refused to believe—he didn't want her anymore. How could that be? After everything?

Her effort to rush through dressing left her all thumbs. It took three tries to get the metal button through the little hole in her jeans. She scrubbed the towel through her hair quickly and combed her fingers through the thick mass of it, but devoted no other effort. She needed to be back in his presence, to touch him, to get answers, to fix whatever was making him act this way.

Before stepping out of her bedroom, she heaved a deep breath that failed to calm, then entered the great room. Owen stood to the side of the front door, stiff-postured, arms across his chest, looking outside through the sidelights. The plastic covering the broken window sucked in and out in response to the wind's command. In her delight at seeing him again, she hadn't noticed he was dressed in black from silky hair to jeans and T-shirt to boots. His aloofness did nothing to diminish his sexy masculinity.

Megan stopped some feet from him. Her arms ached to feel his warmth and solidness; her mouth yearned to taste him again. But he seemed so unapproachable. She cleared her throat.

A beat passed, then another, and he turned his head in her direction. His eyes did a quick scan of her attire, jeans and a long-sleeved shirt, then he motioned toward the couch. "Would you like to sit?"

"No, I don't want to sit. I want you to tell me what's wrong."

He frowned and dropped his gaze to the ground.

Megan forced herself to move, stepped right to him, tilted his chin up with her fingers. His eyes were full of pain and regret and made her heart skip in her chest. "Why are you hiding from me? You're scaring me."

For a moment, he seemed uncertain, torn. He opened his
mouth to speak, but said nothing. Taking a deep breath, he drew
his shoulders up and put a little physical distance between them
again.

"I've come to say good-bye."

Megan heard the words as if they'd been said from
underwater. Her heart plummeted into her stomach. "What?
Why? No."

He nodded once. When they made eye contact, his gaze was
icy cold. "It is what's right."

"Says who? What does that even mean?"

"I just…needed to see you. One last time."

One last time? Panic surged like an electric current through
her blood. "Why are you doing this? I'm sorry for what
happened, Owen. I—"

"No. Stop. Please. I'm the one who should be sorry. It was
not fair to you."

A headache bloomed behind and above Megan's eyes.
"What are you talking about? What wasn't fair?"

"None of it matters now." His expression softened, hinted
at the Owen she'd come to know. The one whose eyes sparkled
with mirth and warmth. A dangerous wave of hope threatened
to swamp her, but then his words continued on so mechanically.
"Thank you for sharing your Christmas with me."

"Owen, stop this. Please. Can we just talk?"

He offered a small, sad smile. "There is nothing to say. And
it's time for me to go."

Fear and panic mushroomed into anger. Anger at herself
for letting things get this far off track. Why couldn't she have
gotten over herself sooner? Anger on behalf of the child in
her belly. No way she was letting the baby lose his father—not

without a fight.

"Are you hurt right now? Is it too warm for you here?" Her gaze bore into him as she spoke.

"No." His tone was almost questioning.

"Good. Then as long as you're not in any kind of danger, you can give me sixty seconds of your immortal life and listen. Right? Please." She cocked an eyebrow at him.

"Fine." He folded his arms across his chest.

She closed the distance between them, gripped his crossed forearms and squeezed, ignored the way he tensed at her touch. *Fix this!* She released a long breath. "I'm sorry for what happened to you. When I came home and saw"—she shook her head, swallowed around the lump that sprang to life in her throat—"I'm so, so very sorry that happened to you."

"Megan—"

Her eyes flashed up to his, half hidden beneath his hair. "No. You're just listening right now, remember?"

The shadow of a smile crossed his face. He nodded.

"I'm sorry I left. I should've stayed and talked everything out with you. But I was kinda freaking out, Owen. And I needed...I just needed some time alone to think, to process. Finding out you'd hurt yourself for me, that you were vulnerable, too..." She shrugged, not letting go of his arms. "I freaked out. I was back there. On that Christmas night. Listening to two strangers tell me John never had a chance. That he'd gone out to do something for me and wasn't coming back. Ever. And I was right back there again." Megan groaned. She leaned her forehead against her hands on his arms. "Shit. This isn't what I want to say," she murmured to herself.

"What do you want to say, then?" he whispered.

Something touched her hair, sent a tingle of want down her

neck and spine. She lifted her gaze again. Took a deep breath and said the only thing that mattered, "I love you, Owen. I love you." She stepped closer, until her breasts pressed against his folded arms, drawn in by the glassiness that bloomed in his eyes. "I already knew I loved you, even before I left, but I couldn't let everything go. Being apart from you made it all so crystal clear. As soon as it hit me, I came back, so happy to tell you…" She swallowed. Reached both hands up to cup his face. "I love you. I want you. I choose you, if you'll have me. If you'll stay. Please stay, Owen. Choose me back."

He shook his head. "Megan."

"Please. Love me." One hot tear spilled down from her right eye.

He swallowed so roughly, she could hear it. "I do," he whispered.

Joy threatened to burst forth, restrained only by his continued hesitation. "Well, then, what's—"

"I don't want to have pressured you into this. For you to have been guilted into this by what happened."

"No, I'm not. I told you. I was coming back to tell you. Before. I was ready to choose you, Owen. Before."

"Megan." His deep voice trembled. "Be sure."

She couldn't stop the smile that broke across her face. She would reassure him 'til the end of time if she had to. "I am. So sure. I love you. I'm *in* love with you. And I want you, forever. Just like you said."

ℰℋℬ

Owen heard the words, felt their pull deep within his soul. Almost six days in the healing waters of the River Acheron, one of the five rivers of the Underworld, had healed his body and restored the strength of his godhood. But the trade off—for one was always required where the gods were concerned—was the letting of his secret sorrows into the currents of the river known for providing passage of newly dead souls into the afterlife. The intense reliving of those memories was the token Owen had to pay to be ferried back to the Upper World.

For an endless moment, his psyche was buffeted by the remembered anguish of losing his family; his soul forced to re-endure its endless solitude; his heart broke anew at Chione's recalled betrayal.

Perhaps he shouldn't have come directly to Megan. He should've waited until the soul-depressing effects of the forced remembering eased, but all he could think of was the warmth and solace Megan's arms provided. When he'd seen her, though, all pink and wet and alive under the streaming water of the shower, he realized how unfair he'd been to try to cajole her love the way he'd done. Boreas had pushed through a cold front so Owen could return, but the Supreme God wouldn't be able to hold out long against Zephyros's greater power. Spring's life had always been stronger than winter's death. So Owen wouldn't have long here. Certainly not long enough to court Megan, to win her love the way he needed to, the way she deserved. The whole project had been a god's folly from the beginning.

But then, here she was, wanting him, loving him, choosing him.

Her soft, slim fingers stroked his face. "Please, baby, come back to me."

Owen sucked in a breath, her words pulling him out of his tortured thoughts. He found her eyes, sparkling blue and full of determined life, brimming with promised love.

Then he was on her. All primal instinct, the desire flooding his body aligned with the soul-deep need of his heart.

Arms around her small shoulders, body pressing, pressing hers until they stumbled backward into the front door. His lips rained down on her eyes, cheeks. "Oh angel," he breathed as his mouth claimed hers. He moaned and pushed his tongue into her, needing every ounce of connection between them. Gods, this was where he belonged. Right here. With this woman. In these arms wound so tight around his neck they almost made it hard to breathe. He didn't mind; he reveled in every bit of Megan's touch.

When her right leg wrapped around his thigh, his hands released their knotted hold on her hair and snaked down her body to pick her up. They both groaned as the new stance positioned his hips between her legs. He was already rock hard.

"I'm sorry. Didn't mean it," he rasped around the edges of a kiss. There was so much he wanted to say, but he just couldn't let her go long enough to say it. Only moments before he'd convinced himself he had to let her go and now she was offering him everything, forever.

"Shhh, we're okay. Right?" Her voice was high, breathy.

"So much more than okay."

"I missed you," she whispered against his lips.

The words grounded him, anchored him to the world. He leaned his forehead against hers. "Let's never have a reason to miss each other again."

"Deal." The joy she unleashed on him was like the sun dawning on a freezing-cold day. The heavy weight of ancient sorrow lifted off his soul.

Their hands tugged at one another's shirts. Owen set Megan back on her feet and fell to his knees to undo her jeans. Her hands felt so good stroking his hair. The button and zipper undone, he kissed Megan's stomach as he pulled the denim down over her hips.

Lips pressed just below her belly button, Owen froze.

CHAPTER TWENTY-SEVEN

Owen gasped. Life grew within her.

Words spilled from him in the ancient language. Eyes fixed in wonder, he skimmed his hands over the silky skin of her abdomen.

Megan slid down the door, straddled his lap. She dug her teeth into her bottom lip, her eyes searching his. "So, um, I take it you can, uh, tell, too?"

"You're pregnant," he whispered, awe stealing his voice.

"Yes."

He pressed a hand against her belly, held it there. "I feel him within you." My child. *My son. Our* son.

Megan grinned. "Yeah?"

He nodded. "Gods, Megan. I'm to be a father?"

"Yes." Her breathing hitched.

"And you…you are the mother of my child."

"Yeah," she whispered. "Is all this okay?"

Okay? Owen's head reeled at how miraculous, how momentous, this news truly was. "Second to you saying you love me, it's the most incredible thing I've ever heard." His chest expanded and eyes stung with the force of his emotion. "Oh, however was I fortunate enough to find you?" He placed a worshipful kiss against her forehead.

"I'm the lucky one," she said, then released a long, weighty sigh. "God, I'm so happy you're happy about him."

He sucked in a breath, pulled back so he could see her eyes. "Oh, angel, were you worried?"

"I don't know, I…" She shrugged.

He pressed a chain of tiny kisses all over her face. "Be assured I want all of you. Every part of you. And this is more than I ever hoped for." The joy that brightened her face was his greatest reward. Then something she'd said occurred to him. "Hey, what did you mean by 'could I feel him, *too*?'"

A blush colored her face. How he'd missed that lovely tell. "Boreas was here."

"What? When?" The Supreme God appearing to a human was beyond unusual. It was unheard of. Boreas had always kept to himself, ensconced within the Realm of Gods.

"The day you…disappeared." She shuddered and her eyes glassed over. "I tried to bring you back by building a new snowman. The snow was too wet, though, and it wouldn't stay together. And I, uh, I guess I passed out in the snow." She waved her hand. "Anyway, he found me and brought me in. He said he could feel the baby, too."

A torrent of responses erupted within Owen. Her effort to resurrect him. Putting herself in harm's way, especially in her condition. Boreas' rescue of his beloved. Mother of Gods, much had happened while he was gone. And she'd had to handle so much of it on her own. He kissed her again, poured his thanks and love, his heart and soul into it. "I love you, Megan."

"I love you, too, so much."

"Then take me to bed. Make love to me. Claim me once and for all. Root me in this world for all time."

Megan pulled back from their constant kisses and whispered words. "What do you...what are you saying?"

"We must declare our love while I'm inside you. That was what the gods agreed would prove you'd chosen me, that is what will make it possible for me to stay here, with you, as a human." Owen wrapped his arms around her and brought them both to their feet. He kissed her one last time, giddy with excitement at what was about to happen—not just the sex, but the humanity.

They fumbled their way to the bedroom, kissing, removing clothes, touching, laughing, exchanging sweet declarations of love and need. Together, they climbed onto the bed. Megan lowered her back to the cool covers and beckoned his body to come to hers. Owen settled his body between her thighs and uttered a long low moan of relief and desire. He was home.

Then he sprang up from her. Looked down at her stomach. "I will be too heavy on you...and the baby."

Her giggle drew his gaze away from the part of her that would soon swell with his child. A demigod. Part him. Part her. She carded her fingers through his hair, and he leaned into the touch. "You're sweet for being concerned. But we'll both be fine. Now, come here."

He crawled up her, found her lips with his. His hand dropped between her legs and stroked and circled, but found her already wet and wanting. His cock twitched and throbbed, ached for their joining. Eyes fixed on hers, he pushed forward, filled her in one slow, slick stroke. "It feels so right when I'm in you," he said against the shell of her ear. "Like I'm right where I belong." His body moved in long, deep strokes.

"You are," she whispered. "Oh, God, I love you so much I might float away." Her arms tightened around him, nails bit into his skin.

"Don't worry, angel. I've got you. And you're not going anywhere."

"Not without you."

"Not without me." Never again.

She groaned. Wrapped her legs around his lower back. "I need more."

He grunted. Kissed her ear, neck, cheek. "Anything for you." He thrust harder, faster, angled his hips to hit right where it would drive her wild. "Aw, gods, I love you."

"Love you, too," she panted, her breath coming in shallow gasps and throaty moans.

Pleasure clawed up Owen's spine, ripping him apart, pulling him back together again, preparing to reassemble him into a new man. Into a human man. It was the most beautiful torment, and he chased it with every wet stroke, every open-mouthed kiss. His release would be like no other—for it would not only be physical, but psychic.

Ecstatic pressure pooled low in his belly, gathered, intensified. Her body tightened around his length, one by one severing the ties to his sanity. "I love you, Megan," he ground out like he couldn't stop saying it.

Megan groaned and sucked in a breath, released just enough air to whimper, "I love you" back. And then she screamed his name. Her whole body pulsed with the force of her orgasm. Head wrenched into the pillow, back arched, thighs clenched, her muscles milked him over and over.

He buried his shout in her neck. His orgasm hit like a tidal wave, tossing him around until he didn't know which way was up, dragging him down and then right back to the heavens again, stealing his breath until he dangled near the brink of unconsciousness.

Peace descended on Owen, body and mind. One beat passed, then another.

The tingling, like standing too near a live electrical current, started in his extremities and worked inward. Body still shuddering, he rolled off Megan and looked at his hands, but couldn't see the phantom presence making its way up his arms, up his legs. His heart set off at an even wilder gallop. When the preternatural sensation hit his chest, his whole body seized against the mattress. His back arched unnaturally, like someone was pulling him upward by the heart.

In the far-off distance, he imagined he heard Megan calling for him, yelling his name over and over. His brain conjured the soothing feel of her hands on his face, his chest. He wanted to tell her not to worry for him.

But then he wasn't with her anymore. Wasn't in their bed in the cabin.

One glance down at the cold white marble below his feet and he knew instantly where he was. He'd walked the halls of Boreas' primary residence many times, but he was moving through the space like he was in a dream. He felt in it, but not of it.

"That's because you're not really here."

Owen pivoted toward Boreas' deep voice, found him sitting on the deep ledge of a wide window that looked out over the pristine tundra. The white marble, the animal furs, the floor-to-ceiling jeweled mosaic of a compass rose, arrow pointing to the calligraphic 'N' at the top... Boreas' private chamber materialized around him, as if out of a fog. He bowed his head. "My Lord?"

"I have a proposition for you."

Glancing down at his nakedness, he resisted covering himself and instead thumbed over his shoulder. "Now? I was kind of in the middle of something."

Still gazing out the window, Boreas chuckled. "Yes, I gathered. Thus our need to talk, now, before the change is finalized."

That strange current continued to flow through him, and now adrenaline born of curiosity joined the sensation. "I am, of course, willing to hear anything you have to say."

"Congratulations on your son."

Owen's confusion didn't keep the pleased grin from dominating his face. "Thank you. It is wonderful news."

"Indeed. Which is why I think you should consider maintaining some of your powers. Instead of becoming a mortal human, I would like to propose a demotion of sorts. To demigod."

His mind raced over the implications of Boreas' words, began to compile lists of pros and cons. What he mostly saw were the pros—his ability to protect Megan and his son, his ability to teach him, by example. "What about my vulnerability to heat?" he asked. He couldn't tolerate such weakness ever again.

Boreas nodded. "Unlike now, as a demigod you would possess the strengths of your human and god natures, while bearing few to none of the weaknesses of either. The trade off is you won't have the full strength or variety of power you now possess."

Owen's main concern allayed, he nodded. In that very first

conversation regarding John's request for help, Owen had in part been attracted to the idea of finding a way free from the unendingness of immortality, to the idea of finally experiencing firsthand the many joys it seemed humans did on a daily basis. Boreas' proposal would get him much of what he'd wanted, while also offering other benefits he didn't know enough to realize he'd need. He frowned. "What's the catch?"

"The boy. He will work for me upon majority. After he's been trained in his powers, of course."

A fierce protectiveness shot up Owen's spine. "You will not speak of taking my son from me before he is even born." His raised voice echoed around the marble. He would make sure his son never experienced the pain of familial loss like he had.

Boreas held his hands up. "Fear not. Hear me out. He will work for me within the human realm, as a human. We are losing, Owen. Every year, Zephyros gets stronger and stronger, and the gods of winter lose small increments that in the blink of an eye will add up to catastrophe for the planet we all share. We need more people from our team working on issues of climate change, to stem the current damage, to try to turn it back."

Owen's hackles settled some, but he was still on the defensive, waiting for the next shoe to drop. "And?"

Boreas smirked. "And I will set up and fund a foundation to bring together the greatest thinkers, policy analysts, and scientists of the day. You will run it. And then you will pass on stewardship of it to your son."

Owen scowled, but didn't mind so much for himself the idea of a useful occupation. And what better for him to do? He knew firsthand the devastating effects of deforestation on the Earth's atmosphere and polar ecosystems, how much less Arctic sea ice formed every year—soon it was likely no ice would form in the summers at all. "How about this: I'll run this foundation for you, but first I get a whole year to enjoy my life with my new family. And the child will have the foundation as one occupational choice among many he might choose on the issue of climate change."

"Are you negotiating with the Supreme God of Winter?"

Owen nodded, confident he was on an acceptable path because of the twinkle of humor illuminating the ancient god's silver eyes. "I am."

"Fatherhood agrees with you."

"It does."

"I can accept these terms."

"And what of Megan?" As demigods, they wouldn't be fully immortal, but his and his son's aging would be so slow as to extend their lives well beyond the normal range of a human. His stomach clenched at the thought of Megan growing old, dying. No. There must be a way.

Boreas leaned back against the wide stone molding, crossing his arms and looking totally self-satisfied. "Already taken care of. While a god of any rank, all of your bodily fluids will remain infused with the healing powers of the River Acheron. As long as the two of you are *together*, the river's elixir will pass through you to her and bestow upon her the health and longevity you and your son will enjoy as demigods."

Owen gasped. Son of a— He'd planned this all along. "Sure of yourself, eh?"

"No, son. I'm sure of you. Sure you are the kind of man who would do what is in his family's best interest. And if my causes are helped along the way, why, that is all the better."

Hope and excitement to begin this new life infused Owen's entire being with an incredible levity. He couldn't see the downsides, though these weren't decisions he could fully make on his own. "I would like you to give Megan the opportunity to discuss any other details I haven't thought of with you, later, but otherwise I would be all too pleased to accept your proposal."

"Done. Tell Megan hello from Grampa."

Before Owen even had the chance to reply, his whole body sucked backward through time and space. He collapsed into the mattress at their cabin. The breath whooshed out of him and he coughed and rolled to his side, his head finding Megan's lap.

"Owen, Owen, are you all right?" She stroked his hair and shoulders. "I thought you were having a seizure. Can gods have seizures?"

"Don't...worry," he panted, worked to regain his equilibrium. Part of his struggle was the sensation of trying to see the world through a new pair of glasses with a radically different prescription. Supernatural power still flowed through Owen's body, but it hummed where before it had vibrated in its intensity. Then again, the air in the bedroom felt cool against Owen's body, proving his part-human nature. "I'm better than all right. Now."

"Are you... did it work?"

Pushing himself up so he could brace on one arm and face her, Owen cupped her jaw in his hand. "It worked. I'm yours. Forever."

Her eyes danced, the bright blue heaven in a stare. She pressed a kiss against the palm of his hand. "And I'm yours. God, I love you so much." She grasped his other hand and placed their palms, together, on her bare belly. "Both of you."

He leaned in for a kiss. Slow and gentle, he communicated with his lips every bit of the love and gratitude and hope flowing through him. "I promise to make a wonderful life for you, for the both of you."

She nodded. "We'll do it together. Oh, Owen, it's so exciting imagining the future now. I can't wait to meet this little person. I wonder what he'll look like. What he'll enjoy. What he'll want to be when he grows up."

Owen felt the unusual heat of a blush spread across his cheeks. "Yeah. So, about that…"

EPILOGUE

Almost One Year Later

Megan rolled over in the big bed and reached out a searching hand. When she didn't find what she was looking for, she begrudgingly opened one eyelid. She was alone. Her ears perked up as they always did now—in constant listening for even the smallest sign of distress from her child, motherhood made her suddenly cognizant of every little noise. But all was quiet.

Her eyes adjusted to the light and scanned over the ceiling above, finally fixing on the new grouping of stars in the corner by the window. The small constellation of the dove had appeared out of nowhere. Owen had been just as surprised as Megan. A good-bye from John, a reassurance he'd found his peace. Because she'd found hers.

Megan luxuriated in a body-awakening stretch, then propped herself up enough to see over her pillows to the alarm clock: 10:30 a.m.

She gasped and whipped her legs out of bed. She couldn't remember the last time she'd slept so late. Well, yes she could. She'd spent a lot of mornings lounging in bed with Owen right up until September fifth, when their son, Theodore Eoghan Winters, came screaming into the world. When she'd learned the name Theodore was Greek for "gift of god," she couldn't imagine anything better for the baby who had truly been just that. Owen couldn't have agreed more, and Megan had loved his suggestion of using the ancient spelling for her new husband's name for Teddy's middle name.

But, jeez, this wasn't just any other morning. She shrugged into her robe and hurried out into the cabin's great room. "Why did you let me sleep so late?"

Owen turned from where he sat on the floor in front of the huge Christmas tree they'd bought and decorated together, bouncing Teddy on his lap and pointing out the colorful lights and ornaments. "Figured sleeping in a little would be a gift in itself," he said, his voice warm and pleased.

Wasn't that the truth? Teddy had only started sleeping a six-hour stretch through the night a few weeks before. She knelt down beside them. "Well, it was wonderful. Thank you." She pressed a lingering kiss to Owen's mouth. "Merry Christmas, baby."

His smile was playful and so sexy. "Merry Christmas to you, too."

"And to you, too, little man. Happy first Christmas." She kissed the super-fine mass of black hair that already covered her son's head. He responded instantly to her nearness, squirming in Owen's grasp and reaching out for her. "Oh, oh, what's this?" She lifted him and snuggled him into that sweet spot against her chest. He immediately opened his mouth and gummed his fist. "Somebody's a hungry bugger."

"I gave him a bottle earlier, but he sucked it down in like two minutes."

"That's because somebody inherited Daddy's appetite. Yes he did," she said. "How 'bout I feed him, and then we can make some breakfast for us?"

Owen stretched over and kissed her cheek and then his son's head. "You feed him and I'll make us breakfast." He helped Megan off the floor.

She settled into the soft comfort of the leather couch and positioned some pillows to hold Teddy's big body. Of course, demigods couldn't be small babies. Oh no. Megan still managed to wrangle favors out of Owen by reminding him of their son's ten-pound, eight-ounce weight at birth.

Owen asked her questions about what she wanted to eat as she nursed Teddy, who grabbed tight to a finger with one little hand. She laughed and cooed and talked to the baby while he ate, all the time staring into his beautiful mismatched eyes. The only difference between his and Owen's was that Teddy's blue eye was brighter, more like hers. Otherwise, the boy appeared a near carbon copy of his father. She often wondered if the striking resemblance was the result of Owen having dominant genes or her decorating that little snowman the night she'd tried to bring Owen back to her, but, really, it didn't matter. She was glad their son looked like his father, glad they had that connection.

"Here we go," Owen said. He placed an overflowing tray of toast, scrambled eggs, bacon, yogurt, berries, and bananas on the coffee table.

"Wow. That's quite a feast. Thank you."

"Hungry?"

"Starving, actually." Megan reached for a plate he'd set on the pillow next to her, but couldn't quite reach without jostling the baby.

"Here, let me help." Owen grabbed a slice of toast with butter and jelly and held it up to her mouth.

She took a big bite. She looked up and found his eyes blazing, that odd light flickering faintly behind the blue and brown. "What could possibly be turning you on about this situation?"

He popped a berry in his mouth and quirked a playful, cocky grin. "Everything about you turns me on, angel. You know that." He held the toast out again. "Have another bite." She did, feeling a blush heat her face even as she leaned forward.

"You totally have a thing for feeding me."

He tossed more berries between his full lips. "I'm man enough to admit that. I like seeing you healthy and sated, and I like to have a hand in making you that way."

Good God. What he didn't do with his heated gazes or godlike body, he could always do with his words. She laughed and Teddy pulled away from her. "All done?" She tossed a cloth over her shoulder and lifted his chunky baby body up to burp. He gave up a few good ones before Owen offered to hold him while she ate.

Seeing him hold his son filled her heart up to the very top. Owen was always so attentive, so affectionate, so helpful with him. The smallness of Teddy's body against Owen's broad chest made her husband look like the protector he was. Owen's big hand spanned their son's back as he held him gently, assuredly. He was already a great father, and damn if fatherhood wasn't sexy as hell on him.

By the time Megan finished eating, Owen's low singing in

that ancient language and steady pacing around the room had
lulled Teddy to sleep. They nestled him into the travel crib in
their bedroom, complete with a flannel snowman crib sheet
she'd found online and couldn't resist.

Owen pulled her into the bathroom and started the water
in the shower. They slowly undressed one another, taking
advantage of this quiet time alone before the baby was back up
again and needing their attention. Megan stared in wonder as
Owen stepped under the stream of hot water. Her mind could
so easily conjure the image of his hand melting under the heat
of the tub faucet. But here he was, warm and safe in her arms.

The deal Owen and Boreas had struck initially left her
head spinning—especially the part where she'd share in the
longevity of life that both her boys possessed as a result of
their preternatural natures. But it didn't take her long to see
the wisdom of Owen keeping some of his powers. In fact,
knowing he was stronger, and that her son would be too, helped
quell the nagging fear of losing them that sometimes crept
up in quiet, unexpected moments. And she had viewed the
concessions Boreas had demanded as hardly any sacrifice at all.
She supported her new family's business, the idea of saving the
Earth, so strongly she had quit her admissions counselor job
at the end of the spring semester. They didn't need her income
anyway—they'd be able to live off Owen's ancient resources
forever if necessary, and her job had never represented a calling.
She was thrilled to be going to work with Owen part time when
the WinterWatch Environmental Foundation opened its doors
in downtown D.C. on March 1. Her mother had even offered
to watch Teddy while she worked, so she could part from him
secure in the knowledge he was in good hands, family hands.

How Megan had worried about her family's reception of

Owen. Not that she didn't think they'd totally love him—that was never the question. But it had all happened so fast. She hadn't even been able to eat the day she'd gone to tell them she was engaged. And pregnant. They'd met Owen a few times by that point, and all got on so well, but she'd only known him for six weeks when she'd sprung the news. Her family was equal parts thrilled and hesitant, but in the end her obvious happiness had won them over. They'd married in a small, human-family-and-close-friends ceremony on the last day of winter.

In the days and weeks that followed, several of Owen's uncles, she supposed, had popped in to introduce themselves. Polite though reserved, Zephyros had found them immediately after the wedding, though he'd seemed uncomfortable around her and hadn't stayed long. Chrysander, on the other hand, invited himself for a whole weekend and left her feeling she'd known him forever. Using the face of a compass, Owen had long-since explained the Anemoi family tree, with the four cardinal wind gods representing the north, west, south, and east, and the dozen lesser ordinal and interordinal gods. While the father of the Anemoi, a powerful storm god named Aeolus, had sent gifts to the new couple, no one else had appeared. Yet.

Under the hot spray of the shower, Megan and Owen took turns washing each other, the small touches both comforting and stimulating. When they were clean, Owen pulled her body against his. They shared slow, deep, exploring kisses. Their hands skimmed over wet skin, rubbing, stroking. Breathy moans fogged the glass, cocooning them in the small space as they fell apart within each other's arms.

Afterward, they dressed quickly and quietly, stealing kisses and shushing laughter. Then they settled on the floor beside the festive Christmas tree. Megan had unpacked some of the ornaments from her collection, and together she and Owen had bought some more. The day they'd returned from picking their tree at a lot by the general store, they'd found a box in brown paper on the front steps. Two dozen brilliant cut-glass ornaments filled the inside, each one a dazzling, unique snowflake. Boreas. It was just like him to drop in, quite literally, from time to time. She was always glad when he did.

Unlike the tree from last year, the one that stood before them now belonged to a family fully embracing the celebration of Christmas.

"Here," Owen said, holding out a gift-wrapped box. He nearly vibrated with excitement. His enthusiasm for all things was one of his dominant personality traits, one she absolutely adored. "You first."

All grins and ripping hands, Megan removed the paper in no time flat. Thick tissue padded the inside of the rectangular package, and she unfolded it to reveal a beautiful crystal snowman figure. She lifted him out with a gasp. "Oh, Owen, he's beautiful." A snow globe with an idyllic mountain village inside filled his stomach—the miniature scene looked strikingly like the collection of buildings at the summit at Wisp. Tiny inset crystals edging the snowman's top hat, gloves, and coat threw off tiny prisms. "Thank you."

"I just thought…" He looked up at her from under his hair and shrugged.

She dived over the discarded paper and planted a kiss on his soft lips. "I know. And it's perfect. Your turn."

Owen flipped the long thin box around over and over. Shook it. His eyes went wide and he chuckled when the contents offered a muffled rattle.

"Careful! You'll break it."

He gaped and froze.

Megan burst out laughing. "Kidding. You're fine."

He cocked an eyebrow. The front door eased open and a whirl of icy wind shot in and wrapped around her.

"Hey!" She hugged her arms around her body and pouted, chuckling despite herself. "No fair. That's freaking cold!"

Owen's cocky grin was as infuriating as it was sexy. How was she going to handle them both when Teddy came into his powers, too? Luckily she had more than a decade to prepare for that—Boreas explained his powers wouldn't begin to manifest until he hit puberty. The front door gently clicked closed.

"You started it," he said as he made quick work of the wrapping paper. He yanked the two halves of the box apart and the thin rectangular cards exploded out in every direction. They rained down around him and he flinched.

Clapping a hand over her mouth to smother the sound of her own good humor, she mentally high-fived herself—she couldn't have planned that better if she'd tried.

Owen picked up one of the plastic cards. "Ben and Jerry's! Aw, man." He scooped them into a pile. "Thank you, silly girl. How many of them are there?"

"Twenty," she said, giggling at the enthusiastic flash of his eyes. The first time Owen had ice cream from the Ben and Jerry's store in Old Town Alexandria, he turned to her with a sternly serious face and told her she'd been holding out on him. There was little room for actual food in their freezer for the number of flavors of Ben and Jerry's stored there. Seeing his absolute delight as he straightened the stack of cards within his big hands made her giddy and glad she'd gone for the joke gift of five-dollar certificates. "The only catch is you have to share."

He froze mid-shuffle and arched a skeptical brow. "And

why would I want to do that?"

"Because you love me."

His answering smile lit up his whole face. "I do." He set the cards aside and rubbed his hands together. "Okay, here's another one for you."

Megan bit her bottom lip and tore into the small, flat rectangular package. She recognized the name of the jewelry store right away and gasped. "What did you do?" She eased the fancy blue case open and this time her hand flew to her mouth when she gasped. Nestled on the dark velvet bed inside the jewelry box was a necklace in her favorite color she had absolutely drooled over on their honeymoon. The pink natural conch pearls were among the rarest in the world—which is why she'd resisted Owen's encouragements to buy the piece even though she adored it. So few of the pearls were harvested each year they cost a small fortune. Four of the variegated pink pearls hung down from a white gold drop necklace. The piece was exquisite. One of a kind. "When did you go back for it? I can't believe you did this."

He crawled on his knees and slipped the fine chain from her hands. "That afternoon, while you napped."

She held her hair up while he did the clasp and remembered that warm, wonderful day they strolled the streets of Philipsburg, ducking into every colorful, quirky shop that caught their fancy. After getting married at her childhood church near their new home in Fairfax, they'd flown that evening to Dutch St. Maarten, where they had a private villa right on the beach. When Megan had learned Owen had never been to a beach before—had never been *able* to go to a beach before—she knew exactly what kind of honeymoon they had to have. She gathered up information on a few possible destinations and let him choose.

So, for a month, they'd made love and sunbathed and shopped and saw the sights in paradise, but being four months pregnant often left her in urgent need of an afternoon nap. Sneaky demigod of a husband.

He ran his fingers over the pearls where they hung down from her collar bone. "You so rarely want anything for yourself, I couldn't resist. So I bought it and debated the right moment to give it to you. And then I thought of Christmas, and decided to wait."

Megan grabbed his hand and pressed a long, heartfelt kiss against his palm. "I don't want anything, because you've given me everything I ever dreamed of having. Just you. And Teddy."

Their kiss started slow and sweet, with gentle pulls of lips and soft, breathy sighs.

"I'm so grateful for you every day, Megan. I'd give you the world if I could."

"You do," she moaned around the edge of a kiss. She pulled away and leaned her forehead against his. "Ready to open another?"

He grinned and nodded. Accepted the small box. This time he pulled the lid off more gently. Megan's stomach flip-flopped as his eyes settled on the contents. His mouth dropped open as he uttered something in that ancient language. He smoothed the pad of his thumb over the markings. "This is from the Realm the Gods. How did you get this?" His eyes flashed to hers.

"I had a little help," she whispered. Boreas, of course. She'd told the ancient god in passing she wanted something really special and meaningful for Owen for Christmas, and on his next visit he'd handed her a small cloth-wrapped bundle. When she unfolded it, she'd found a very old iron pendant with a designed stamped into it—a snowflake with symbols she didn't understand or recognize surrounding it. At Boreas's suggestion, she'd added a leather lanyard so Owen could wear it. "Do you recognize it?" Adrenaline in the form of pins and needles tingled over her body. She hoped this went over well.

"No. Well, I know the symbols. It says, 'Without the death of winter, there is no rebirth of spring.' It's ancient."

"Yes. Owen?"

He pulled his gaze from the amulet.

"It was your father's."

Owen's eyes grew large. Preternatural light flashed low in their depths. "How?" he whispered.

"Boreas found it. That's all I know."

Reverent foreign words spilled from him again. "Gods, Megan. This is…this is beyond…" He shook his head. His Adam's apple bobbed as he swallowed.

Megan chewed on her lip, her heart throbbing at the emotion rolling off him in waves. "Is it…is it okay? Are you okay?"

He looped the leather over his head, nestled his only possession from his native family under his shirt against his chest. The leather and iron looked so perfect against his skin. His eyes flashed up to hers. "I have existed an immeasurable amount of time, and never been more happy, more content, than I am with you. You are the light of my life, Megan Winters."

His lips crashed into hers before she could form a response. So she poured every bit of her love into the heated interweaving of her tongue with his, the needful exploration of her hands over his muscled back.

From the other room, the baby's shrill cry sounded. They both pulled away from the kiss breathing hard and smiling.

"To be continued?" she asked.

"Your wish..."

Her face heated and she shook her head. "Let's go see what woke him already."

They entered the bedroom to find the Supreme God of Winter hovering over the crib. She'd almost gotten used to his dropping in. Today, she'd expected it. Megan laughed out loud at the sheepish look on his face, though. As if he were in trouble.

He grimaced. "I couldn't resist touching his hand. Didn't mean to wake him, though." Teddy totally owned Boreas, and it squeezed Megan's heart with joy.

"It's all right, Grampa. Merry Christmas." When she pushed up on tiptoes, Boreas leaned down, way down, to receive her kiss on his cheek.

"Merry Christmas, Megan," came his deep, pleased voice.

Owen and Boreas shook hands and exchanged Christmas wishes as Megan scooped their chunky bundle from his crib. He didn't settle down like he usually did when she picked him up, so she patted his back and bounced him gently. Then his face went bright red. All of a sudden, he stopped crying. Cooed. The smell that rose up was suffocating. How in the world did something so little make a smell so lethal?

Covering their noses, the men both chuckled. Megan turned and held Teddy out to Owen. "Your turn."

"What? No. Besides, you're so much better at it than I am."

Megan pressed their son against his father's chest and patted his big mountain of a shoulder. "That's complete crap" — she laughed at her unintended pun — "and you know it. Besides, I would think between the two of you, you could handle one stinky diaper. You are gods, after all."

Grumbling and looking a little green, Owen gathered the changing supplies and laid Teddy on a pad on the bed. Boreas stood next to him and winced as Owen's removal of layers intensified the smell. When Owen unhooked the diaper's tabs, both men reared back, groaning. Teddy kicked his feet up in delight.

"That's impressive," Boreas said.

Owen caught a bit of his father-figure's good humor. "That can't be natural, can it? Aw, pass me some more wipes."

As the two men fumbled their way through, Megan watched in complete admiration. A year ago, she wouldn't have been able to imagine this kind of happiness. Never would she have even dared to think she could have so much. She'd been twenty-nine years old and, truth be told, was already counting herself out, had already decided she'd had her chance at a happy life and lost it.

Owen folded the dirty diaper in a way that ensured minimal skin-to-diaper contact for himself, then dropped it in a bag and tied the plastic off. "There you go, little man." From there, he made quick work of the new diaper and redressing the now giggly baby. "You feel better, huh?" Owen tickled Teddy's chest and Ted's toothless smiles drew both men in.

The sight of the three of them together, so natural and affectionate, swelled Megan's heart where it beat in her chest.

Owen picked Teddy up and hugged him close. Boreas stroked his big hand over the baby's fine black hair.

And Megan knew it couldn't get any better than this. These men were her family. Her love for them was unending, and she knew they felt the same for her. Love, family, a safe place to belong. With her snowmen by her side, she now lived the true meaning of Christmas. Every day of the year.

And what could be better than that?

ACKNOWLEDGMENTS

As I was sitting alone in a hotel room one November night, Owen Winters took his first breath. Since then, a lot of people helped me bring him, Megan, and their love story to life. I have the great fortune to belong to the best critique group ever, and two fantastic author friends in particular—Joya Fields and Christi Barth—read the whole manuscript and offered frank and engaging advice. I also have to acknowledge Heather Howland, whose enthusiasm for Owen and his story from our very first conversation was the stuff of which authors dream. Thank you to her and Liz Pelletier for the incredible undertaking that is Entangled Publishing—I'll be proud to say "I knew you when." And, finally, much gratitude to my editor, Marie Loggia-Kee, for making Owen and Megan shine. And, as always, I have complete love for the readers, who welcome characters into their hearts and minds and let them tell their stories over and over. ~ LK

"WEST OF WANT is steamy, spellbinding, and a
must-read for all romance fantasy fans."
– Elisabeth Naughton, author of *Enraptured*

HEARTS OF THE ANEMOI
BOOK TWO

WEST OF WANT

Betrayal is all he's ever known,
but in her, he'll find a love
strong enough to be trusted...

LAURA KAYE

Keep reading for a sneak peek of
WEST OF WANT
book two in the Hearts of the Anemoi series
by Laura Kaye

*Betrayal is all he's ever known, but in her, he'll find a love
strong enough to be trusted…*

When Marcella Raines' twin brother dies, she honors his
request to be buried at sea, never expecting the violent storm
that swamps her boat. Though she's gravely injured—and still
emotionally damaged from her recent divorce—Ella fights to
survive.

Zephyros Martius is the Supreme God of the West Wind
and Spring, but being the strongest Anemoi hasn't protected
him from betrayal and loss. Worse, he's sure his brother Eurus
is behind it. When Zeph's heartbreak whips up a storm that
shipwrecks a human, his guilt forces him to save her.

Ella is drawn to the vulnerability Zeph hides beneath
his otherworldly masculinity and ancient blue eyes. And her
honesty, empathy, and unique, calming influence leave Zeph
wanting…everything. When Eurus threatens Ella, she and Zeph
struggle to let go of the past, defend their future, and embrace
what they most want—a love that can be trusted.

In stores everywhere July 10th, 2012!

CHAPTER ONE

Ella Raines knelt on the varnished deck of the sailboat's cockpit, her dead brother's ashes in her hands, and stared out at the dark green chop of the Chesapeake Bay. The cold March breeze kicked up sea spray and rippled through the sails, but all Ella could feel was the metal urn turning her aching fingers to ice. She had to let him go—she knew she did—but with everything else she'd lost, how could the world be so cruel as to expect her to give up her twin, too?

She twisted open the urn's brass lid and stuffed it in the pocket of her windbreaker. Sailing had been the passion over which she and Marcus had most bonded, not just as siblings, but as best friends. A day spent cruising on the bay, blue skies overhead and warm winds lifting the sails, had been Marcus's favorite thing to do. He wasn't a religious man, but said he most believed in God when he was out on the open water. So a burial at sea made sense, and it was time. When she'd woken up this morning and seen the clear forecast, she resolved today was the day. After all, it had been two months, and the first day of spring seemed a fitting time for starting over.

Leaning over the stern, Ella tilted the brass container by slow degrees until fine ashes spilled out, swirled on the wind, and blew away in a sad gray ribbon that blurred from her silent tears. Choppy waves splashed against the transom, soaking Ella to the elbows, and the boat heeled to the starboard. She braced herself on the backstay. The fixed steel cable bit into her hand but steadied her enough to empty the urn.

"Good-bye, Marcus. I love you." She barely heard herself over the sudden gusting of the wind that roared through the sails.

Ella locked down the grief and despair that wanted to claw out of her chest and climbed to a standing position. The boat heeled again, hard, the forty-five-degree angle nearly catching her off guard. She stumbled. The urn dropped with a brassy clang to the deck of the helm and rolled lopsidedly as the sloop tossed.

She turned, her brain already moving her hands and body through the motions of furling the mainsail and tacking upwind. A bright flash caught her gaze and a gasp stuck in her throat.

An enormous dark cloud sprawled low over the water to the southwest. Mountainous black plumes protruded from the top, creating a tower through which brilliant explosions of yellow-orange streaked. Inky fingers reached down from the storm's edge as the squalling winds lashed at the sea.

Where the hell had *that* come from?

A long growl of thunder rumbled over the bay. Ella felt it in her bones. The boat tossed and heeled. Waves pounded the hull, sloshed over the sides, and soaked her sneakers. A spare glance at her instruments revealed thirty-knot winds. Thirty-five.

A four-foot wave slammed against the port side. Ella slipped on the wet deck and went down hard on one knee. She grasped the wheel just as the boat lurched sideways. Thunder crashed above her, the sound vibrating through the whipping wind. Bitter cold rain poured down over the boat in a torrent. Tendrils of Ella's hair came loose from her long braid and plastered to her forehead and cheeks.

She needed to turn the boat and reach shore if she had any hope of escaping the wind. Ella wrestled the steering wheel hard to windward, the rudder fighting her every turn. Damn, how could she have been so reckless, so unobservant? Storms like this didn't just develop out of nowhere. A sailor never trusted the weathermen over her own eyes and ears. How long had she been kneeling on the deck giving in to her woe-is-me routine, anyway? And here she was, in the literal eye of a storm, sailing single-handed without life jacket or tether on. She locked the wheel into place. At least she could remedy *that* problem.

Ella reached for an orange vest and slipped her arms through the holes. A final glance at her instruments revealed forty-knot winds now. Dread threatened to swamp her. She disconnected the electronics, leaving only the compass to guide her. Her mast was a forty-foot lightning rod, so she did what little she could to combat the likelihood of a strike.

The windward course was a short-lived pursuit as the wind direction changed again and again. Eyes on the compass, she adjusted to the wind as best she could. She couldn't see squat through the deluge, and the hovering gray sheets of rain and spray and six-foot waves obscured the horizon. She'd have to ride it out. With shaking, bone-cold fingers, she connected the bottom of the three buckles on her vest. Small *clicks* sounded from overhead, got louder, more frequent. Hail pelted down the size of dimes, then nickels. Ella crouched against the wheel and shielded her head with her hands and arms. The falling ice ripped into the plastic of her jacket and bit into her knuckles.

Thunder crashed right above her and the storm-darkened sky exploded in ferocious jags of electricity. Rain and hail lashed her body, and wind and waves battered her ship like it had a personal vendetta to settle. With her. A tremendous wave crested over the starboard side, shoving her head against the metal spoke of the wheel. Spots burst across her vision. She cried out, the sound swallowed by the wind.

When she could focus again, her gaze settled on the lidless cremation urn wedged fore of the wheel pedestal. Marcus. What she wouldn't do to have him with her. She reached around the huge wheel to grab the container, just grasping for something, anything to make her feel less alone. She couldn't reach. Shifting her hold on the wheel, she stretched, her fingers straining, yearning to feel the cold brass. Not quite.

She lunged for the urn, grabbed it up, and hugged it to her chest.

Thunder and lightning blasted the sky above her. A wall of wind shoved at the side of the sailboat. It lurched. Spun. An ominous crack reverberated from below. A wave pounded Ella's shoulders and back, flattening her atop the urn onto the deck of the cockpit, holding her hostage with its watery weight. Seawater strangled her, stole her breath, and receded.

The boat reared over a peaked wave and bucked. Ella slid into a free fall.

Not releasing her death grip on the urn, Ella's right hand shot out and clutched the steel backstay. The ligaments of her shoulder wrenched apart in a sickening, audible pop just as her lower body whipped over the transom and hit the frigid water. The jolt stole her scream, allowed her only to moan long and low. Icy wetness soaked through her heavy clothes and the drag tugged and pulled at her destroyed joint.

Triple bolts of lightning illuminated the gunmetal sky in quick succession. Shaking nonstop from cold and pain and adrenaline, Ella stared up at her hand clutching the metal cable. One strike and she'd be done. Her mind laid out the choices. Ship or sea. Urn or ship. Drown or fry. Life or death.

A wave swamped her. And another. She choked and gagged. The next slammed her head against the fiberglass transom.

Her hands flew open from the impact. She plunged into the storm-tortured water, sucked down nauseating mouthfuls. Her body whipped feet over head, side to side. Impossible to determine which way was up. The violent churning of the sea ripped the lifejacket off one arm, but the orange padding held just enough to finally guide her head to the surface.

Despite her daze, survival instincts had her gulping oxygen, precious oxygen. Her successful fight against the urge to vomit left her shuddering, the sour bile almost a welcome respite from the cold salt. No matter. The next cresting wave forced her to drink more.

Panic jolted through her body, shook the drunken haze from her mind. Kicking and paddling, she spun around and around, until she'd done several three-sixties. The boat. Gone.

As her body crested the top of wave after wave, she strained to see some glimpse of white in the thick, dark gray. At thirty-four feet, the *True Blue* was not little, but the sea was too rough, the wind too forceful.

No. No, no, no. Not their sailboat, too. Not the last place that truly felt like home, the last place filled with memories of laughter and love and honesty.

Deafening thunder rumbled over the world. Jagged electricity flared over the monstrous seascape.

Ella tilted her head back, squinted against the blinding rain, and screamed. "Is that all you got? Well, fuck you! Fuck you and the cloud you blew in on! I've got nothing left to lose, so take your best shot!"

A wave smacked her in the face. She gagged. Coughed. Laughed until sobs took over.

Exhaustion. Pure and utter. Like she'd lived a thousand lives.

Debris thudded against her ear. She howled as the jarring hit rang through her head.

Please don't let it be pieces of True Blue.

Her eyes focused on the sea next to her. Nothing. She propelled herself around. The urn. Ella gasped and irrational joy filled her chest.

She half-swam—a nearly impossible feat against the thrashing waves with one useless arm. Each leaden stroke sapped what little energy she had left.

She grabbed the urn. Held it in her numb hands.

"I knew you wouldn't leave me," she whispered against the brass, all she could manage. "We're true blue."

Together, the churn carried them up one side of a wave, then plunged them down the other. Ella's head slumped against the flat base of the upside down container. Her eyelids sagged.

And everything went black.

CHAPTER TWO

A life force was fading.

The sensation tugged at Zephyros's consciousness, embattled as it was as he raged over the sea. Caught up in his own thoughts, his own pain, his own loss, he writhed and tossed, howled and lashed out. The wind and rain—nature's very energy—were his to control, even when he was out of control. But, still, the wrongness of the sensation tugged at him, demanded redress. In his elemental form, he felt the call of life and birth and renewal most strongly. He could ignore it no longer.

He forced himself to embrace the calm that had once been the truest manifestation of his nature. Around him, the clouds dispersed, the rains thinned, the winds settled to a bluster. The sea, black and roiling a moment ago, eased into the early spring chop typical of the bay.

Zephyros allowed the tranquility of the open water to fuel the return of his composure. He focused. Scanned for the soul decrying its unnatural end. Commanding the West Wind to carry him down from the heavens, he soared on the gentle gusts. The only thing nearby was a lone sailboat, floundering in the wind.

He glided around the fine boat. No life resided on its decks or within its hull. A sour pit formed in his gut as he began to suspect what had happened.

Rising up to gain a broader view of the sea, Zephyros searched, the dwindling life a beacon he latched onto. Pursued. The thrum of its force vibrated within him. Closing in, he descended toward the surface, the waves passing under him in a blur. There! A flicker of orange upon the dark gray-green.

Flashing into corporeality, Zephyros assumed the form of a giant water kingfisher.

Slate-blue wings exploded twenty feet out on either side of his body. He plunged head-first toward the bobbing figure, the wind ruffling through the crown-like crest of blue feathers atop his head. Rarely did he ever have the need to shift into his sacred animal form, but it was a power all the Anemoi possessed.

Glaring down at the water, Zephyros braced himself. Extreme temperatures pained and weakened him, and he'd be lucky if this water was in the fifties. He skied into the water's surface, spread wings gentling his landing. No such luck. Mid-forties if it was anything. But this wasn't about him, was it?

Just ahead, the human bobbed face down, tendrils of long hair floating in strands of silk like a halo. He smelled blood. Best hurry. His senses told him time was short.

Zephyros plunged his regal, avian body into the water, came up with the dead weight draped over his neck. With a shove of a wing, he pushed the legs of the body up, resituating the length along his back. He took flight.

Frigid water shook off him in a fantastic spray as his massive wingspan flapped and lifted them away from the bay. His gaze lit on the sailboat and he banked in its direction. He circled the boat once, twice. The metal cables connecting the mast to the deck would not accommodate his wings. He couldn't land on the boat.

Taking extra care not to jostle the victim, *his* victim, Zephyros landed behind the sailboat. Instinctively, he commanded the change and shifted into his human form. The biting chill of the water tormented his naked flesh, but more important matters demanded his attention. Grabbing onto one delicate hand, he ensured his hold on the person draped across his back before turning and cradling the body into his arms.

He sucked in a breath. Mother of gods. A bruise mottled the whole left side of her face, from cheek to eyebrow. A nasty gash along the cheekbone oozed a thin line of blood. Her bottom lip was busted open, swollen. But even the severity of her injuries couldn't hide her beauty.

That sour pit in his stomach grew, suffocated. He'd caused this. Damn it, could he never do anything right? Ancient turmoil roiled through him, threatening to turn him inside out. No, of course he couldn't.

Zephyros adjusted the woman's weight in his arms and reached up over the transom. His fingers searched for and found the release, and the swim platform folded out toward them. He lifted the woman above his head and settled her on the glossy wooden surface, then hefted himself up beside her. With solid footing beneath him, he gently lifted her again. He stepped around the massive wheel to the seating area to the fore, and laid her out on a long bench.

Her head lolled to the side. Wheezes morphed into a weak cough. Her whole body seized. Water expelled from her throat. Zephyros supported her shoulders, held her up until she quieted. Her eyelids creaked open, revealing the rolling whites of her eyes.

They sagged again, and her whole body went limp.

Zephyros released a breath as unexpected relief flooded him—followed quickly by guilt. His suspicions about what had happened to her were confirmed by an imprinting on her life jacket. The words "True Blue" matched the dark blue calligraphy painted on the back of the boat. She'd been thrown overboard in the storm. *His* storm.

He shivered, a combination of guilt, shame, and the wind against his wet body. Well, the latter problem he could address. He materialized jeans and a T-shirt and made himself decent.

Like a magnet, she drew his gaze. He reached out and stroked his fingers over the reds and purples coloring the side of her face. Her hair appeared deep brown, but he suspected the darkness was an effect of the water still drenching her.

Shaking his head, Zephyros debated. He should leave now. The Coast Guard would find her. The bay had patrols. He could even command the current to carry the boat, with her upon it, to shore. Even as he agreed with himself, agreed leaving her would be for the best, he searched the boat for information he could use to help her. Storage lockers filled the space beneath the bench seats. Empty. His gaze scanned. He'd look below.

Down the companionway steps, he descended into the cabin and stepped in a few inches of sloshing water on the galley floor. All warm wood and white accents, the space was surprisingly spacious and bright. Far forward there appeared to be a berth. Aft of that bedroom, a large sitting area centered round a table. To his immediate left, a small galley kitchen, and to his right, a chart table. Compasses and instruments hung above it on the hull wall.

Zephyros stepped to the desk and opened the top drawer. Maps and paperwork sat in skewed stacks. He flipped through the pages until he found a name and address. That the name was male brought an unexpected frown to his face, but at least he had a lead on where to take her. Surely someone so physically attractive had a significant other, someone who would care for her and see her mended back to health.

As he moved to return above deck, a small aft berth caught his eye and he reached in and yanked a blanket from the bed. Up top again, he tucked the red comforter around the woman. The loose strands of hair around her face had air-dried to a light golden-brown. Peaceful in her unconsciousness, her face appeared delicate and young, unmarred by cruelty or pain—except for what he'd done to her, of-fucking-course.

Ignoring the rock of guilt in his gut, he considered the problem of actually getting the boat to harbor. Sailing was a foreign language to him. He had no need for the knowledge. He could soar on the wind, even glide on the currents for short times. All he knew was a sailboat with furled sails wasn't going anywhere.

No matter. He stepped around the wheel and down onto the swimming platform. The clothing would just be a drag, so he disappeared it and jumped. The cold water sucker-punched him. He gasped and willed his muscles to cooperate. How long had the woman suffered with the freezing waves battering her damaged body? He bit down on his tongue to keep from roaring out. The pain focused him.

Arms extended beside him, he closed his eyes and called the current. As a wind god, Zephyros was most at home in the sky, but marshaling sea currents worked on the same principle. The rush of water pushed behind him, just as he directed, and scooped up the boat's hull in the grip of its gentle forward motion. One hand on the platform, he floated behind the boat, guiding its heading, adjusting as necessary, shivering until he thought his bones might snap. Luckily, the storm had chased away other maritime traffic.

The bay was wide open and empty. Nice to have one thing going for him. Occasional gulls cried out high above, their pale bodies nearly camouflaged against the gray-white sky.

Within an hour, they were in sight of Annapolis. Above the town proper, a large steeple and a tall domed cupola framed the colonial seaport. But Zephyros's destination was a bit closer. The address he'd found should be on the neck of land just south of the town.

An inlet emerged up ahead. All along the shore, clusters of masts stood up together, sentinels on the water. He guided the boat toward the creek. A sailboat with a large blue mast sail glided past. Zephyros submerged into the cold, but not before noticing the confounded expression on the other captain's face. Of course. The boat he guided moved without aid of sail or motor.

He resurfaced long enough to see the other boat coming about, the captain on the radio. Damn it all to Hades.

This situation was about to become shit meets fan. For gods' sake, he currently didn't have clothes, and until he warmed he'd be lucky to hold a conversation. Naked, nearly incapacitated, with no ability to dock the boat, and with a gravely injured woman on board, he had little likelihood of contriving a convincing story about how they'd gotten that way.

His presence was a liability here. He was useless. Again.

As the blue-masted boat neared, the captain called out, asking whether the *True Blue* was in distress. No one answered, of course.

And it was time for him to go.

Zephyros released his grip on the platform and eased the created current until it dispersed altogether. He sank beneath the surface, shaking nonstop, and hesitated just a moment. His gut clenched. He hated the idea of not seeing her to safety. Okay, in truth, he'd done that. But what he *wanted* was to see her to health—awake and conscious and warm and happy.

Happy? What did her emotions have to do with anything? Fluttery panic ripped through his chest. The fact he was even thinking about her feelings was a major get-the-hell-out-of-there red flag. Getting involved was the last thing he needed. Hadn't he learned that? Again and again and a-fucking-gain?

No more.

The rescue sailboat came alongside the *True Blue*. A man's voice rang out above the water's surface. There. *He* would make sure she was safe, cared for, got everything she needed. The thought had Zephyros grinding his teeth in frustration. In self-defense.

In want.

No.

He wanted nothing and no one. And, in truth, no one wanted him either. So didn't that work out just perfectly, thank you very much.

Zephyros turned and, without looking back, swam to the opposite shore.

He broke the icy surface gasping for breath and shaking so hard his bones hurt.

"Job well done, Zephyros. Very good. And on the first day of your season, too," came the last voice Zeph wanted to hear in that moment. Or any moment.

Zeph wiped the water from his eyes and climbed the small embankment opposite the marina where he could hear a small crowd gathering. The clothes he materialized didn't begin to compensate for the consequences of over an hour of exertion in a forty-degree sea. Grinding his teeth together to keep them from chattering, he faced his younger brother Eurus, Supreme God of the East Wind and Harbinger of Misfortune. Evil in a pair of $900 dress shoes. Zeph ignored the comment intended to pluck at his guilt and rile him up. "You have no business here, Eurus. Leave. I don't have anything to say to you."

Standing on the shore in his I'm-dark-and-mysterious black leather getup, Eurus stared across the water through the black wraparound sunglasses he always wore. His lips twitched. "Be that as it may, I have something to say to you." He turned away from the drama unfolding across the inlet and faced Zeph, but didn't speak.

Striking a careful indifference as emergency vehicles poured into the marina parking lot, Zeph glared at his brother. He'd paid his debt to Eurus, and then some. Not that Zeph truly believed he owed that fucker anything, but he'd wanted to make nice, keep the peace. Problem was, Eurus didn't agree. And never would. "For the love of the gods, Eurus. What do you want? I'm freezing and don't want to stand here arguing with you."

Eurus laced his hands behind his back. "Fine. I'll get right to the point. I plan to submit a petition."

Gods, he hated how Eurus made everything so damn dramatic. "About?"

"I will propose that, lest you beget an heir by the end of your season, my son Alastor be installed as your heir." Zeph gaped as Eurus plowed on. "Only Boreas and I have addressed issues of succession." He shook his head and tsked. "And it's very dangerous, Zephyros. Very dangerous indeed not to have an heir in place."

Maybe Zeph's ears were frozen and the words had gotten garbled. No way his brother had just proposed— "You can't be serious."

Eurus arched an eyebrow.

"You're out of your mind." As if that wasn't stating the obvious. "A god of the East could never do the job of a god of the West." Not to mention the fact Alastor was a complete recluse and, more

importantly, Zeph would never trust anyone of Eurus's line with...
anything.

"Alastor could."

Zeph turned away and climbed the rest of the way up the
embankment. "Whatever. I'll get around to having an heir when
I'm good and goddamned ready." When that might be, he had
no idea. After all, someone had to stick around long enough first.
"Besides, Father would never approve an eastern god as the heir
of my line."

"He would if he had the blood of spring in his veins."

Going stock still, Zeph heaved a breath. Icy fingers crawled up
his spine. He schooled his expression and turned on his brother.
Glared, but kept his mouth shut.

Eurus's smug expression went glacial. "Oh, come now. I know
you want me to explain."

Despite the way his skin crawled and his gut squeezed, he'd
freeze out here before giving Eurus the satisfaction of asking.

Leaning forward, a smile that could only be described as
wicked curled the edges of Eurus's lips. "Your *wife*, Chloris," he
sneered, voice dark and satisfied. Then he was gone.

The words cut through the air and crashed into Zeph so hard
he couldn't breathe.

CHAPTER THREE

Words disconnected from meaning. Sounds out of context. Numbness like floating. And always the darkness.

Sometimes she surfaced. Nauseating light played behind eyelids she couldn't force open. Shooting pain accompanied the smallest shift in her position. A world-spinning ache throbbed beneath her face and ear. An odd, distant keening sounded in those moments, bringing a rush of relief through her veins that would pull her under into merciful oblivion once more.

Consciousness returned in the quiet of night. Ella blinked her dry, crusty eyes again and again. The dim room took shape before her. Sage-green walls. A mounted television. A movable tray. Gentle, rhythmic beeps entered her consciousness. Rolling her head just a little, she found the source of the sound. Monitors and medicine drips on metal stands lined the side of her bed. A hospital, then.

She opened her mouth, but knew instinctively she wouldn't be able to talk. Her tongue lay thick and unused. Her lips burned with dryness. She tried to lick them.

"Here. Take a sip."

Her gaze tracked the new sound, setting off a wave of dizziness. Her lips found the straw first, held right where she could reach it. She sucked the life-giving water into her mouth. It was the best thing she had ever tasted. She could've cried.

"Welcome back," the deep voice said.

Ella had almost forgotten someone was there. She released the straw and with effort made herself look up.

The nurse stood next to the side of her bed. She blinked and squinted. Focus slowly returned. He towered above her. His hair was short and dark, unruly curls just at the ends. Close-trimmed facial hair set off an angled jaw and lips pressed in a concerned line.

"More?"

She frowned. The straw stroked her bottom lip. She opened, eagerly drank more of the water. Her throat rejoiced.

"Thank you," she mouthed, no sound emerging.

"Don't try to speak. Just rest. And be well."

She sighed. And slipped into nothingness.

In the early morning gloom, she awoke again. A man, all broad shoulders, stared out through the slats in the blinds. Green scrubs. Her nurse again?

"Water," she croaked.

He was at her side so fast, she must've blinked. A couple of times. She hadn't seen him move.

This time when she offered her thanks, she could manage a rasping whisper.

His lips curved up, the smallest bit. "You're welcome." Intense slate-blue eyes stared down at her. "How are you feeling?"

"Dunno." She licked her lips. "What happened?"

His brow furrowed. "You don't remember?"

She closed her eyes and concentrated. A lump formed in her throat and swelled. "Marcus." Flashing images of a ferocious storm joined the memory of her brother. "Dead." She swallowed hard, the sound thick and tortured in her own ears.

"He died?"

Something in his voice begged her attention. She blinked up at him. He'd gone totally still next to her, his expression grave and alarmed. Ella frowned. "Yeah."

"When this happened to you?"

She opened and closed her mouth. The hair on her arms raised, the air taking on a warm, electrical quality. Obviously, some good drugs dripped into her veins. Still, his intensity did seem weird. Why was he so upset?

He grasped her hand. "Ella, did he die when this happened to you?"

Her gaze fell to his engulfing grip on her fingers. So warm. Her skin tingled where they touched.

The big man leaned across the path of her vision to capture her attention. "Gods, woman, answer me."

Her head swam. From the effort of remembering the question. From exhaustion. From the roiling power behind his piercing blue eyes. She shook her head once. "No, not then."

His whole body sagged. The air in the room cooled and calmed. He stood up and turned away, lacing his hands on top of his head. Ella missed the warm connection immediately, but was equally consumed with watching him. For a moment, he muttered and paced along the length of her bed, roughly scrubbing his palms over his face. He had the slightest sprinkling of gray at his temples.

His every movement radiated power. The green scrubs pulled across the muscles of his shoulders, back, and thighs with each step.

His very presence took up the whole side of the room in which he paced. He exuded a raw masculinity her body recognized, even if she was in absolutely no position to respond to it.

"You okay?" she scratched out.

He whirled on her, eyes guarded, muscles tense.

The movement was so unexpected, she gasped. Her heart raced, unleashing a series of throbs in her shoulder, neck, and head. She groaned.

"Damn it!" he bit out. He rushed to her and pushed a button on the side of the bed. A big hand smoothed over her forehead. "I'm sorry."

Ella's eyes clenched shut against the pounding torment rooting itself behind her eye and ear. But his touch helped. How amazing the power of human touch.

Then it was gone.

Her gaze scanned the room. Empty. A ball of panic bloomed in her gut. Where had he gone? And why had he left?

The door to her room pushed open and a woman with brown skin and pink scrubs breezed in. "Well, welcome back, Ms. Raines. It's good to see you awake."

Ella could only manage a drawn-out moan. The nurse was pretty, her smile open, and she wore her black hair in a curly natural style. The woman made pleasant small talk with her while she checked her vitals and entered her findings into a computer on a swivel stand.

"Don't you worry, now, we'll get you feeling better in no time. Can you tell me your pain level on a scale of one to ten, with ten the worst pain of your life and one pain-free?"

Licking her lips again and forcing herself to focus, Ella considered the question. How did one judge pain? Her shoulder was a good solid six. The throb vibrating through her skull, a seven.

But her heart, oh, her heart might never recover. A ten for sure. But Ella supposed that wasn't the kind of pain the nurse was asking her to describe. "Maybe a seven," she rasped.

"Okay, honey. Let's see what we can do about that." The woman inserted a needle into the IV. Cool solace slid into her veins and tugged at Ella's consciousness. She almost gave in, before she thought to ask. "The man? The male nurse?" she slurred.

The woman smiled and shook her head. "Musta been a good dream. Only us ladies on this unit." She went right on, explaining procedures to Ella in case she needed anything, but Ella's attention drifted away, stolen by the pain medication and the memory of a man who didn't exist.

Read on for a sneak peek of Inara Scott's
sexy contemporary fantasy,

Radiant Desire...

Kaia Verde is one of the four Faerie Handmaids of Zafira,
Queen of the Fey. To redress an ancient wrong done to Zafira by a
human king, the Handmaids make sport of mortal men, seducing
and humiliating them. When Kaia sets out to seduce Garrett
Jameson, but ends up being the one surrendering to pleasure,
Zafira is furious. Kaia's punishment is simple: make Garrett fall in
love with her by the summer solstice, then break his heart, or face
eternity without her wings—or her soul. To make the task harder,
Zafira tells Kaia she cannot use her faerie magic or charm to lure
Garrett into her bed.

Kaia thinks her task will be relatively easy—as a faerie, she
understands lust, and can love be much different? But once she
is living among the humans, Kaia discovers the race she once
disparaged is far more complex and beautiful than she imagined.
She learns before she can break Garrett's heart, she must find a
way to heal it. And eventually, discovers that losing her wings may
be a far easier price to pay than losing her heart.

Chapter One

Kaia took her place in line with the rest of the court, across the room from the gleaming marble dais that held Queen Zafira's empty throne. Today, she had to be perfect. Her hair had to flow in sunlit waves, her body curve with pure, radiant sensuality. She had to exemplify beauty, desire, and sex. She had to be the fantasy of every living man.

For today was the Anniversary.

A tall sprite with enormous ears and long teeth raised a crystal bugle to his lips and began to play the ancient processional hymn. There was a flurry of activity as the crowds of Fey—tiny pixies, gangly sprites, hundreds of imps and their darker cousins, the boggles and dakini—jostled for position closest to the silk rope that separated the queen from her subjects.

The queen's court began its slow march toward the throne. Each move was carefully orchestrated. Zafira had little pity for those who disrupted the perfection of her ceremonies. First down the aisle came the dryads, with their narrow faces, thick, tangled hair, and slanted eyes. The water nymphs followed, their voluptuous bodies barely clothed, clouds of blonde hair floating around their piquant faces. The night faeries came next, with glowing, moonlit skin, white hair, and sad, dark eyes. Just before the queen came the light faeries, represented by the four Faerie Handmaids: Analise, Talia, Kaia, and Mina.

When the procession reached the dais the Handmaids—each wearing a crown made from her birth plant—took their places in formation around the throne. Kaia looked to her sisters. Even among the Fey, they were a breathtaking quartet: tough-as-nails Talia, with her inky black hair and red lips; sweet Analise with her blonde hair and startling blue eyes; rebellious Mina, her voluptuous body topped by a shock of curly red ringlets and creamy skin. Together, their iridescent wings shot rainbows around the hall.

The crystal bugle sounded again, a high trill that always brought a shiver to Kaia's spine. This was Zafira's call, the call that had brought together the Fey since the beginning of time. Kaia bowed her head, spread her wings wide across her back, and bent one knee. A cloud of silver sparkles flared, then faded to reveal Zafira, light faerie and Queen of the Fey, her arms flung wide in a dramatic gesture intended to elicit a gasp from the audience.

Zafira's long, black tresses danced about her head and shoulders on the breeze of the sylphs, the tiny, butterfly-like creatures that surrounded her. She'd enhanced her stature for the occasion until she stood at least a head above the tallest faerie in the room.

"Tonight," Zafira boomed, "is the night we recall the infamy of man."

"Tonight is the Anniversary," Kaia and the other Handmaids chorused in response.

No matter how many times she had said the words, they

never grew rote. As a child, Kaia had watched Zafira's previous Handmaids say these same words, and had felt a wave of giddy pleasure and awe every time she saw the beautiful light faeries. Now, it was hard to believe that *she* was one of those symbols of the grace and power of the Fey.

Zafira nodded solemnly. "On this dark night, we recall how man's treachery is unbounded by conscience or honor, and how he has sought to destroy Faeria and claim dominion over the land of the Fey."

Zafira raised the Willow Scepter, its bulbous head rubbed smooth from the generations of queens that had come before, and the crowd roared in response. The Scepter's sinuous length twisted to symbolize that the ways of the Fey were not straight and predictable like men, but creative, curved, and impossible to control.

"Let us begin," intoned the Handmaids, and Kaia smiled at the second wave of cheers that followed their words.

Zafira glided down the aisle to her throne. Two male figures followed closely at her sides, bare chests displaying broad shoulders and rippling muscles. Their cloven feet exposed their dual nature: these were satyrs, half-demon and half-faerie, driven only by a need for pleasure and beauty. Zafira demanded obedience from all her subjects, but her hold was tightest around her satyrs, from whom she expected pure, unfettered devotion.

When she reached her throne, Zafira spun around, letting her golden gown flow in billowing waves around her feet. Many of the Fey took an involuntary step back. "Tonight, I will send my Handmaids into the human world to punish men and humiliate them the way they have humiliated us."

Cries of delight filled the hall. Faeries had been seducing men for thousands of years, but for the Handmaids it was a sacred duty.

Stealing the hearts of men and using them for pleasure was the way the Handmaids extracted revenge for the pain Zafira, and all of the Fey, had suffered over the centuries.

"Handmaid Kaia, step forth!"

Kaia paused, startled to hear the queen call her by name. This was not part of the usual ceremony. But then again, Zafira honored tradition when she pleased and disregarded it when it did not suit her. Kaia threw back her shoulders, forced her wings to arc gracefully across her back, and ensured her gentle smile was perfectly intact before stepping up to the dais. Her heart thumped. Had she done something wrong? Somehow displeased Zafira?

She lowered her head gracefully. "My queen."

"Kaia, you know the vow of my Handmaids."

Kaia nodded, her lips automatically forming her response after decades of practice. "My queen, as your Handmaid I vow never to lose control, and never to yield to the wishes of men."

Zafira swirled her staff in a circle, leaving behind a translucent, sparkling image of a man's face. He was as handsome as the satyrs at Zafira's side, with a tumble of blond hair falling over his forehead, cerulean blue eyes, and dark, tanned skin. His white teeth flashed in a smile that was equal parts humor and unspoken menace.

"This man, Garrett Jameson, is the man you will capture next," Zafira said. "You will bring him to his knees as only a Handmaid can. Introduce him to pleasure and the greatest desire he has ever known, and then leave him alone and wanting."

Kaia hid her surprise behind a deep curtsy and swirl of her wings. Zafira had never sent her after a particular human before.

"Yes, my queen." She paused, knowing she should keep her mouth shut but unable to prevent the question from leaving her lips. "May I ask why?"

Zafira frowned, and Kaia froze, terrified she had angered the mercurial queen. A moment later, Zafira's icy features softened and she began to chuckle. The sound danced through the hall like music, as beautiful as everything else about the queen—and just as dangerous.

"Because it will amuse me," Zafira said, her laugh tinkling through the hall. "I have some interest in this particular man. I will enjoy seeing him brought low."

Kaia nodded, feeling a lump in her throat. "It will be done."

Zafira motioned for Kaia to return to her place beside the other Handmaids. "See that it is, Kaia," she said in a quiet voice. "See that it is."

Chapter Two

Kaia shot a glance at the thin gold band around her wrist. Quarter to ten; he should be here soon. Somewhere behind her a band started to play. The music was soft and rhythmic, a saxophone and bass guitar, the smooth crawl of a rute across a snare drum. In the week that she'd been haunting this club, Kaia had come to appreciate the live jazz music featured each night. Of course, no mortal could approach the perfection of the music that filled the halls of Faeria. Still, of all the sounds humans created, she'd found jazz most appropriate to seduction.

Seduction.

Kaia shook her head. She'd been sent to the human world to complete a very simple task. Thus far, she had experienced nothing but defeat. Though the boggles had given her the location of Garrett Jameson's favorite nightclub, the coffee shop he frequented, and his office, she hadn't even managed to talk to him. Every time she saw him he was surrounded by other men in dark suits, or he was talking on his cell phone, or reading thick sheafs of papers with very small print. She had tried bumping into him on the street, but he'd done little more than apologize and stride away, not affording her more than a moment's glance. She had seen him here, at the Blue Hour. He had sat in a booth in the back of the room while watchful bouncers steered her away if she tried to get too close.

Kaia found her failure utterly infuriating, particularly when faced with Garrett Jameson's uncanny perfection. As far as she could tell, her target lacked any visible flaw, with only the unruly lock of hair that fell across his forehead betraying the perfection of his square jaw and arresting eyes. His suits were exquisitely tailored, his voice smooth and deep. Sometimes, Kaia could scarcely believe he was human. Yet he had no interest in catching the eye of a beautiful stranger, even one practically glowing with faerie magic.

Every day that she failed to achieve her task brought with it a fresh wave of panic. At first, it seemed laughable—a man resisting her attempt at seduction? Impossible! As the days passed with no sign of progress, Kaia's worry began to mount. Zafira had given her a direct command. She *had* to succeed. Zafira would show no mercy to a Handmaid who could not meet her expectations.

She had vowed that tonight would be different. She'd finally caught a break while following Garrett in line for his morning coffee, when she'd overheard him agreeing to meet someone named Ted here at ten. Arriving early, she'd positioned herself at a table near the entrance to the club. At around 9:30, the bartender called a man with curly red hair and soft hazel eyes Ted.

She'd shamelessly eavesdropped on Ted's cell phone call a few minutes later. It started with him asking someone named Rachel where she was, and quickly devolved to begging and pleading for her to come to the club. She'd heard "my love," "the wedding," and "whatever you want," followed by a deluge of words from the other end. After a few minutes, he slapped the phone closed. His face was mournful, his eyes drooping at the corners like a sad Irish setter.

He was needy, and if there was one thing Kaia understood, it was needy men.

She had introduced herself a few minutes later. She tried not to turn on so much charm that she'd scare him away, but there wasn't much she could do about her appearance. She'd found a tissue-thin silk dress at the hotel boutique that morning, and it draped across every one of her curves like a gleaming, silky spider web. The hazy light from dim strobes and tiny votives danced across her skin, leaving behind a perfect golden glow. Men from every side of the crowded bar were watching her, earning dirty looks from their female companions. Kaia deliberately shielded the red-haired man across the table from some of her heat. She wanted to seduce his friend, not him.

Yet her efforts were seemingly unnecessary. Ted didn't even glance at her perfectly positioned cleavage. All he wanted to do was talk about his fiancée, Rachel.

"I asked her out the first time we met," he said dreamily, staring into space. "I knew from the start we had something special. It took only one date before I fell in love."

"So what happened?" Kaia stole a sideways look toward the door, hoping Garrett would arrive soon. Anticipation licked down her spine. Tonight, they would meet. He couldn't avoid it if she was talking to his friend.

And when his eyes finally met hers, she would unleash all the power of faerie on him.

He didn't stand a chance.

"I don't know," Ted said miserably. "She's nervous about the wedding, I suppose. It's a big step. Anyone would be scared. But we love each other, we really do. She's perfect. The perfect woman." He launched into a litany of Rachel's angelic qualities.

Kaia masked her irritation with a patient smile.

He shook his head. "I'm sorry. Look, I should let you go. I have a friend coming in a few minutes. I didn't mean to drag you down this way. I'm sure you could find someone much more interesting to talk to."

Kaia's heart skipped at his not-so-subtle attempt to get rid of her. She *needed* to stay with Ted. He represented her only chance to get close to Garrett. "Please, I could really use the company. I'm just in town for a night." She shook her hair and let a hint of faerie magic trickle to him. "The last thing I need is some oaf trying to hit on me. I'd much rather hear more about Rachel."

Ted's mouth dropped open and for a moment he stared at her, transfixed. As soon as Kaia let off on the flow of magic, he sank back into his memory of Rachel. "Well, she's the most beautiful woman in the world. I mean, not beautiful like you, but beautiful in her way. Some people think she's bossy, but truly, she's the kindest person you'll ever meet. You can see it in her eyes. She just opened up a flower shop. Rachel's Roses." He sighed. "Everyone told her how hard it would be to open her own store, but she made it happen. She's amazing."

"So what's the problem?" Kaia asked, her gaze sliding briefly to the door. "Why is she having second thoughts?"

"She does a lot of weddings, and they don't always go well. She doesn't want to turn into Bridezilla or get too worked up about the whole thing. She said she wanted to elope, but I couldn't do it. A couple of weeks ago she started saying maybe we should wait, maybe we went too fast. Her parents had a messy divorce, and I think she's scared to get married. I don't know how to convince her to trust me."

Kaia wanted to believe Ted loved his fiancée. Unfortunately, she had a long history of watching men like him pledge their devotion to unsuspecting wives and girlfriends minutes before they succumbed to Kaia's charms. They used every excuse in the book to justify their unfaithfulness, but it came down to one thing: men were treacherous, dangerous creatures.

Kaia and the others used faerie magic to entice the men, but the magic wasn't irresistible. It simply took willpower. Willpower most men weren't interested in exercising.

She started to say something soothing and understanding, but the words caught in her throat when a tall figure appeared at the doorway.

Garrett Jameson had finally arrived.

He wore a rumpled linen shirt, open at the neck, and a dark blue blazer, managing to convey the appearance of both enormous wealth and utter lack of care. Square, rangy shoulders topped a narrow waist and long legs. The bouncer at the door motioned toward Ted, and Garrett stopped, surprise flickering across his face.

He crossed the floor to where they sat. Kaia forced herself to drop her eyes. If this week had taught her anything, it was that she would have to play this man very carefully.

"Ted, is that you?" Garrett asked in disbelief.

Kaia slowly met his gaze, her pulse racing as she waited for him to react to the burst of faerie magic that transformed her in a matter of seconds into the object of every man's desire. Instead, his startling aquamarine eyes surveyed her without emotion, raking across her bare shoulders and plunging cleavage with clinical precision.

No! He could not ignore me now.

The shock left Kaia reeling.

"Garrett!" Ted jumped up from his seat, looking for all the world like a guilty child. "You're here."

"Right on time." Garrett held up a heavy silver diver's watch.

"Ten o'clock."

"I was talking." Ted's face flushed as he glanced nervously at Kaia. "I guess I lost track of time."

"Understandably so," Garrett drawled. "You'll have to introduce me to your new friend."

"Garrett Jameson, this is Kaia... er... " Ted trailed off as his flush deepened. "I don't think I got your last name?"

Kaia rose languidly and offered her hand, leaning forward just enough to give Garrett a peek down her dress. She wasn't giving up that easily. "Kaia Verde," she purred, giving her voice enough throaty appeal to make Ted take a step back and adjust his collar.

Garrett did not react. He shook Kaia's hand and treated her to another thorough visual examination. He maintained a relaxed smile, sliding one hand to rest casually in the pocket of his pants. For all his easy posture, he pinned her with his gaze like a butterfly in a display case. She had the sinking feeling he had already decided something about her, and it wasn't good.

"Where did you and the lovely Ms. Verde meet, Ted?"

"Kaia's in town for a conference. She was asking me about things to do while she's in Miami and we got to talking." Ted shrugged helplessly. "I suppose I was boring her senseless."

Kaia placed a hand on Ted's arm. "No, absolutely not. I was enjoying the company."

Garrett smiled knowingly. "In town for a conference, you say? Which one?"

Kaia bristled at the tone. Mistrust was not a reaction she was used to receiving from men. Sometimes they were regretful, sometimes shy, but never had she had a man look at her the way Garrett Jameson did. She threw a lock of hair over her shoulder and focused on radiating charm and sensuality.

"It's for work," she said. "Nothing exciting. Ted was kind enough to share a table with me. We were just getting to know each other."

Men stopped and stared from across the dance floor at the renewed rush of faerie magic. Garrett only shook his head, turning back to Ted. "So where is Rachel? I thought she was meeting us here."

"She's at home," Ted replied. "Before we left I asked her about the wedding and she went a little berserk. She said she needed some time by herself."

Garrett frowned. "As in, she's moving out?"

Ted's mouth dropped open. "I hadn't even thought of that. I assumed it was more of her usual wedding panic. You don't think she would *really* move out, do you?"

Garrett sighed with exasperation. "Ted, this is Rachel we're talking about. Once she gets something in her head, she's impossible to reason with. You know that."

"It just never occurred to me… I never thought… "

"Well, think about it," Garrett said. "I've been listening to you moaning about losing her for weeks. You can't very well ignore something like this."

"But what about—" Ted glanced in Kaia's direction. "I sort of promised I'd keep Kaia company."

Garrett followed his gaze and raised his eyebrows. "Seriously? You'd risk Rachel for *that*?" He rolled his eyes. "Go find your fiancée."

Kaia gasped at the direct insult. She had never, *ever* been on the receiving end of such derision.

Ted winced. He turned and gave Kaia an apologetic smile. "He can be a little bossy sometimes."

Kaia narrowed her gaze. "Bossy? Is that what you call it here in Miami?"

"Go," Garrett said again. His disapproval surged at her, but he directed his words at Ted. "You shouldn't be here anyway."

"Ahem." Kaia cleared her throat. She turned to Ted and dropped her voice. She needed to preserve a relationship with Ted, just in case she needed to use him again later. "I understand if you need to leave. I would hate to get between you and Rachel."

Ted glanced back at Garrett. "Garrett, she's all alone," he pleaded. "Any chance you can keep an eye out for her?"

Kaia masked a rush of satisfaction. Ted might think himself in love with Rachel, but he was hardly immune to her faerie charm. If she had wanted him to stay by her side all night long, he probably would have.

Silly men.

"Sure," Garrett said, flashing her a mocking smile. "I have the feeling Kaia doesn't like to be lonely."

A quiver passed down her spine as his gaze bore into her, full of warning and a deep-seated, distinctly unfriendly suspicion. She focused on keeping her back straight and the faerie magic flowing.

Zafira herself had sent Kaia after this man.

She could not fail.

Read on for a sneak peek of Jess Macallan's
sexy urban fantasy,

Stone Cold Seduction...

"Elle. It's just Elle."

When a regular night of Robin Hood-ery results in the manifestation of some, um, unusual paranormal abilities, perfume-maker Elleodora Fredricks realizes the normal world she lives in isn't quite… normal. And neither is she, thanks to her father, king of the shadow elves. Not only is he evil incarnate and the reason Elle moonlights as a burglar—someone has to take care of all his victims—he's stolen her memories.

And only reading her fate can fix that.

Good thing she's got a trio of hotties willing to help her find said fate. Saving her oracle BFF's fiancée, falling in love with the gargoyle, and making up for breaking the phoenix's heart ought to be a piece of cake for the princess of the shadow elves.

If only the king didn't want his daughter dead…

Chapter One

The worst day of my life began with a double mocha, extra whipped cream. I burned my tongue, spilled whipped cream on my black top, and then dumped the whole thing when I tripped while walking up the stairs to my second-floor apartment. It got worse. Like a bad country song, I broke things, lost things, ran over things, and hurt things—mostly myself.

If it had stopped there, I could have slept it off with a little help from a bottle of cabernet. But, naturally, it didn't.

Now, a little past one in the morning, I'm balancing on a stone ledge outside a building that doesn't belong to me, trying to get away with gems that don't belong to me. An employee who does, sort of, belong to me, has just opened the nearest window and casually said hello.

Being caught stealing by my newest employee—who happens to be a hottie—tops my list of Worst Situations Ever.

Yes, I've had better days.

My name is Elleodora Fredricks—Elle for short. I'm not a fan of my name, especially because it comes from my paternal line. By day, I'm a small business owner, the proprietress of an organic soap store. By night, a cat burglar. I'm moderately talented at both professions. In my defense, I do my part to spread good karma. I donate pet food and blankets to the local animal shelter, I collect donations at my shop twice a year for the food bank, and the only person I ever steal from is the biggest son of a bitch in town.

My father.

I typically refer to him as the jerk who mistakenly donated DNA. He never earned the title of dad. It's safe to say we have father-daughter issues.

A small bead of sweat slid down my jaw and disappeared into my collar. It was a cool October evening, but a combination of nerves and leather had me perspiring. Face first, I pressed my weight against the building and gripped the decorative stone that surrounded the window. It had rained earlier, so the stone was slick, but the swirls and pattern in the stone made it fairly easy to grip, despite the rain.

The ledge under my feet was another matter. The eight inches of concrete I balanced on were not nearly enough to make me feel safe from the potential five-story drop. Heights made me queasy, but the gorgeous man staring at me from the window I'd just crawled out of unnerved me.

For starters, he hadn't taken his eyes off me. For a brief moment, I wondered why I'd listened to Teryl and worn the black catsuit. I was a walking cliché for cat burglars, clinging to a ledge with gemstones hidden between my breasts, wearing a freaking black leather catsuit. I'd only wanted to blend into the shadows and avoid leaving a scrap of identifiable clothing behind. Teryl had sworn the neck-to-ankle black one-piece made me look dangerous and sexy.

Teryl was a liar.

However, Teryl is a liar who also happens to be my best friend, and a key component to this failure of an operation. He's the one and only informant I have inside my father's business. Without him, I wouldn't have access to any of the information I need to stay one step ahead of dear old Dad. Too bad Teryl was striking out tonight. Big time.

Excuses to explain my position to my hot employee began to run through my mind, but as quickly as they formed, I dismissed them. It was as bad as it looked. Catsuit, theft, and all. Tonight's cache included fifty-two carats of flawless Paraiba tourmaline gemstones. It really doesn't hurt my father's bottom line—he's loaded—but it keeps him distracted. More importantly, it prevents him from murdering any more innocents. The money goes back to the families of those who weren't so lucky, and to the small few who've survived, but wished they hadn't.

Breathing deeply, I prayed for strength and slowly turned my head to look at Jaxon West, otherwise known as Jax. I'd hired him two months ago to help with deliveries, shipments, and all-around handy man tasks.

The man was hot, sweaty, bring-the-roof-down sex poured into jeans.

Jax stood a solid six feet tall, with broad shoulders, a tapered waist, and every inch of him threaded with muscle. His hair was cut short and an honest-to-God black. It's so black, it has a gorgeous blue sheen in certain light. And then there were his eyes.

Oh, his eyes.

They're a steely, flint gray. I swear, at times I've seen them shimmer with streaks of silver. Most days, they reflect a sense of calm and knowledge that you associate with the very old, very patient, and very wise.

The strange thing: he's only thirty-four.

While I stared at him, unable to form a coherent explanation, he leaned out of the window and softly cleared his throat. "Hi, boss."

His voice reminded me of my favorite chocolate. Dark, smooth, and so delicious, you can only eat one small bite at a time, because you want to wrap it around yourself to savor every little bit. Too bad this was the wrong place, wrong time.

Thankful for the dark of night, I offered him a stiff smile he probably couldn't see. "Hi, Jax. Fancy meeting you here."

He crossed his arms and settled against the window frame as if he had all night. One black brow lifted, but he said nothing.

Jax was good at silence. There were days he'd work for hours without saying a single word. I didn't get the impression he was anti-social, just quiet and observant. He didn't miss a thing, but he rarely offered his two cents. His silent presence was usually calming. Right now, I felt anything but calm.

Gritting my teeth in disgust, mostly at myself, I lifted my gaze toward the dark October night sky. He was going to be difficult, and I didn't have time to offer up the harsh details of why I was here. Plus, I really wanted to get out of this catsuit. Sweat accumulated in uncomfortable places when wearing leather.

Teryl would have to die for this.

"I know this looks bad, but if you'd let me—" I bit off the rest of my words when Jax's head whipped around to look at something in my father's office. He put a hand up to silence me.

I heard the voices, and my blood ran cold. My heart began to pound hard against my chest. If my father's men found me... I couldn't even finish the thought as my stomach began to churn. I wondered if jumping would be a better option.

Jax motioned for me to remain quiet, and he carefully climbed onto the ledge without making a sound. He managed to close the window most of the way before the men walked into the room.

I inched my way over, so Jax could slide beside me on the slippery, narrow brick ledge.

At least I'll die with a gorgeous man, I thought morbidly, trying not to panic.

I could hear the men shuffling around in the room, their voices tense and angry. Holding my breath, I kept as still as I could. I'd never been this close to being caught. I felt knots forming into hard, heavy lumps in my stomach as I pressed into the stone wall.

"Mr. Warlow is gonna be pissed if another one goes missing," a raspy voice pronounced.

"That's an understatement" was the sarcastic reply.

I didn't recognize the first voice, but I knew the second.

It haunted me.

I hadn't seen Luke for over ten years. Hearing his voice…it was as if the nightmare had ended only yesterday. Except it hadn't really ended. I'd merely been given a reprieve.

Luke is my father's right-hand goon. He is pure nastiness behind an ugly mug of a face. Built like a tank, Luke enjoys inflicting pain in ways that go far beyond disturbing. No amount of therapy or medication would ever get through to him. Some people are born evil, and Luke fit that description to a T. I had nightmares about that man more often than I liked to admit.

If he was involved tonight, things were going to get ugly, soon. I pushed distant memories into the furthest corners of my mind and laid my cheek against the cold, wet stone. It would be embarrassing if I got caught and cried in front of Jax in the same night.

On the bright side, if Luke was on the job, my father must be getting irritated. Maybe I was finally getting results. It thrilled and terrified me at the same time.

"Seriously man, we've got to find this bastard." The raspy

voice sounded slightly panicked. "This will be the third one in four months. You know how Mr. Warlow is. Heads will roll."

Luke's reply was muffled, and I sent up a quick thanks. I didn't want to hear anything he might have to say about what he'd do when he caught me.

I could hear the men moving things around, probably looking for the small bag of gemstones I had secured against my chest. Were the police on their way? I pressed closer to the stone face, trying to make myself as small as possible. It was a futile effort. You can't hide a five-foot, eight-inch tall, catsuit-covered woman on an eight-inch ledge.

Did I mention I'm not great under pressure?

Jax put an arm around the back of my waist, for comfort or safety, I wasn't sure. I shifted slightly, distracted with the close contact. His arm was warm and hard, and a small part of me enjoyed the touch. Jax was an innocent in all this. I still didn't know why he was there, but I did know he should have never been caught up in my mess. I drew in a breath to whisper that I was sorry, but he stopped me.

"Hush." His breath felt warm against my ear as he whispered the command. "They will see the open window soon."

I ignored the shiver his words conjured. I'd rather jump from five stories than let Luke find me.

Almost on cue, that raspy voice called, "Hey, did you check the window?"

I heard someone scramble toward the window. As it slid open, I was desperate for the night to swallow us whole. Bile rose in my throat as the thought burned through me.

I saw a shaved head poke out and look both directions. Luke's cold eyes scanned the area, and I could almost feel that sharp gaze cut over me. His image wavered as I forgot to breathe, and I waited for the pain and oblivion that always followed Luke. I squeezed my eyes shut as fear wrenched me back to the past.

I stood before my father, hands clasped in front of me, eyes on the floor. He was angry again.

I tried not to cry. He hated it when I cried. He called me a sniveling weakling. Not fit to share his blood. Mom said I had to be here because we were blood. My seven-year-old mind didn't understand.

But I did understand his anger. It meant pain for me.

I heard a door creak open and dared to look up. A terrified whimper escaped before I could stop it. Father would be furious at the sound.

His fists clenched until the knuckles were white.

He never hit me. I always flinched, waiting for his blow. But he never hit me. I could see in his eyes that he wanted to.

"Luke, make sure the child understands her place," Father bit out, raking me with one last, scathing look. Shaking his head in disgust, he walked out.

Luke watched him leave, a small, cruel smile playing at his lips. His eyes were lit with an unholy gleam, and he smoothed a hand over his bald head. "Well, well, Princess. Shall we play?"

Seven-year-old legs trembled, unable to run. No longer caring about Father's wrath, I opened my mouth to scream. I knew I shouldn't. Luke loved it when I screamed.

His smile grew wider.

Tears streamed down my face and I wondered how long it would take for the darkness to come this time.

"Anything?" the unknown voice inside called, jarring me back to the present. I dared to open my eyes. This time, they were clear and dry.

"Nope." Luke's shaved head disappeared. Moments later, their voices trailed away, still grumbling.

I remained still, confused. Luke never walked away when his prey was in sight. Maybe this was a new, sick twist of his. Psych out the prey before you torture and kill it.

I hated him with every fiber of my soul.

Almost choking on my rage and fear, I held still, waiting to be discovered. He'd be back. He always came back. Maybe he'd left to call the police. I waited for the sound of a security alarm or sirens.

After a full two minutes of quiet, I worked up the courage to whisper, "What the hell just happened? Are they gone?"

Jax was silent. His body stiffened at my question. The darkness made his fierce expression even harsher. It was not a happy look.

When he finally spoke, his voice stretched between us, low and deadly. "How long have you been able to shadow?"

I wasn't sure what he meant, so I didn't answer. I was still shocked we hadn't been seen.

With a muttered curse, he grabbed me around the waist with both arms and jumped. I didn't have time to draw in a breath to scream before he gently set me down on the street, five stories below.

I gurgled and stared up to where we had just been standing. "What…I…I…"

His expression was grim when he faced me. "We need to talk."

"Buh…buh…but how did you…" My words trailed off as I looked up and down the street, at a complete loss. Was I going crazy? How had we gotten to the ground in one piece? How had Luke not seen us? Maybe I'd finally gone off the deep end. It sounded like a viable option.

I brushed a shaky hand against the small, velvet bag that was nestled against my chest, inside the suit. It was still there. My heart thundered against it, and I swore I heard the echo of the beat. The stress of the past few moments caught up with me, and I felt my knees begin to buckle.

I was in another nightmare. Except Luke didn't have a starring role, and I couldn't seem to wake up from this one.

Jax grabbed me around the waist before I crumpled to the pavement. He strode away from the building, half-dragging me beside him. "Let's get you home and get you a drink. We have a lot to discuss."

I stumbled along and felt my breath coming in short gasps, suddenly feeling uncomfortably awake and wishing I weren't. Jax had caught me breaking and entering, we'd barely escaped my father's sadistic enforcer by jumping from five stories up, and now he wanted to go get a drink?

The cool night air held the lingering scent of rain and the undertones of a flowering tree, but thankfully, no sound of sirens or alarms. I couldn't remember the name of the tree, but the soothing ritual of identifying scents helped calm me down.

We arrived at my apartment on Seattle's Capitol Hill a half hour later. My neck hurt from constantly looking over my shoulder for Luke or the police. I'd cringed at every shadow, real and imagined. Despite my paranoia, I hadn't seen anyone on our walk beyond the late night partygoers.

I loved the area. It had a fun, funky feel and suited my business perfectly. My building was plain, but my neighbors were great. I had a Thai restaurant to the left and an accountant's office to the right. Directly across the street was my favorite yoga studio. I didn't have to venture far for anything. My shop was downstairs, and my apartment was upstairs. As an employee, Jax already had a key to the shop. Now, he held out his hand and demanded the key to my apartment.

Don't ask me how I managed to fit a key in a leather catsuit. I did.

My limbs felt heavy with exhaustion. The long walk home hadn't helped, but public transportation hadn't been an option. I remained silent until Jax had pushed me inside and locked the door behind us.

"Am I dreaming? Because not one moment of the last twenty minutes has made much sense."

Part of me was hoping he'd lie. Maybe Teryl would jump out from behind my favorite overstuffed chair and yell "You've been *Punk'd!*"

Life is never that easy.

"Elleodora," Jax began.

"It's *Elle*. Just Elle," I grumbled. I've been telling him for two months to call me by my nickname. Only my father and my mother called me Elleodora. My mom had only used it when she was mad at me. My father used it as an insult.

Jax sighed and pinched the bridge of his nose. Putting extra emphasis on my name, he said, "*Elle*, I need to know how long you've been able to shadow."

I still had no idea what he was talking about, so I turned away and walked into my small kitchen, and sagged into one of the chairs at my breakfast table.

I love my little kitchen. It smells like an herb garden. I keep pots of lavender, basil, thyme, and lemon balm on the counter. My favorite place to be is sitting at my table, holding a cup of hot tea. I'd found the round table at an antique shop and refinished it myself. The scrollwork on the pedestal leg shows old-fashioned craftsmanship at its finest.

The warm mocha color of the kitchen walls wraps around me like a cozy blanket. I can read the paper, eat in peace, or stare out the small window and watch people rushing by on the sidewalk below. I always find comfort here.

Tonight, that comfort eluded me. Instead, I felt cold and numb.

Folding my hands on the table, I let my head sink onto them. My breath shuddered through me as I tried to let the weight of my tension slowly slip away.

If my father had Luke on the job, it would only be a matter of time before he found me. I was certain Luke had never, ever come up empty-handed in a hunt. And fool that I was, I had taken on this crusade like some misguided, modern-day Robin Hood. The problem was, I had no Little John to back me up, and I was completely inept.

Who was I kidding? I'd been playing a dangerous game, and I'd known the potential outcome. I had let my ego get the better of me. Seeing Luke today had brought reality crashing down around me.

Lost in a moment of self-pity, I jumped when Jax sat down in the opposite chair.

He watched me with his calm, knowing eyes.

I took another breath and stared at my hands. "What shadows are you talking about?"

Jax leaned forward and stared at me intently. "You really don't know what shadowing is." It was a statement, and he was waiting for my reaction.

Some of my hair had escaped the ponytail I'd pulled it into earlier. I wearily tucked it behind my ear. "Since you showed up tonight, nothing has made sense. I don't understand what you're asking me, and I don't understand how we got off that ledge. If Luke had caught me tonight, neither you nor any shadows would have been much help." My voice had risen with each word, and Jax sat back at the volume of my last word, "help."

Fear had overridden my good sense once again. Jax didn't

know a thing about my father or Luke or our history, and I didn't want him to know. The fewer people on this planet who knew how screwed up I really was, the better. "Never mind. Scratch that. I don't know what shadowing is." And I didn't really care at this point. I had enough on my plate that I couldn't handle. The police worried me a hell of a lot more than Jax's shadows.

His voice was soft when he replied, "You're coming into your powers, and one of them is obviously shadowing. How else would they not have seen us?"

I dropped my head to my hands once more. Powers? Shadowing? Maybe he'd had a good idea with that drink suggestion. I also needed to get out of this catsuit.

One crisis at a time.

I decided to tackle the simplest one first. With effort, I pushed myself to my feet. "I need to change. I have no idea what's going on, but I sure hope it was a really, really bad dream. I'll see you in the morning." I turned to walk away. Hopefully he'd let himself out, because I just didn't have it in me to play hostess. My terror had gone as quickly as it had come, and it had burned through my energy reserves. I was wiped out and wanted to be alone.

Jax gently stopped me with his hand on my arm after I'd gotten only two steps out of the kitchen.

A banging at my door made me jump. Heart racing again, I stared at Jax.

How had they found me so quickly? Luke must have called the police. I could hardly believe he'd decided to let the authorities handle this, but if Luke was at the door himself, he wouldn't be bothering to knock. I had to hide the stones. Crap, I had to answer the door. I had to—

"Elle, open up! It's colder than shit out here."

I let out a strangled laugh when I recognized the voice. Teryl had the worst timing.

He's been my best friend since we were ten years old. He's my partner in crime and the worst fashion advisor a girl could have. I leaned against the doorframe of the kitchen while Jax went to the front door.

He'd barely turned the lock when Teryl pushed his way in. "What in the hell happened? I tried to…" He stopped short when he saw Jax standing halfway behind the door. "Hey, Jax. I…um… this must be a bad time."

Pivoting quickly, he turned to leave.

Jax grabbed his arm. "In the kitchen. Now." Gone was the soft, steady voice. Hard steel, coated with menace, Jax all but growled at Teryl.

Eyes wide, Teryl pivoted again and brushed past me into the kitchen. He looked like he'd stepped out of a clothing ad. Dark wash jeans fit his slim, lanky figure great. A black jacket hung unzipped over a wildly-striped polo. He looked as comfortable as I wanted to be. He sat at one of the four chairs and watched Jax nervously. I took the seat to his right, too tired to argue about shadows or leaping off buildings, and too confused to care.

Jax said nothing. He stared at Teryl, while Teryl did his best to look anywhere and everywhere but in Jax's direction. He jumped when Jax said his name.

"Teryl."

Even in my weary state, I recognized the command in Jax's tone. I slapped a hand on the table with irritation. "Can someone please explain what is going on?"

Neither man answered right away. They were too busy staring at each other, communicating silently.

My hands slapped on the table as I stood up. "Have your silent *man*versation outside, but right now, I want words!"

"Manversation?" Teryl's smile was brief. "Is that even a word?"

"I suggest you start kissing the ground I walk on because you will pay for the rest of your miserable life for tonight. And for your information, a manversation is a conversation men have where only grunts, growls, and manly looks are exchanged."

"Is that so? I had no idea we did that." Teryl's cheeky grin pissed me off even more than his sarcasm. Normally, I found his sense of humor a little twisted, but a lot funny. I found nothing funny about what had happened tonight.

His smile faded as he realized I was serious. "Hey, I think you look freakin' amazing in that leather."

I dropped into the chair, slumping back. "Start explaining what you're trying to avoid telling me. Now."

Teryl began to fidget, which was never a good sign. He fidgeted, but he didn't say a word. I looked at Jax, who was equally silent.

It didn't matter who spilled the beans, but they'd better start talking. Now.

Jax sighed and leaned back so his chair tipped against the wall, facing us. He folded his arms across his chest, causing the muscles in his shoulders to bunch. Not that I'd notice such a thing at a time like this. Not that I *should* notice such a thing.

Jax's sigh strummed across my last nerve.

"You know what? To hell with you." I let my glare slide over Teryl's guilty face. "You, too. Luke almost caught me tonight, Teryl."

His face blanched and he reached across the table and grabbed my hand. "Luke? He's in town? Are you okay?" He squeezed gently.

Teryl was one of the only people alive who knew my history with Luke. Because I wanted to keep it that way, I tilted my head slightly to remind Teryl that we had an audience.

He cleared his throat and let go of my hand. "Right. Uh, what happened?"

I rubbed my temples. A headache was beginning to develop behind my right eye. I pulled the ponytail holder out of my hair and let it fall loose around my shoulders in an effort to ease the tightness along my scalp. "I don't know what happened. We weren't caught, and we didn't die after stepping off the ledge, and if one of you doesn't explain, I'm going to start crying. Big, fat, hysterical woman tears."

"Elle shadowed," Jax said to Teryl.

There was that word again. *Shadowed.* It sounded like something a superhero—or supervillian—would do. I caught another meaningful stare between the two of them.

"Explain. Now."

The chair squeaked against the floor as Teryl scooted back and stood up. "How about a drink?"

"I don't want a damned drink." Well, I did, but that could wait.

"I meant for me," he grumbled, as he began rummaging around in my cupboards. He found a bottle of whiskey in my small liquor stash and poured a shot. I watched him grimace as it went down. Teryl rarely drank.

Unease slithered through my irritation as I watched him drink a second shot. He coughed when the alcohol hit his throat, and then turned back to us. "She doesn't know about it."

The word Jax muttered under his breath startled me. I'd never heard the man curse before, not in that deep, sincere voice of his.

"Doesn't know what?" I asked, eyeing the bottle of whiskey Teryl carried to the table. He sat down and poured two more shots, handing one to me.

Jax spoke for him. "Your father is a shadow elf king, and you're his heir."